The Night Man

The Night Man

JØRN LIER HORST

Translated by Anne Bruce

MICHAEL JOSEPH

MICHAEL JOSEPH

UK | USA | Canada | Ireland | Australia
India | New Zealand | South Africa

Michael Joseph is part of the Penguin Random House group of companies
whose addresses can be found at global.penguinrandomhouse.com

First published in Norway as *Nattmannen* by Gyldendal, 2009
First published in the UK by Michael Joseph, 2022

001

Copyright © Jørn Lier Horst, 2009
English translation copyright © Anne Bruce, 2022

The moral right of the author has been asserted

Set in 13.5/16pt Garamond MT Std
Typeset by Jouve (UK), Milton Keynes
Printed and bound in Great Britain by Clays Ltd, Elcograf S.p.A.

The authorized representative in the EEA is Penguin Random House Ireland,
Morrison Chambers, 32 Nassau Street, Dublin D02 YH68

A CIP catalogue record for this book is available from the British Library

HB ISBN: 978–0–241–53379–6
OM ISBN: 978–0–241–53380–2

This book has been published with the financial support of Norla

NORLA

www.greenpenguin.co.uk

For Aras Ali, wherever you are.

Overnight, the fog had come rolling in from sea, settling heavy as lead and changing everything around her into murky silhouettes.

Hoisting her bag on to her shoulder, Vera Kvålsvik focused intently, staring into the greyish-white blur. She had walked the same route nearly every morning for almost thirty years now and would have found her way to the little bookshop in the pitch dark, but this fog was worse than darkness. It transformed everything familiar and formed new shapes, shadows and fuzzy edges. It was like a silent predator that came sneaking up on you from behind.

She bowed her head and concentrated on her feet. With every step she took, her heels echoed on the paving stones of the town square. Apart from that, she was surrounded by solid silence.

Pushing away the uneasy feeling, she tried to concentrate on the week ahead. A number of new books would be coming in. Books were her life and the mere thought of a good book waiting for her at home made the day easier.

Somewhere in the distance, a dog was barking. She could hear how it craned its neck to sound a warning or note of caution. She stopped and automatically clutched her shoulder bag with both hands as she looked around. All she could make out was the outline of the tall buildings that loomed around the square. Fifty more steps and she would be at her destination.

The dog was silent now but fear still had her in its grip.

She was not alone. Somewhere out in the mist a door creaked open and light footsteps approached the street. A car door slammed and an engine fired up. Not far ahead of her, a crow squawked loudly. Everyday sounds had become harsh and discordant.

Vera bit her bottom lip. The cool, damp air held a taste of salt from the sea.

The crow squawked again. The fog was heavy and sticky, clinging to her and making her feel clammy and sweaty under her jacket. She took one step, rummaging in her bag to get the shop key ready before she moved on. Then she stopped again, hesitating. In the midst of the grey-white haze she could see the contours of something she had not noticed before. It looked like a bust or a memorial stone that someone must have placed in one of the raised flowerbeds over the weekend. At the same time she realized that could not be the explanation. It was something else, something terrifying.

Taking another few steps forward, Vera Kvålsvik squinted into the mist, feeling her heart thump convulsively in her chest. Then she opened her mouth into a scream.

2

It was Monday 10 November 2008 and William Wisting was sitting at the kitchen table with a cup of coffee and some toast with strawberry jam. The time was 6.57 a.m. and he had already been awake for almost two hours.

He woke earlier and earlier these days. To begin with he had stayed in bed, staring at the empty space beside him, but after a couple of sleepless months he had realized he was not going to be able to drop off again once he was wide awake and had decided to get up.

He swallowed down the dry bread with his coffee. Outside, the morning fog had taken over from the night darkness. It was one of those rare days with no breath of wind. The foghorn howled like an abandoned animal in the distance, reminding him of how quiet it was inside the house.

Although he had not noticed it before, he saw that the leaves on the green potted plant on the windowsill were drooping.

He got to his feet, stuck his finger in the pot and stood rubbing the dry earth between his thumb and forefinger, wondering whether to give up on it. It deserves a second chance, he decided, and moved to the sink, where he filled a glass with water. He poured it into the pot and picked off a couple of brown, withered leaves.

The morning paper was open in front of him at the property pages. Compact modern apartments with no garden or need for regular maintenance. He had begun to think of moving when summer began to wane. He had felt at home in the house with its large garden and view over Stavern and the sea beyond. Passing it on to anyone else had seemed almost like a betrayal, but the more often the thought of moving had struck him, the more comfortable he became with it.

The phone rang, breaking into his train of thought. Automatically, he glanced at the time before picking up the receiver as soon as he recognized Line's number.

'Hi, it's me,' his daughter said at the other end. 'How are things?'

Clearing his throat, Wisting tried to analyse her tone of voice, listening to hear if anything was wrong.

'Fine,' he replied. 'What about you?'

'I'm on my way down,' she explained.

Wisting felt her words immediately raise his spirits. Six months ago, Line had put a shaky relationship behind her and moved to Oslo when she was offered a temporary post at *Verdens Gang*. It made him proud that the biggest newspaper in the country had hired her. He regarded it as a real achievement. But then Line had excelled more in two years at the local newspaper than most other journalists did in the course of their entire careers. She possessed something of the same hunger that had driven Wisting in his work as well as a virtually clairvoyant ability to be in the right place at the right time. It had been noticed.

'Are you working?' he asked.

'I've been given a couple of days to follow up the suitcase story,' she told him.

Wisting frowned. He never liked it when his daughter was writing about investigations he was working on, but this time the furrowed brow came from sheer curiosity. *The Suitcase Mystery* had been splashed on the front pages of all the newspapers a fortnight ago but the inquiry had been at an

4

impasse from day one. It was a case he was really keen to see cleared up.

'I've got an interesting tip-off,' Line continued when she heard her father's silence. She knew him well enough to know the thoughts that were running through his head. 'There's a woman I'm going to talk to who might know something.'

'Oh?' He forced out the question but refrained from asking anything further.

'It's no secret,' Line added, as if she had read his thoughts. 'I'm sure you'll be able to talk to her too.'

'Or else I can just read about it in the paper.' He stood up and opened the fridge, studying the contents. 'How long will you be staying?'

The sound of the fridge door made the cat, lying curled up on the rug, react. It raised its head, sprang up and snuggled into his legs.

'Just until tomorrow.'

Wisting took out a pack of cooked ham and dropped the last slice on to the floor before shutting the fridge door.

'Buster will be glad to see you,' he said, scratching the cat behind the ear.

Line laughed at the other end. 'Don't go to a lot of bother, though,' she said. 'I only need my bed.'

'Not at all,' he assured her, stealing a glance at the clock. He would have time to vacuum before he went to work. Also, he would have to do some shopping. Bread, cold meats and milk. Line drank milk. And something for dinner. He found some notepaper and made a list.

Fruit as well, he thought, scribbling that down. Line liked green apples. He could leave work an hour earlier than usual. He would also manage a trip to the grave and get that tidied.

'When will you arrive?' he asked.

'About five?' she suggested.

The phone signalled that another call was waiting.

'Then I'll see you later,' Wisting concluded, taking the receiver from his ear, looking at the display and recognizing the number of the police switchboard.

3

She had looked at the world through clear, green eyes.

Wisting cocked his head. As her empty gaze fixed on his and held it fast, he took a step back but could not stop staring.

'Is it real?' he asked in an unsteady voice.

Espen Mortensen, the crime-scene technician, nodded.

Wisting swallowed audibly. Long experience had given him knowledge and insight into most forms of brutality and violence, but he had never believed in pure evil or the idea that people existed who were wicked through and through. Not until now. The crime he was now faced with could not have originated anywhere other than a very dark mind.

The girl with the green eyes could be around twelve years old. Her head had been severed from her body and placed on a wooden stake.

He could see parts of the smooth, whorled musculature in her oesophagus and the rings of cartilage in her windpipe. The surface of the wound was uneven and ragged, with bloody fibres and fragments of skin hanging down on the stake.

Her facial expression bore traces of the fear that had been the last of her emotions. Fear and distress. It contrasted starkly with her youthful features. Her black hair was still gathered into a ponytail.

Something silvery glistened on both her cheeks. Eyes that had cried until they were dry. Salt tears that had dried out. He thought he could see fear, torment and pain in her green gaze, as if she had known the fate that lay in store and had begged for mercy.

In the course of his almost thirty years as a police officer, Wisting had often encountered sudden, violent death. Corpses that were swollen and discoloured, decayed and partly devoured by animals. He had seen dead people with their bowels and intestines hanging out. Bodies with axes or knives plunged deep inside, brain matter smeared over the walls. In a sense he had trained himself to put up with what he saw and pushed the brutal impressions aside with the aid of rational thought and a methodical approach to investigative work. When it came to children, though, it was always different. It was invariably senseless and incomprehensible. When a young person died, it shattered the professional shield he had constructed. The experience tore him up and paralysed him. It was as if all hope and belief in humanity was ripped away.

In this case, however, there was something that unsettled him even more. This was not an irrational act committed in the heat of the moment. The dead girl's head had been placed almost as if on a pedestal, something the killer was proud of. He wanted to put her on display and that revealed a plan and intention behind the act.

Wisting noticed how this line of thought made him feel breathless, and he had to force himself to get to work, to think methodically.

He let his eyes wander in an attempt to form an overall impression and not lose sight of individual details that either alone or in sum total could tell him something about the killer.

The wooden stake on which the head was placed was about two metres in length and the thickness of a forearm. Stripped of bark, it had been dried by wind and weather. Down below the bushes he saw traces of footprints made by someone tramping around in the flowerbed. A regular pattern of little ridges, slightly smaller than his own shoe size. A spider had managed to spin a rough net between two branches that had sprung up after being trampled down. Dewdrops were clinging to the white threads.

On the ground beside it he spotted a couple of cigarette butts, a crumpled scrap of paper and a flattened piece of chewing gum that anyone could have thrown away. Everything would be routinely gathered up, packed and labelled. Nothing of what he saw gave any real hope of leading the investigation in a definitive direction. All the same, he believed that the disparate fragments in this case would eventually, slowly but surely, fall into place, just as newly fallen snow builds into a wall, flake by flake.

Shivering, Wisting took a step back. A heavy blanket of gloom, fear and confusion settled over the site, just as dense as the fog that swirled around them.

'What do you think?' he asked, turning to face Mortensen.

'She doesn't look Norwegian,' the crime-scene technician answered, staring at the face. 'I don't think she's from this part of the world.'

Wisting nodded. The initial phase of the investigation would centre on finding out who she was. He knew that death could distort facial features and make it difficult to recognize someone. Eyes became hollow, soft tissue puffy and skin discoloured.

'Several hours have passed since she was beheaded,' Mortensen went on, pointing at the reddish-brown blood that had congealed along the edge of the wound. 'I'd estimate she was killed some time early last night.'

'Beheaded,' Wisting repeated, mostly to himself. The word was almost as brutal as the act.

Mortensen was getting his camera equipment ready. Wisting turned around and surveyed the square. The fog was lifting and he could see the rear view of a couple of uniformed policemen in front of the red-and-white crime-scene tape that had been rolled out. Small groups of inquisitive onlookers had gathered. Snippets of whispered conversations full of amazement and disquiet reached across to him.

The noise of heavy traffic made him peer into one of the side streets and he watched as two of the fire brigade's large tenders trundled into the square. One of the police officers directed them to park at an angle in order to block the view.

Wisting cast one last glance at the girl's head before plodding away with a heavy, slow tread.

4

The first rays of sun broke through the grey, overcast sky as she passed the exit road for Tønsberg.

Line sat up straight in her seat, leaned forward a little and peered into the rear-view mirror. As she pushed aside a couple of stray hairs of her flyaway fringe, she wondered whether she had cut it too short, but then decided it suited her.

She relished the tingling in her stomach that always came when she was working on an intriguing story and she had no idea where it might lead, except that it would end in huge headlines.

Her sharp blue eyes looked into the mirror again and she smiled.

When the newspaper ran in-depth profiles of well-known people, they sometimes asked the interview subjects to make a graph of their lives. A red curve that formed waves, showing highs and lows. This showed that life was not plain sailing, even for people who had achieved success. Right now she felt that her own life was on the crest of a wave. Admittedly, the curve was filled with fluctuations from the two years she had lived with Jacob Loe, but she had now put all that behind her. The lowest point on the graph was the summer two years ago when her mother had died while employed as an aid worker for NORAD in Africa.

The high point until now must have been when she had, as a newly appointed journalist on the local newspaper, made headlines that had spread beyond national borders. Chance events had sent her on the trail of one of the world's most wanted men. Chasing the story had put her life in danger, and the red curve could have come to an abrupt stop. Instead it had given a solid start to her career and was one of the reasons she now sat with a press card from *Verdens Gang* – Norway's largest newspaper with more than a million daily readers – in her bag.

Leaning back in her seat, she hummed along to a song on the morning radio show. Her best time lay in the future, she was sure of that. If there was anything that prevented the red curve from reaching the absolute heights, it was the lack of a romantic partner. She missed having someone to share her life with, but at the moment she had no time for that sort of thing.

She cast a glance at the notes beside her. She had printed out the pictures of the blue suitcase adorned with Mickey Mouse stickers from the photo archives. They had been taken at a press conference in one of the meeting rooms at the police station in her hometown. Her father was depicted in a couple of them. With his dark eyes staring into the camera lens, resting one hand on top of the suitcase, he looked good. Line understood that, behind his authoritative gaze, he was feeling perplexed.

He had lost weight, she thought, as she concentrated on the road again. Her father had always been fit and healthy, and when the first few kilos had dropped off, it had suited him. Now he was starting to look gaunt, his face more rugged, and his cheekbones were clearly defined in his angular face. Although his dark hair was still thick, it was now increasingly streaked with grey.

She looked down at his photo again. In a sense her father was the focal point of her life. He had always been working on some case or other but had invariably made time for her. Even though he would turn up at the last minute, he had always attended end-of-term events at school and come to handball matches. And, without exception, he had taken the time to listen when there was something she needed to talk to him about. He also had a special talent for understanding and coming up with good advice.

He had, in addition, appreciated why she had broken off her studies and jumped into a temporary post at the local newspaper, even though it was far from problem-free when she was assigned to cases he was working on. Anyway, she knew he was proud of her and, actually, their jobs were not so very different. If you wanted to achieve above-average results, you needed to put in extra effort. It demanded creativity, intuition and social intelligence as well as the ability to create a connection with people, to unearth details, to coax and even outwit people to some degree into giving information. These were not skills you could learn from reading books. For the average journalist, the job was just a source of income, but for her, it was becoming a way of life. She had a great deal to thank her father for.

Her mobile phone rang in her bag just as the newsreader was introduced on the radio. She dug out her phone with one hand and only half listened to what was being said. The morning news had so far dealt with the presidential election in the US and the international financial crisis.

Then she sat bolt upright. Something had happened in the course of the morning. The headline item had changed.

'Police in Vestfold have launched a murder investigation following the discovery of a dead body in Larvik's town square,' the radio journalist announced.

Glancing at her phone, she recognized her editor's number, but let it go on ringing while she continued to listen: *'Police have cordoned off an extensive area and will not be releasing any further details at this stage.'*

She answered the phone call, now aware what it would be about.

'Change of plan,' the chief news editor announced from his office in Akersgata, Oslo. 'A body's been found down in your neck of the woods. When will you get there?'

Line glanced at the dashboard clock. 'In twenty minutes.'

'Then you'll be the first of our crew to arrive.' She heard paper rustling at the other end. 'Our tipster heard it from his mother. She was the one who found the body. Apparently it's a severed head on a wooden stake. It's not been confirmed yet, but it seems solid. They've closed off half the square and no one in the police has time to take phone calls.'

'Shit,' Line sighed.

'Yes, if it turns out to be right, this is big. To start with, we're sending a team from here, plus a team from the local office in Skien. The online paper will send their own people but we need a story from you the minute you have something.'

Line felt her hands grow clammy as she eased her foot off the accelerator. All of a sudden it felt as if she had put on shoes that were a bit too big.

5

Chief Inspector Wisting had been to the supplies store to pick up a new writing pad. There was something special about blank sheets of paper and a newly sharpened pencil.

Setting it down at the head of the conference table, he confidently ran his pen down the first page and divided it into two columns. On the left, he wrote *racism* and, on the right, *honour*. Two immediate thoughts regarding what could lie behind the grotesque crime. Then he sat back in his chair, watching as every investigator in the entire department streamed in and found a seat.

He nodded to Torunn Borg, who sat halfway down one side of the table. Tiny lines surrounded her brown eyes and he could see that what little she had learned of this case had made her anxious. She had been involved in many of the major cases they had investigated in the past and he regarded her as one of the best tactical investigators he had. She was efficient, committed and a skilled professional, but her most important quality was her ability always to ask questions about the actions they were taking.

Nils Hammer put his notebook down on the table across from her and drew his chair in closer. These two detectives were exact opposites. They neither complemented nor attracted each other, but both were his first choice when he had to assemble an investigative team.

Hammer was six foot three and weighed just under sixteen stone. Broad-shouldered, he had fair hair on the backs of his large hands. Having come through the ranks, he had worked his way from being an undercover detective to the head of the Drugs Squad and was one of the most respected investigators in the country in that field. At the same time, there was no one who knew the local street scene better than him. However, all his years in the narcotics section had made him tired, at times flippant, and perhaps taught him to cut too many corners.

Superintendent Audun Vetti sat on Wisting's right at the head of the table. In charge of the prosecution service, he was the formal leader of the investigation. Although a couple of years younger than Wisting, he looked older. His bony face had a broad forehead, a strong chin and hollow cheeks. What little grey hair he had was combed over his bald head. His suit jacket was thrown over the chair back and a small pot belly hung over his belt. The smell of sweat and after-shave wafted around him.

For one reason or another Vetti must like seeing his picture in the newspapers. He was more than happy to talk about cases that were ongoing investigations and had a tendency to use long words and to say more than was strictly necessary. This had led to good relationships with certain crime reporters but also caused friction between him and Wisting. The superintendent lacked understanding of tactical judgements made by the police and had on more than one occasion come close to damaging criminal inquiries. Simply telling the press that footprints had been secured at a crime scene could upend an entire case. Criminals also read newspapers and would not be slow to get rid of the shoes the police thought might help clear up a crime.

Vetti ran his fingers along the edge of his shirt collar as he cleared his throat, but Wisting spoke first.

'Thank you all for coming,' he began, glancing at the printout of the message logged with the switchboard less than two hours earlier. The information he intended to run through was already known to everyone around the table, but they sat up attentively and prepared to take note of significant points, important details and the assignments handed out.

'At 6.59 a.m. we received a phone call from a woman on her way to work at the book and stationery shop in the town square,' he continued.

'Ark Farris,' said the detective sitting on his left, naming the bookshop. Jan Osther had been in the department for just over a year and had distinguished himself with his painful precision, a quality that was important in a competent investigator but could also prove irritating.

Wisting nodded as he leafed through to the end of the printed records.

'Vera Kvålsvik, born 16 August 1958,' he read out to be equally precise. It struck him that there was something familiar about the name, but he could not think why.

'She reported discovering a severed head, placed on a stake in one of the flowerbeds in the square,' he went on. Raising his head, he looked out of the window. The distance from the police station to the crime scene was a little more than one hundred metres. If it had not been for the surrounding buildings, they could have been sitting there watching the ongoing forensic work.

'Was the stake already there or was it brought to the square?' one of the investigators asked.

'I assume the perpetrators carried it with them,' he replied, realizing why the man had asked. An unusual object left at the scene gave them an extra lead to follow up.

'Perpetrators *plural*?' Nils Hammer repeated, sounding puzzled. 'Is there anything to suggest there was more than one?'

'Just a theory of mine,' Wisting answered. 'I imagined it

took two of them, one to carry and plant the stake and the other to dispose of the head, but I suppose it might not have been like that.' He waited for further comments before adding: 'Mortensen is still working at the crime scene, but we think the victim is a young girl of minority ethnic origin, probably from one of the countries in Central Asia.'

'Kristallnacht,' Jan Osther commented.

Wisting made a note in the *racism* column. He had made the same observation as the young policeman but let him go on to explain what he meant.

'The night between 9 and 10 November 1938 fired the starting pistol for the persecution of Jews in Nazi Germany,' Osther explained. 'Several hundred Jews were killed, synagogues were torched and shops vandalized. Thousands were carted off to concentration camps. That night was given the name Kristallnacht because of all the broken glass left in the streets after the Nazi storm troopers had razed the Jewish quarter to the ground. The Night of Broken Glass.'

The detective leaned across the table as if to emphasize that he was coming to the point.

'In recent years, right-wing nationalists throughout Europe have celebrated Kristallnacht. It's still a night of violence when neo-Nazis beat up their political opponents and other targets of their hatred.'

'You think this crime could be racially motivated?' Hammer asked.

'Unfortunately, fascism, Nazism, racism and ethnic cleansing are not things that belong only to the past,' Osther said. 'They are still alive and well. Hatred of Muslims and "non-Westerners" has fed a new wave of racist and neo-Nazi organizations. Every year in European countries these extreme nationalists are behind a number of assaults and murders of people with minority ethnic backgrounds.'

Audun Vetti straightened up in his seat. 'Are you thinking of the Patriotic Front?' he asked.

Wisting could see that the idea of a racist motive and the resulting copious media coverage had energized the superintendent. He jotted down the name of the neo-Nazi group that had local adherents. Until now they had confined themselves to causing damage and vandalism at Muslim mosques and distributing racist propaganda, but Jan Osther was right to say that the reach of this type of organization was on the increase. The Patriotic Front played on Old Norse mythology and fed antipathy towards immigrants, attracting young people who were already on the fringes of normal society and who were drawn to the organization's racist and violent ideology. Young people who might be willing to go to great lengths to bring attention to themselves and gain acceptance they could not otherwise achieve in society.

'It's too early to point the investigation towards individuals or any particular group,' he said. 'We need to spread our net wide. Right now the most important thing is to find out the identity of the deceased.'

Wisting glanced across at Torunn Borg, who had made good use of the time before the meeting by checking the records.

'We have no local reports of missing girls that fit the description,' she said, thumbing through the papers. 'In Haugesund there's a girl who has run away from her foster home, but obviously not for the first time. Also, in Oslo there are a couple of girls missing, but they got in touch with their parents by phone last night and it seems they're in Denmark.'

Wisting, nodding to show his appreciation of all the comments, made some notes and turned to a new page to allocate the various assignments.

'I'll handle the media,' the superintendent volunteered before Wisting had resumed speaking. 'This is a case in which we'll be dependent on excellent cooperation with the press to encourage the public to come forward with information.'

It immediately crossed Wisting's mind that the superintendent would also be able to exercise his own hankering for personal publicity but dismissed the thought. This case would cause an endless hue and cry in the media. Numerous press conferences and countless phone calls from journalists in addition to pressure from the chief of police and the top brass. National politicians were sure to put their oar in. He was only too glad for someone to relieve him of all that.

'In consultation with the police chief, I've called a press conference for twelve o'clock,' Vetti went on, turning to Wisting. 'We'll have a meeting in advance of that. If the girl hasn't been identified before then, *that* has to be the main focus.'

Wisting nodded. Clearing his throat, he fixed his gaze on Nils Hammer: 'Door-to-door inquiries,' he said, ticking that off on the pad in front of him. 'You can take four officers,' he added, pointing along the table. 'We have to talk to everyone who lives in the apartments around the square and in the neighbouring side streets, as well as everyone who was out and about last night – taxi drivers, security guards, paper boys and suchlike. I want a list of all sightings.'

Hammer nodded and Wisting used his pen to indicate Jan Osther.

'Electronic traces,' he said, noting that the enthusiastic investigator seemed disappointed to be allocated such a routine task. 'You can have two people to assist you. I want an overview of all mobile phone calls in the town centre during the night, all bank card usage and video from all CCTV locations: petrol stations, banks, web cameras, everything.'

'You're forgetting about the fog,' Jan Osther objected.

'Just get hold of the footage,' Wisting insisted before going on. 'If we're lucky, the perpetrator might have popped into a petrol station to buy a packet of cigarettes or something.'

He issued several more assignments and one chair after another scraped along the floor as the investigators rose to their feet and got cracking. In the end he was left on his own with Torunn Borg.

'I'd like you to stay here at the station with me,' he said. 'I'm going to need someone to help me keep on top of everything.'

6

Line turned off the motorway and drove towards the town. Keeping one hand on the wheel, she fumbled in her bag for her laptop. The pictures of her father with the blue suitcase slid down on to the rubber mat in the passenger footwell, reminding her that she had an appointment she would have to postpone, and she found a convenient layby in which to park. She left the laptop lying on the seat and picked up her mobile phone instead, writing a brief message to say that something had turned up and she would get in touch later in the week. Locating the name Suzanne with a 'z' in her list of contacts, she sent the message. Ten seconds later she received a reply: *OK.*

The computer took half a minute to start up. The fingers of her free hand raced over the keyboard and soon she was into *VG*'s web pages.

The story was headline news.

BODY FOUND IN TOWN SQUARE was the caption, illustrated with a slightly unclear photo a reader had taken with a mobile phone. It showed a uniformed police officer she did not recognize rolling out a reel of crime-scene tape. In the background she could make out a fire engine and two police cars.

She clicked on the story. In addition to readers' photos, the online editor had also included a map showing Larvik pinpointed with a red marker. The police spokesperson had confirmed that *a murder investigation has been initiated.* He had *at present no information about the sex or age of the victim.*

The online journalist had obviously been unable to confirm the tip-off phoned in that the body found had in fact been a severed head.

The police have cordoned off a large area and have arranged for fire engines to be parked in order to screen the discovery site, Line read on. To amplify the story, it said that the police were *very reticent about further details*. And at the foot of the page the final words were: *VG Online will be back with more news.*

Line gulped. Her assignment was to update the more than a million readers who were waiting for more information.

She clicked her way through the other major online newspapers. *Aftenposten* had spoken to the same police spokesperson and had an almost identical headline. *Dagbladet* had not yet covered the story. *Nettavisen* quoted *VG*. She then moved on to the pages of *Østlandsposten*. The local newspaper managed to update their webpages surprisingly often. They carried the same headline as *VG: BODY FOUND IN LARVIK TOWN SQUARE*. The story was illustrated with photos from the newspaper's web camera on the roof of one of the buildings facing the square. *Follow the police at work*, urged the text. The image had been updated less than a minute ago. It had been taken from an appropriate distance and showed a crowd of rubberneckers huddled together at the far corner of the square and also afforded readers a glimpse of the area that had been closed off. However, the detail was too blurred to see exactly what the police were working on.

The overview image also told her that the easiest way for her to reach the cordoned area would be to park at Lilletorget and walk down the pedestrian street. Closing the lid of her laptop, she drove off, heading for the town centre, where she manoeuvred through a couple of side streets until she reached the town square.

She lifted her bag, opened the car door and stepped out.

For a brief moment she stood still and got her bearings. It was four months since she had been in her hometown of Larvik – even though she had visited her father a few times, she had driven the quickest route to his house in Stavern. She took in the shabby, sad facades of the buildings and listened to the wind rippling through the beech woods that towered like a roof above the town. Her town. A couple of grey stone walls had acquired a few new tags from the town's graffiti artists and a new hairdresser's had appeared. Apart from that, everything was the same as before.

She slammed the car door behind her and walked to the square. A dark cloud drifted over the sun, fading her surroundings into shadow. All the same, something was different, she decided; it was as if an unfamiliar, sombre uneasiness hung over the streets.

She approached the barriers. An older woman emerged from the group of spectators at the end of the pedestrian street and walked towards her, a familiar face with a serious expression. Line took a moment or two to place her as the mother of one of the boys in her primary-school class, who worked in the shoe shop she and her mother used to frequent. Normally they would have said hello, smiled at each other and maybe stopped to exchange a word or two. Today they both contented themselves with a nod.

In the crowd of inquisitive onlookers, there were a number of people she had seen before, familiar faces that belonged to the town. A cold gust of wind ruffled her hair. The thought that the person who lay behind the police cordon might also be someone she knew sent shivers down her spine.

Garm Søbakken from *Østlandsposten* was also present. She had worked with him when she was employed at the local newspaper but he had not yet spotted her and she avoided approaching him.

On the steps beside the Narvesen kiosk she saw another man who must also be a journalist. He had a bulky camera slung over his shoulder and was talking intently into a mobile phone, but she had never seen him before. He was about her age, slim with broad shoulders and sandy hair. His fringe was spiked straight up like a shark's fin.

She turned her back on him and headed towards the barrier. Frank Kvastmo was standing on the other side. The burly policeman had worked at the station as long as her father had, but still in the uniformed branch. He stood with his hands clasped behind his back, rocking slightly on the soles of his feet. His eyes wandered then looked down as he moved a few paces, turned and marched back to his post.

Line had to hide a smile of satisfaction. This was going to go in her favour. Frank Kvastmo had always been Santa Claus at the Christmas parties held in the canteen at the police station when she was little. With continuous bursts of deep, ringing laughter, he would appear with a sack full of goody bags and dance in a circle around the Christmas tree with the children. On 17 May, Norway's National Day, he would be the barbecue chef, cooking the sausages and making sure the families of the staff had plenty to eat and drink. Kvastmo had no children of his own and always made a big fuss of his colleagues' youngsters.

Pinning her press badge to her lapel to avoid having to introduce herself as a *VG* journalist, she knew at the same time it would warn Kvastmo that she was on the job. She left her notepad and tape recorder in her bag.

Once she reached the barrier, she caught his eye and smiled. Frank Kvastmo gave her a broad smile in return as he approached her.

'Line Wisting!' he exclaimed, looking as if he wanted to draw her into a hug but was prevented from doing so by his police role and the present circumstances. 'Long time no see. You're looking great!'

'Thanks, you too.'

'I read about you all the time in the newspaper,' Kvastmo said. He glanced at her press badge. 'That is to say, the articles you've been writing. I think you're really good. Your father must be proud of you.'

Line thanked him again and peered into the distance, past the hefty policeman. In addition to the huge fire engines, a tarpaulin had been set up like a sail, blocking all view of the actual crime scene.

'Have you found the rest of her body?' she asked in an undertone so that no one in the vicinity could hear.

Frank Kvastmo shook his head, sighed wearily and adopted a serious expression, without realizing he had just confirmed that the victim was indeed female, that the body had been mutilated and that only part of it had been found. Line was already forming sentences in her head. *From what VG has learned, part of a young woman's body has been found.* This sentence was not quite right. She would have to work on it. Also, the age had not been confirmed. *Young woman* was too imprecise.

'Do you know who she is?' she went on to ask.

'No idea.'

'But someone must have reported her missing,' Line said. 'Her parents, for instance?'

'Well, they haven't done that yet,' Kvastmo told her. His voice had taken on a mournful tone.

'How old is she, then?'

Kvastmo shrugged. 'Twelve or thirteen.'

Line was ready with her next question but stood with her mouth open. The gruesome reality of the crime was suddenly dawning on her. She felt ill at the thought of a child's

26

body parts lying only metres away from her and that the killer could have stood exactly where she was now standing.

She dismissed these thoughts and focused on being professional.

'Is Kripos coming?' she asked, referring to the National Criminal Investigation Service.

'I doubt whether the police chief will request their support,' Kvastmo answered. 'We're meant to be self-sufficient these days.' As he glanced again at her press badge, a frown was etched on his tanned forehead. 'You can ask your father. He was here not long ago.'

Line replied with a nod, appreciating that she had reached the limit of questions she could ask.

'Are you going to write something about it?' Kvastmo asked, rocking on the soles of his feet again.

'That's my job,' Line said, with a disarming smile. 'But I'll have to talk to the prosecutor in charge of the case. Who is that?'

'Audun Vetti,' Kvastmo replied. 'He's the one you should talk to.'

'I'll do that,' Line assured him, taking her camera out of her shoulder bag. The newspaper had its own photographers and a couple of them couldn't be far away, but she never ventured out to cover a story without her own camera. 'I just need to take a couple of photos,' she said, excusing herself.

Frank Kvastmo nodded, adjusted his uniform cap and moved a few paces back so that they could both get on with their jobs. It was not her best picture. The sun had appeared again, casting shadows that made the contrast too stark but also giving the image drama and depth.

She drew back from the barriers, took out her press notebook and jotted down key words from the conversation. She had made use of the old police officer but was not sure he would realize that once it was in print. By the time he had the chance to read the paper, the same details would have been issued at a press conference and spread to other media outlets. But she would be the first journalist to reveal them.

Taking out her mobile phone, she rang the police station number and asked for Audun Vetti.

'Hello,' she said in her smoothest voice when he answered. 'This is Line Wisting.'

'Line,' he repeated. She could hear that he was busy but taking the time to speak to her when he recognized her name.

'I work for *VG* now,' she said, knowing him well enough to understand that he would have nothing against his name being mentioned on the front page of the country's largest newspaper.

'Yes,' was all he said in response.

Line decided to go on the offensive.

'The head of a young girl was found in the town square,' she summarized. 'You don't know who she is or where the rest of her body is.'

'We're in the very initial stages of the investigation,' Vetti countered.

'But her head has been severed?' Line pressed him.

'There will be a press conference at noon,' the police superintendent replied, after clearing his throat. 'We're going to ask the media for assistance to identify the victim.'

'What do you know about her?'

She heard him riffle through papers at the other end. 'At present, very little.'

'Approximate age?' Line ventured.

'She is probably in her early teens, and of minority ethnic origin.'

Line clamped the phone tightly under her chin as she took some notes. The information that the victim was from a minority ethnic background could give the story a different slant.

'What kind of minority ethnic?'

'It would be slightly dangerous to specify any particular country, but most likely Central Asia.'

Line pictured a map in her head: Afghanistan, Pakistan, Iran and several of the former Soviet states.

'A Muslim country?'

'We can't say anything . . .'

'But nobody fitting her description has been reported missing?'

'Not so far.'

'Could it have been a case of domestic violence?' Line asked, her thoughts racing. 'Since the family haven't reported her missing, I mean. Could they be the ones behind it?'

'As I said, we're at a very preliminary stage . . .'

'But is that a theory you're considering?'

'We don't know who she is or what kind of family relationships she had,' the superintendent reminded her, sounding discouraged. 'We have to keep all lines of inquiry open.'

Line nodded to herself. Her article was beginning to take shape in her mind, but she still lacked the detail of the wooden stake.

'Can you say anything about the circumstances of the discovery?' she asked, giving him little choice: 'About her head being placed on a stake?'

Silence ensued at the other end while the superintendent gave this some thought.

'We'll deal with that at the press conference,' he said finally.

Refusing to give up, Line asked, 'Isn't it true?'

'It's at twelve o'clock.'

She tried out a few more questions but soon realized that

29

the superintendent either knew nothing more about the case or wanted to withhold information to avoid the press conference being nothing but a presentation of old news.

She thanked him for talking to her and headed towards one of the vacant tables outside the Kaffebryggeriet café. At this time of year, the outdoor tables were reserved for smokers, but they afforded her a view of the cordoned area and a sense of still being able to keep up with events. She took the time to go to the counter inside to buy a latte before sitting down, taking her laptop out of her bag and starting to write.

Ten minutes later, she had seventy lines written, with the title *ONLY HEAD FOUND*. The introduction was short and punctuated with key phrases such as *macabre find*, *severed head*, *teenage girl* and *minority ethnic origin*. She had also suggested four subtitles: *Placed at night*, *Unknown victim*, *Search for more body parts* and *Challenging investigation*.

She read it through quickly, redrafted a couple of sentences and sent the text to the online editor before leaning back to take her first sip from the paper cup. It could be that the news editor would liven up the story by adding a few sentences along the lines of *Police have no leads* or that they were *fumbling in the dark*, but it would still be substantially her story.

A text message ticked in. A photographer and journalist from the local office in Skien had arrived. The hunt for fresh headlines had already started.

Typing had chilled her fingers, so she blew on them and rubbed them together before clicking to see what *Dagbladet* had come up with.

SEARCHING FOR KILLER AND HEADLESS TORSO was the headline. She frowned as she read on. The newspaper quoted Audun Vetti and used the same facts as she had. Details she had thought she alone knew. One or two of the sentences were actually more dramatic and more precise than her own wording. Swearing under her breath, she noted that the article had been published at 9.38 a.m. and had already been updated once. *Dagbladet* had beaten her by thirteen minutes.

Shifting her gaze back to the top of the article, she noted that the byline read *By Erik Thue*. She knew most of the *Dagbladet* reporters but she had not seen that name before.

'Fucking terrible business,' a voice behind her said.

Line turned to look up into the suntanned face of the journalist with the shark's fin hair.

'Erik Thue,' he said, stretching out his hand. 'You're Line Wisting, aren't you?'

He sat down before she had a chance to say a word, smiling expectantly, revealing a row of white teeth and fixing a pair of dark brown eyes on hers.

'*Dagbladet?*' she asked.

'*Dagbladet.no,*' he corrected her, with a nod in the direction of her laptop.

Line wanted to ask him what he was doing here and how he had managed to release his story before hers, but kept silent. Instead she glanced at her watch as if to excuse herself.

'I have to run,' she said, shutting her laptop.

7

Wisting had left the office door open a crack. He liked to hear the sound of footsteps hurrying past in the corridor beyond. It gave him a reassuring feeling that the machinery of the investigation was running smoothly.

The sight that had met him that morning was worse than anything he had seen before. This investigation would affect everyone working on it for a long time. It was the type of case that left very deep wounds.

He had followed the development of criminality over the past thirty years and did not like what he saw. Thoroughly negative elements were emerging, an explosion of drugs and violence. The investigative work was becoming increasingly complex and demanding. Alongside this, there was also a completely new kind of public to contend with. Almost ten per cent of the country's populace now came from an immigrant background. This meant the police were working more and more within cultures of which they had no significant knowledge. Investigations took place in environments to which they had no connection and where the police met with no trust. This made the work even more challenging and placed fresh demands on their methods and skills.

Picking up his pen, he gazed at the writing pad open on the desk in front of him. The left-hand column was filled with questions and the other side was blank.

His authority as head of investigations had always been anchored in personal abilities, experience and, not least, professional competence. Various aspects of multicultural society were unfamiliar to him, and the investigation team might well require expertise from outside their own ranks.

Various police reports began to come in, but none of them contained anything to lead them in any specific direction. The dog patrol had completed their search around the discovery site, but they had found nothing but litter and a dead seagull. A couple of tip-offs had been given concerning sightings of cars and individuals behaving oddly, but nothing that could be linked directly to the case.

The paved square where the crime had been committed had become a major nightmare for the business community. It was always deserted, even on Saturday mornings. The police could not expect anyone to have been there and seen something on a foggy night.

Wisting was used to cases in which the amount of information was so vast that it made the task of investigation impossible to grasp. Disparate pieces of information had to be organized and broken down into individual elements. Only then could the team make sense of them. This time, however, they had nothing. The incident they had begun to investigate was incomprehensible in itself. He had no idea where they should start looking for an explanation for what had occurred.

He put the plastic cup to his mouth and forced out yet another swig of the thin coffee. He knew how crucial it was for motivation to home in on a specific direction at an early point, to have some kind of lead, no matter how vague.

Espen Mortensen appeared at the door with a sheaf of loose sheets of paper under his arm that would hopefully contribute something new to the inquiry.

'Are you finished already?'

The crime-scene technician shook his head.

'Just a short break,' he replied. 'It's not every day we work within walking distance of the police station.' He sat down opposite Wisting and gave him a fleeting smile. 'I was keen to hear whether you'd made any progress in here. Have you found out who she might be?'

It was Wisting's turn to shake his head. 'How long has she been dead?' he asked.

'The murder took place last night,' Mortensen said firmly, taking a couple of photographs from under his arm and placing them on the desk between them. They had been printed out on the faulty printer in the workroom, but the details were still unpleasant and grotesque.

'As I said before, it's only been a matter of hours since she was beheaded,' he explained, pointing at the shredded neck in the picture. Brownish-black crusts of blood overlaid the smooth skin. 'Her internal brain temperature is thirty-one degrees.'

Wisting rolled his eyes and leaned back in his chair. 'Internal brain temperature?' he repeated.

'Standard procedure,' Mortensen clarified. 'The temperature of the body is measured with the aid of a thermometer inserted up through the nose. It doesn't have to go all the way up to . . .'

Wisting held up his hand to show that he did not need to hear the details. 'What does it tell us?' he asked instead.

'After death the body temperature drops by one to one and a half degrees an hour,' Mortensen said. 'Roughly speaking, that means the girl was killed around midnight.'

Wisting took a few notes and looked at the time. That was less than twelve hours ago. He had solved cases in which the killers had had a considerably lengthier advantage.

'Forensics will probably tell us more,' Mortensen continued. 'I'm not sure if the calculations can be done in the same way when we only have part of the body.'

Wisting waved that aside. 'Any trace of the perpetrator?'

Espen Mortensen nodded. 'I think that person may have a splinter.'

'Splinter?'

'The stake is fairly rough and jagged.' Mortensen pointed again at one of the pictures. 'I've found some traces of blood and skin around the middle of the stake. I think whoever was holding it has sustained a minor injury.'

Wisting felt encouraged by that thought. 'Enough for a DNA profile?'

'If it's the perpetrator's blood, we'll have his profile.'

Wisting drummed his pen on his notepad. 'Can you say anything more about the actual incident?'

Espen Mortensen pushed a close-up of the open wound towards Wisting. 'A great deal of coagulated blood,' he said, putting his finger on the image.

Wisting forced himself to look at it. 'And?'

'That means she was probably alive when she was beheaded. You could imagine she might have been killed in some other way and then the head removed from the body afterwards, but then the loss of blood would not have been so massive. The actual crime scene must look fucking horrendous.'

Wisting pushed the photograph away.

'I just read that beheading is a quick and almost pain-free way to die,' he said, indicating the browser on his computer screen. 'Death happens as a consequence of a tremendous drop in blood pressure and total lack of oxygen supply to the brain. Unconsciousness is normally immediate and the beheaded person is brain dead after only a few seconds, max.'

Espen Mortensen gathered up the photos. 'Beheading might not be the right word in our case. At least, it's not a clean cut,' he said. 'The surface of the wound is pretty ragged.'

'What does that mean?'

'It means I think whoever killed her used a saw and it wasn't particularly sharp.'

Wisting stood up and walked to the window. He was glad he was not the one who would have to speak at the press conference.

'What could she have done wrong?' he asked aloud, gazing out over the fjord, where the masts of two fishing boats were silhouetted at its mouth.

'She was only a child,' Mortensen answered quietly as he got to his feet. 'No matter what she had or hadn't done, she didn't deserve this.'

Wisting remained at the window, staring out.

'At the far edge of Citadelløya Island there's a small promontory called Kariodden,' he said, pointing to the fjord. 'You won't find the name on any map, and really it's only a bleak pile of stones with a couple of windswept pine trees. The fjord beyond it is full of shallows and people never go ashore there. But that little promontory bears witness to a gruesome old story.'

Espen Mortensen took a few steps towards him and they stood together, gazing out at the fjord.

'It is named after Kari Mathiasdatter,' Wisting went on. 'She was a poor young girl who lived at the beginning of the nineteenth century. She owned nothing more than the clothes she had on but her sister had married well and she got work as a servant on the farm belonging to her and her husband. She moved up into the attic and was given board and lodging in return for her labours. After eleven months she gave birth to a baby girl in secret. The baby lived for only ten minutes before Kari drowned her in a washtub, wrapped her in rags and went outside to bury her. She encountered her sister and had to confess what she had done. Her brother-in-law was the child's father. She killed the baby in desperation at the thought of the shame and punishment in store for her after having an illegitimate child. The judges unanimously agreed that she should lose her head and that her head should be placed on a stake to strike fear in others and provide a warning. It was planted out there on that promontory. It took only a fortnight for the gulls to hack her head to pieces, but the stake is still said to be out there.'

Wisting turned away and returned to his desk.

'What about the baby's father?' Mortensen asked.

'His name was Haldor Magnussen, and he escaped with a fine,' Wisting answered. He was about to add that the reason he knew the story was that Haldor Magnussen had been Ingrid's great-great-grandfather, but he decided against it. People around him had a tendency to feel embarrassed when he mentioned his dead wife.

Mortensen remained standing there for a while until he turned and moved towards the door. Then he stopped and asked: 'What did they do with the rest of her body?'

Wisting shrugged. 'The story says nothing about that.'

8

The usually spacious canteen had been rearranged as a make-
shift media briefing room in preparation for the press
conference. Wisting sat behind the table at the end of the room,
alongside Superintendent Audun Vetti and Chief Superintendent Eskild Anvik. His two colleagues were wearing stiff
uniforms and sat hunched over the table, leafing through their
folders.

Wisting watched as the room filled up. There were not
enough chairs. They were all talking over one another. The
room was cramped and the air was already becoming stuffy.

In the course of a few hours the town had been invaded
by members of the press. Sitting with all the cameras focused
on him made him feel uncomfortable and his hands were
clammy. His heart was beating faster and harder and his chest
felt constricted. Reaching his hand out for the glass on the
table, he drank deeply and felt the cold water clear his head.

The pressure that arose when what was defined as a major
news story exploded into the public arena was enormous. It
was like splitting a news atom, he thought. A colossal suppressed energy was released and moved in directions that
were difficult to predict. He already thought he could read
the fear of losing the battle for the latest news in the eyes of
the nearest journalists.

The major media outlets had already launched their own
independent, ambitious investigations. Equipped with a var-
ied array of techniques and tactics to outsmart sources and
witnesses, they searched out people with information and

knowledge. In the years Wisting had worked in the police, a journalist's role had changed from simply recording events to moving increasingly closer to situations and bringing readers in contact with people in distress and crisis. He pretty much understood that was how things were. Crime had become a social problem in its widest meaning. Following the process from the time the police arrived at a crime scene until the perpetrator was found guilty in court gave people an important insight into central aspects of society. In many ways, journalism was the glue that held society together, but crime reporters continually operated in a minefield where it was easy to take a wrong step. In a country that is praised with some justification for having a media with both high ethical standards and civilized behaviour, he more and more often encountered journalists who seemed to forget that press ethics also applied to the gathering of information and not simply to the dissemination of it. Far too often he had seen that the role of society's guard dog had morphed into that of a snapping hunting dog. Some slip-ups were perhaps only to be expected in the highly competitive field in which journalists worked, but it seemed as if ethical judgement was under pressure – with the steadily increasing number of media outlets and the concomitant stiff competition and demand for financial returns.

Wisting glanced at the clock. It was now one minute past twelve. Five hours had passed since the discovery of the body. They still had no idea of the identity of the victim. For the moment, the journalists had only the police as targets for their attack. He almost dreaded finding out who she was, at which point the race to uncover the victim's story would begin. Reporters would invade the personal lives of vulnerable people in a state of shock and grief, people who would be used without realizing the impact their statements would have.

Audun Vetti sat up straight in his seat, drew his chair closer to the table and theatrically cleared his throat. Silence settled over the room. All the camera lights were already red.

'My name is Audun Vetti,' the superintendent introduced himself, spelling out his name. 'I have here with me Chief Superintendent Eskild Anvik and Chief Inspector William Wisting.'

He paused for a few seconds before continuing.

'I can inform you that Vestfold police have launched an investigation into an apparently premeditated murder, committed in particularly aggravating circumstances by an unknown perpetrator.'

It crossed Wisting's mind that the sober wording of the legal text had seldom been more appropriate. He cast his eyes down as the superintendent gave an account of the background on the case, the details and circumstances already known to most of the assembled journalists.

The information that the severed head had been placed on a wooden stake triggered a tumult of camera flashes; it was a detail that added to the horror of the crime.

They had decided who would say what in advance of the meeting. Vetti wrapped up his contribution by stating that the victim had not yet been identified and handed over to Wisting. In this way, the superintendent avoided being the one to announce to the public that the investigation had not yet taken any specific shape or direction.

Wisting counted silently to three before he went ahead.

'We have no indication of the identity of the murder victim, as Superintendent Vetti has said,' he began, running his eyes over the audience. Suddenly he noticed Line at the very back of the room. Her hair was cut short and she now had a fringe that made her look more like her mother than ever.

A couple of photographers caught the anxiety that crossed

his face and blinded him with camera flashes. Like all the others in the room, Line must have had to change the plans she had made for the day, but he did not like the thought of them both working on the same case.

Clearing his throat, he looked down and found some key words on his notepad.

'This concerns a young woman from a minority ethnic background,' he explained.

They had agreed not to give a more detailed description. Age, height and weight were difficult to estimate. However, a limited description could constrain people from coming forward as witnesses.

'No one of this description has been reported missing and we ask anyone with possible information about the identity of the victim to make contact with the police.'

Adding some standard comments about the wide-ranging nature of the investigation, he gave a brief description of the discovery site and explained about the door-to-door inquiries and other general steps being taken before turning to Audun Vetti and nodding that he was handing back to him. The superintendent passed the baton to the chief superintendent, who gave an account of how the investigative work was organized, how well prepared the police district was for such a task, and ended by saying that so far there was no requirement for support from Kripos or any other external agencies.

Then the conference was opened up for questions. The first of these revolved around the age of the murder victim. The journalists tried to gain clarity on whether or not she was a child but had to content themselves with the information that the forensic examinations would provide more specific details the next day. These vague answers were followed up by a fresh round of questions that were not so dissimilar to the ones the investigators were asking themselves: where had the actual beheading taken place? Where could the rest of the body be located? And what could be the motive for such a crime?

After twenty-five minutes the superintendent finally drew a line under the press conference. Wisting got to his feet and rushed out the side door as Vetti stepped forward for television interviews.

9

At present the newspaper had two news teams working on the story as well as the online newspaper's crew on the ground. Line was teamed up with Morten Pludowski, who had come down from the editorial offices in Akersgata. He had brought a photographer who had set himself up at the square, waiting for the severed head or any other important evidence to be removed from the discovery site. Line and Morten P. sat on opposite sides of a café table.

Morten P. was a skinny, ungainly man in his mid-forties with a weather-beaten face, narrow shoulders and a long neck. He sported a beard and his black hair was far too long at the back. Line had said hello to him on a couple of occasions but knew him mostly by reputation. It was said that he had a special talent for reading police investigations and catching certain aspects the authorities were keen to keep hidden. He had worked as a crime reporter for a number of years and could have papered his office walls with front-page splashes carrying his byline.

His press pad was filling up with notes, thoughts and ideas while Line gave an account of the five hours she had been covering the story. He seemed interested, curious and in no way pompous or dissatisfied about having to work with a young temp. For all she knew, he could have requested to work with her. This was a story that could keep them going with front-page news for a long time to come. Although her father's position in charge of the inquiry could give the newspaper an advantage, it could also cause some conflicts over impartiality, exactly the dilemma she had been keen to put behind her when she had applied for posts outside the local area.

'I've spoken to Lynge,' she said, referring to the editor in charge of the news desk. 'We agreed that someone other than me should communicate with the police.'

Morten P.'s thin lips formed a good-natured smile.

'The local office will deal with that side of things,' he said. 'With stories like this they always find a crack for information to leak out. Some people always feel a stronger need to give information to the public than others. Just be aware that the most important thing for both us and the police right now is to find out who the victim is.' He put his finger on his laptop screen where all the reporters working on the story were logging in new information. 'The police superintendent says they are still considering whether or not to issue photos of her. Photos of the severed head. That tells us they don't have a handle on the case and reveals how desperate they are for details. We also need to be ready and willing to use unusual methods to get hold of her name. We want to tell her life story. It's short, but also probably one of the most powerful we've printed in a long time.' Morten P. lifted his coffee cup and leaned back in his chair. 'It's our job to let our readers meet the people affected by this tragedy, the ones with immediate experience of it. A young woman's murder will no longer be news by the time the newspapers are stacked up in the news stands tomorrow morning. It's the people *behind* the news we have to get hold of.'

Line cradled her cup in her hands.

'I'm writing a story about the woman who found the head, Vera Kvålsvik,' she told him, putting the cup down again without drinking. 'I've already spoken to her once and have arranged to meet her this afternoon.'

'That's likely to be the nearest we'll get to a victim or a relative for the moment,' Morten P. replied approvingly, but she could see that he was knitting his brows. They had to come up with something more substantial.

Line began to pack up her belongings.

'Have you heard of an online journalist on *Dagbladet* called Erik Thue?' she asked.

'I've seen the name and read some of his articles, but I don't know him personally,' Morten P. replied. 'It's my impression that he's one of these young online journalists who know a lot about the Internet and new technology but not so much about journalism, with no experience or commitment. It's a kind of fast-food journalism. Quick and easy delivery, but the stories are superficial, lacking any insight or perspective.'

Line smiled. She was familiar with the opinions some of the more experienced reporters held about online media. Just as the Internet was growing as a channel for news and online editors were hiring more personnel, printed newspaper sales were plummeting dramatically and staff cuts were being made. However, it seemed that many of her older colleagues preferred to take redundancy rather than change to a different branch of media.

Morten P. shut his laptop and looked at her.

'This could take a long time,' he said. 'I've booked a room at the Grand. Where do you plan to stay?'

Line had not considered staying at a hotel. 'I was thinking of staying at home,' she answered.

Morten P. revealed his crooked teeth in a broad smile.

10

Line returned to the crime scene. The press presence besieging the police cordon had increased considerably and she counted five camera teams and more than ten reporters. In the side streets she saw vans and minibuses with satellite antennae on their roofs, ready for broadcasts.

Frank Kvastmo was nowhere to be seen, but two younger officers she had never encountered before had taken up position inside the crime-scene tape that surrounded the area like some kind of perimeter barricade.

Garm Søbakken was still there. In the last three months she had spent at the local newspaper, they had shared the evening shifts. She had got to know him as a colleague who believed that leading-edge journalism was synonymous with close-ups of bloodstains on an asphalt road where yet another human being had become the victim of a road traffic accident. He lacked the inquiring mind and critical faculty necessary for the job.

Approaching him, she gave him a smile and said hello. 'Any news?' she asked once they had exchanged a few pleasantries.

Garm shook his head.

'They backed a van in behind the tarpaulin half an hour ago. Since then, nothing's happened.' He fished out a half-full pack of chewing gum from the pocket of his crumpled jacket, squeezed out three tabs and dropped them ostentatiously into his mouth, one by one. 'What are you working on?' he asked, without offering her any.

'The same as everybody else here,' she replied, looking around. 'Trying to find out what's happened.'

A stringer from TV 2 was preparing to make a broadcast.

'The online paper has been broadcasting directly from here via one of the web cameras since early this morning,' Garm explained. 'The server nearly collapsed.'

'Brilliant,' Line said with a smile, without mentioning that she had taken a look and seen those photos herself. 'Do you have footage from last night?'

Garm shook his head. 'The webcam footage isn't stored. The police have already –'

He broke off, lifting his camera and moving forward a few paces. The tarpaulin had been swept aside, provoking hectic activity among the press contingent. Garm's jaws were working furiously on his chewing gum. The freelancer from TV 2 was talking excitedly into his microphone, accompanied by a flurry of camera clicks. A white delivery van drove slowly out of the closed-off area. The opening in the tarpaulin screen briefly revealed three white-clad crime-scene technicians hunched over a table discussing something or other before the grey cloth dropped back into place again.

One of the young police officers lifted the tape to let the van pass through. At the same time a man approached, riding a bike, wearing a black leather jacket and a blue baseball cap. Bags hung on either side of the handlebars. The man stopped in front of the young policeman and was about to say something but was brusquely dismissed and waved aside.

The van passed through and the policeman allowed the crime-scene tape to fall back into place. The man on the bike asked a question of some kind but the officer merely shook his head and moved across to join his colleague.

The man shrugged, turned around and trundled the bike into a side street, where he disappeared into an entryway.

Line had recognized him, even though it was years since she had seen him. At school they had simply called him 'Danish Tommy'. He had moved here with his mother when Line was in Year 4 and they had been in the same class at school until Tommy had dropped out halfway through Year 9.

He had been a cold, indifferent boy who seemed a bit mysterious and dangerous, the kind of guy that many of the girls had somehow found very attractive.

He was not really the sort of person to chat to the police for no good reason. On the contrary, she assumed he had run into them often enough to prefer avoiding them. Did Danish Tommy have something he wanted to tell the young policeman?

Stepping away from the huddle of journalists, Line crossed the square and slipped into the entrance where Tommy had disappeared. Six mailboxes of different colours and sizes were lined up on the wall. Some of the names were scored out and new ones written in marker pen as the apartment block had acquired new tenants. After locating the name Tommy Kvanter on a white sticky label, she looked back and saw that the distance to the crime scene was less than forty metres.

There was an overpowering smell of decay in the backyard. Dark patches bloomed on the discoloured plaster, punctuated with sprayed graffiti. Rotting timber was peeling off the window frames and a row of overflowing rubbish bins stood at the far end. A dog lay dozing on an old mattress that must have been flung out of one of the windows higher up. Apart from that, the yard was tidy.

The bike was fastened with a chain to the wrought-iron rack beside the stone steps. The door bore traces of failed break-in attempts or kicks delivered in frustration because of the lack of doorbells or nameplates.

Line tugged the door handle and found it open. She stepped

into the lobby and spotted the same white sticky label bearing Tommy's name on the first door to her right. She knocked, received no answer and knocked again.

She heard someone inside, deliberate steps moving across the floor. A shadow slid in front of the peephole and a chain rattled before the door opened and Danish Tommy suddenly filled the doorway. He was still wearing his cap but had taken off his jacket and stood there in a tight white round-necked T-shirt that stretched around his upper arms. His angular face was unshaven and he had a pair of narrow glasses perched on his nose. He stood holding a bottle of beer and a motorbike magazine in one hand.

With a quizzical tilt of the head, he took off his reading glasses. His brown speckled eyes looked bemused as his lips formed a warm smile.

'Line,' he said with a chuckle. 'It's been a long time.'

She was about to say something, but Tommy stepped back a couple of paces and beckoned her in.

The apartment was very different from what the grey walls of the exterior had suggested. The hallway was bright and cheerful with a tiled floor and the small living room beyond was furnished in a style that made the room seem airy. It was all tidy and clean. The walls were painted a pleasant shade of beige and the curtains, in a slightly deeper colour, were drawn all the way back, making the room seem wider than it actually was. Tommy sat down on a roomy settee and motioned for her to sit in an armchair, as if it was nothing out of the ordinary for an old classmate he had not seen for ten years to come knocking on his door. Between them, an old chest served as a coffee table. He set down his beer, put the magazine beside him on the settee and, taking off his cap, ran his hand through his black hair. He looked unkempt but there was a lovely scent, not too strong, of masculine aftershave wafting through the air around him. Giving her a playful look, he seemed totally relaxed. For the first time she realized what her friends had seen in him in their schooldays.

'Can I offer you anything?' he asked. Some of the Danish accent still clung to his words to soften his voice.

Line shook her head. 'I was in the square,' she explained. 'I thought I recognized you.'

With a smile, he reached out for a pack of tobacco on the window ledge. His sinewy arm was covered in tattoos. The muscles in his stomach and chest were outlined against the thin fabric of his T-shirt.

'Do you mind?' he asked, holding the tobacco pack up to her with a question in his eyes. 'Do you smoke?'

'No, but it doesn't bother me.'

Tommy took out a cigarette paper and began to scatter the tobacco in it. He had a straight scar, around the size of a matchstick, under his left eye. A reminder of a chequered past etched on his face, she thought.

'How are things with Thomas?' he asked.

Line's thoughts turned to her twin brother. He and Tommy had not seen eye to eye and had always been at each other's throats.

'He's in Afghanistan,' she replied. 'Flies a helicopter for NATO.' All at once she realized that she missed her brother. 'Have you been in the military?' she added.

Tommy Kvanter shook his head.

'I've read a lot of what you've written,' he said, changing the subject. 'Can't say I envy you your job. Prying into other people's private lives, into death and misery and personal tragedies.' Shrugging, he shot her a smile. 'But what can I say? I do like reading about it all, of course.'

She thought for a minute of saying something but decided to leave it.

'I really thought you'd become a lawyer or something like that,' he went on. 'You seemed so prim and proper.'

'Do you think you might need one?' The question slipped out without thinking.

'I have at times,' he answered, but the smile was still in place. 'I moved back to Denmark when I was sixteen. That didn't go so well. I've been living here for two years now.'

'What work do you do?' Line asked.

'Chef,' he replied, licking the cigarette paper. 'On board a Danish factory trawler up near East Greenland,' he added. 'We fish for prawns. Thirty tonnes every twenty-four hours. Fourteen days on, fourteen days off.'

'Greenland prawns?' she asked with a smile, thinking of the five-kilo frozen cartons in the supermarkets.

'They're fresher than the prawns you buy down at the quayside,' he claimed, lighting his cigarette. 'They're boiled as soon as they're caught. Then they're shock-frozen before being packed and put into deep-freeze storage on board. The fresh prawns you buy locally here are usually at least twelve hours old. Our prawns are fresh from the sea when you defrost them in the kitchen at home.'

'I wasn't complaining,' she said, and laughed.

'The water in Arctic regions is crystal clear,' Tommy continued. 'Clean, cold and nutritious. The prawns grow slowly and become extra large and also develop top-quality consistency and taste.'

'You should be in the marketing department,' Line suggested.

'I wouldn't be any use.' Tommy dismissed the idea, letting the smoke leak out through his nostrils. 'I can't stand prawns. They're chewy and horrible.'

Line put back her head and laughed. Laughing along with her, he picked a speck of tobacco from his tongue.

'You're the closest neighbour,' Line said, growing serious again. Her eyes moved to the window overlooking the square. 'Did you see or hear anything last night?'

Tommy took another drag, holding in the smoke before exhaling slowly. He grew reflective as he nipped off the burning tip with his fingers.

'Yes,' was his terse response, before putting the cigarette butt down into an empty ashtray.

Line was unsure whether he was confirming that he lived close to the crime scene or that he knew something about the incident. She leaned forward to demonstrate how keen she was to hear more.

'I thought I should tell one of the police officers out there, but they didn't seem very interested.' He smiled again. 'Maybe that will change if they read about it in *Verdens Gang*.'

'What was it you wanted to say?'

Tommy ran his hand over the lid of the chest a couple of times, as if wiping off some dust before he reached his bottle of beer.

'That I saw something,' he replied before taking a swig.

Line could already picture how the duty editor at the news desk would word the headline: *Eyewitness tried to alert police*. Producing her press notebook, she stared at him incredulously.

Tommy took another drink and swallowed. 'I woke at 6.03 a.m.' He nodded towards a door at the end of the living room. 'I have a clock radio with big red numbers on the bedside table,' he explained. 'There was a car in the backyard. I heard a couple of doors slam before it went quiet. A few minutes passed and I had almost fallen asleep again when they were back. I got up and peeked out from under the roller blind. You see, last time I was home, someone stole my bike. It was locked up beside the stairs, but they just cut the lock right off.'

Line noted some key words in her notebook. Quick quotes that only she would understand.

'There were two men. Foreigners. They got into a car and reversed out. They weren't speaking Norwegian or Danish. Dark-skinned. From Syria or Turkey or somewhere like that. They had beards.'

'What type of car was it?'

'An old Toyota Carina estate. White. I've never seen it or the two men here before. I thought something seemed suspicious, so I looked at the registration plate.'

'You have the number?'

Tommy held up his palm to her as if he wanted to warn her about something.

'Well, I did, but I didn't write it down. Just glanced at it and thought I'd be able to remember it later, but then I fell asleep again and it totally slipped my mind.'

Line became uncertain. This observation could be terribly important to the police. Tommy ought to speak to an investigator who could use the appropriate techniques to prompt him to remember and maybe even recreate the memory of the car registration number. If she asked too many questions, she risked influencing him and planting false memories in his mind.

'But it wasn't a Norwegian numberplate,' Tommy added, putting the bottle to his mouth again. 'Three numbers and three letters.'

'Swedish?' Line suggested.

'Or Finnish, Estonian, even Lithuanian.'

Line bit her bottom lip and cocked her head. 'Wasn't it really dark and foggy outside?' she asked.

'There are two lamp posts out in the yard,' he said, his smile showing his white teeth, as if he appreciated her scepticism and criticism. 'I don't think the fog had found its way into that corner. The buildings here are almost hermetically sealed and the air is usually completely still. In summer it gets boiling hot.'

'What makes you think they had anything to do with the severed head in the square?'

'It's just an observation, something out of the ordinary, and it wouldn't have meant anything if it hadn't been for the blood.'

She stared at him. 'Blood?'

He put down the bottle and got to his feet. 'Come with me,' he said, heading for the door.

Line followed him out into the backyard. Tommy moved towards one of the bins, lifted the lid and took out two plastic bags. Then he nodded his head, telling her to look down into the container.

The rubbish stank to high heaven, but Line bent over and peered down. There was a white rag on top, covered in blood.

'It was lying in the middle of the yard here when I went out this morning,' he explained. 'I hadn't heard the news then. I picked it up and tossed it into the bin. It must have fallen out of the car or something.'

He found a stick and flipped the rag over. Only then did she see that it was a T-shirt. The sight of it made her go cold.

11

Wisting sat with the photo of the severed head in his hands. Every detail of the child's face was becoming seared into his brain. The clear green eyes had streaks of brown that ran out like thin threads from the small pupils. On the right side of her nose she had a small scar from a wound that had not healed properly, and above the right-hand corner of her mouth she had a tiny birthmark. There were two more under her chin. Her ears were close set with a few curling, downy hairs. Her lips were dry and cracked, but the rest of her complexion looked smooth and soft even though it was splattered with dried blood.

'We have to think about publishing this photo of her,' Audun Vetti said. He was seated in Wisting's office, holding the chair's armrests tightly, as if preparing for an important leap. 'Unusual cases force the use of unusual methods.'

Torunn Borg stood leaning against a bookcase lined with ring binders in different colours. Although she said nothing, she was shaking her head.

'That's not going to happen,' Wisting said, putting down the photograph. 'Maybe we can use an illustrator if we know no more by the end of the day, but we're not going to publish photos of a desecrated child's body. It might be that some journalist or other thinks it's a good idea, but no newspaper editor will sanction printing it. I'm not sure whether we should even let all our investigators see her.' He picked up the picture from his desk and stuffed it into the folder along with the other photos from the discovery site. 'This would give anyone sleepless nights. I don't want to be responsible for that.'

'But the clock is ticking,' the superintendent objected. 'The first twenty-four hours are crucial. The perpetrators are getting further and further ahead of us.'

Wisting did not need to be reminded that they were in a race against time. Six hours had passed since the severed head had been found, but experience had taught him that by the time six more had elapsed a great deal could have taken place.

'She can't be all alone in the world,' Wisting said with a sigh. 'She must have had people around her. Why would anyone not report a family member missing?'

'Shame?' Torunn Borg suggested. 'If, for example, she had a boyfriend from another culture and her family's the reactionary type. Or if she's sullied the family honour in some way.' She paused for a few seconds. 'Then maybe they would hesitate to report it if she disappeared suddenly?'

'Well, at least if they were the ones behind it,' Vetti agreed. 'They'd feel that the girl has received her rightful punishment for breaking with her family and their traditions.'

Wisting ran his hand through his hair. They knew far too little about the Muslim religion, the various cultures of Muslims globally and the traditions adhered to by a community of more than a billion followers. To them, it was an unfamiliar landscape in which they perceived parental authority and patriarchal views to be commonplace, developed over generations. Women's subordination to men was assumed to be part of tradition and religion, he knew. Indeed it formed part of the entire foundation of society and losing control over a female family member's choice of values and lifestyle could be considered a violation of the family's honour. The honour killings that took place as a result were not unknown to the

Norwegian police and, paradoxically enough, in tandem with successful integration came increasing numbers of young women exposed to danger. The more individual freedom girls demanded – such as wanting to drive or obtain an education – the more extreme the actions in response could well become. A great deal suggested this could be what they were facing here.

He glanced up at Torunn Borg.

'We have to get in touch with the schools,' he said. 'If the family doesn't report her missing, we might be able to find her through the attendance registers.' He cast his eyes down. 'Somewhere today there is an empty desk.'

'Are we going to go with the honour killing theory, then?' the superintendent asked. He pushed his hands down on the armrests as he rose from the seat.

Wisting sat shaking his head. Locking on to one particular theory early in an investigation was a bad move, a trap into which many investigation leaders had fallen. They caught hold of something that pointed in a specific direction and all subsequent investigation was directed along that route. Every other angle was disregarded in the hope of a speedy solution. Even though it often turned out to be the case that what lay closest to hand was correct, you could not behave as if that was always true. The world was full of criminals who had got away with their crimes because of the one-track-minds of the police.

'There are other possibilities,' he said. 'She could potentially be the victim of some kind of human trafficking.'

'That won't make the investigation any easier,' Torunn Borg commented.

Wisting nodded. They had little understanding of the potential dimensions of that area of criminality.

Only on one previous occasion had he been faced with a

case that had turned out to involve human trafficking, when two Nigerian women had been staying at a camping cabin in the area. The investigation had shown that they were mixed up in sex work and the Oslo police had arrested a minor, but he was not one of the main players behind it. The girls had also been sex workers in their homeland but had been recruited by a cousin to work for more money abroad.

False promises of a better life had persuaded them to cross land borders. They had believed they would be working in the hotel and restaurant industry as domestic workers or even models and had had no idea that threats, violence, and the loss of liberty and any rights over their own bodies would become part of their daily lives. They were held in an iron grip of physical and psychological terror. Beaten, raped, locked up and starved until they fell into line for their captors. In the end they were so cowed by shame and desperation (as well as fear of reprisals on their children and families at home) that they did not dare to break out of the situation. Like modern slaves, they worked to repay the debt forced on them by a human trafficking agent to cover the cost of transporting them and expenses for their stay.

The case had given him insight into a type of criminality that was more extensive than he had been prepared for. He had seen how human trafficking had become a global, transfrontier problem and often a factor in other kinds of serious organized crime, such as the trade in narcotics and firearms. The opportunity for profit was huge, and most of the victims were in a vulnerable situation because of poverty and oppression. The networks were usually based abroad and very difficult to tackle.

It had scared him to see how criminals used the traditionally weak position some women had in their homelands, and how the combination of unemployment and lack of education made it easy for them to be forced into prostitution. In countries where there were huge social differences and widespread poverty, women and children were the losers in the fight for work and money and became easy victims. Being forced into the sex industry was perhaps the worst type of human trafficking but there were also other types of forced labour. The victims could be used for housework, in the restaurant trade, in cleaning agencies, in agriculture, for begging, street sales, theft, drugs activity and even organ donation.

Wisting put his pen down on his notepad. 'We'll have to find out who is at the centre of trafficking and procurement of the illegal workforce in the whole Østland region,' he said.

The others nodded. Three heavy knocks on the door interrupted any further discussion. Jan Osther put his head round the door.

'Vera Kvålsvik is here. The woman who found the head. You wanted to speak to her?'

12

He had thought her name sounded familiar but had been unable to place her. Now that she was standing in front of him, he recognized her at once. The town was not so large that he did not occasionally find himself sitting opposite people he had once known and who had at one time meant something to him but with the passage of time had slipped from his memory.

Vera Kvålsvik was a year younger than him. They had grown up in the sixties in the same street in the part of Stavern called Fjerdingen. There had been some kind of childhood romance between them that had ended when Vera had moved to Larvik with her parents. She had acquired the Kvålsvik name when she married before the age of twenty. He had seen her now and then, sometimes at a shopping centre, and a couple of times her picture was in the local paper, but he had not spoken to her for more than thirty years.

She had moved in the late summer of 1971, when Wisting was fourteen. When he saw her now, the warm days of that last summer came alive for him. He recalled how they had lain on their backs in the tall grass, gazing at the clouds that drifted far too quickly across the blue skies. They had sat on warm stone steps and shared their thoughts of a future together that had come to nothing.

'It's been a while, hasn't it?' Wisting said, smiling. He stood up to greet her. It felt completely natural to put his arms around her and give her a hug. Then he took a step back and looked at her. There were fine wrinkles around her eyes that became more obvious when she smiled. She was wearing a charcoal-grey pinstriped jacket, matching trousers and a white blouse.

'I'd prefer to be seeing you under different circumstances,' she said softly.

With a nod, Wisting reached out for the coffee pot on the desk.

'Coffee?' he asked invitingly as he produced two paper cups from the stack.

She thanked him and sat down. 'Sorry to hear about your wife,' she said. 'So senseless and unfair.'

Wisting frowned. It was more than two years since Ingrid had died and he rarely received condolences these days.

'What about you?' he asked, pouring the coffee.

'Divorced,' she told him. 'It was seven years ago. We separated when the children grew up. I have a small apartment in Olavsgate and can walk to work from there.'

Sitting down, Wisting leafed through to a blank page in his notepad and explained the formal aspects of a witness interview.

They did not know what time of night the head had been placed in the square and he had little faith that Vera Kvålsvik might have seen anything significant in the course of her six-hundred-metre walk through the fog, but for the moment she was the only witness they had.

'Tell me about the fog,' Wisting said, starting with the external circumstances to set the wheels turning in her mind and facilitate the thought processes that might lead to accurate recall of the scene.

'It was thick,' Vera Kvålsvik explained. 'Almost impenetrable. I could only just make out the houses on the other side of the street when I went out.'

Wisting made a few notes to let her see that he was listening and paying attention.

'I don't like fog.' She shifted in her seat, as if the very thought of it made her feel uncomfortable. 'I've read about it somewhere. It's called nebulaphobia. Some folk are scared of spiders or heights. I don't like fog.'

Wisting was reluctant to disturb the mental process that had begun. Instead of asking questions, he leaned back to give her time. Remembering was hard work. It demanded concentration.

'Usually I take about eight minutes to get to work, but today I walked a bit faster.' She put the cup to her lips, drank and set the cup down carefully before continuing: 'Suddenly she was just there. Right in front of me. A big, round head without a body. Staring at me with two sad eyes.'

Her voice had become unsteady. The muscles in her throat were working. She turned her gaze away and swallowed audibly. Wisting could see how afraid she was. What she had experienced that morning would affect her for the rest of her life.

'I screamed,' she said suddenly, as if she wanted to move on. 'Staggered to the shop. A man came and I managed to tell him what had happened. He helped me into the shop and sat me down on a chair before he went out to see for himself. I found the phone and called you. When the man came back, I handed him the phone.'

Wisting thumbed through his papers to find the printout of the statement given by the man who had come to her aid. He had been on his way to his work at the Farris factory and had looked after Vera Kvålsvik, just as she had told him. The report contained nothing of any further interest.

'Did you notice anything else?' Wisting asked. 'Did you see or hear anything?'

'The crows,' Vera answered in a quiet voice. 'They were flying low. I could hear their wings beating and saw that they were making a racket about something.'

'Anything else?'

'Only the usual noises. A dog barking. A car starting up and driving off. All the noises become so extreme in the fog. Amplified, you know.'

Wisting leaned forward. There was a difference between listening and hearing. Listening demanded both attention and concentration. It was a skill he had learned through years of being an investigator.

'A car?' he repeated, sensing an opportunity to stir something.

She nodded, about to say something, but all at once a different expression came over her face.

'There was another car too,' she said. 'Before I arrived at the square. At the Nansetgata crossroads. It came from further down.'

Wisting settled into a sympathetic pose, moving closer and listening.

'I heard it first and moved out of the way across the pavement. Then it emerged from the fog, drove past and continued up the street.'

'Tell me about the car,' he said, encouraging her with an open question.

'I turned to look at it,' she explained. 'It was driving fast – at least, it seemed fast in the poor visibility.'

Wisting wanted to interrupt with a question but held back to avoid disturbing her train of thought. Vera Kvålsvik stared past him at the wall, as if she could picture the whole scene again in her mind's eye.

'There were two people in it,' she went on. 'I saw the backs of their heads. It was white, some kind of estate car.'

'Old?'

She nodded. 'A bit bashed and dented, I think. One of the side mirrors was hanging off.'

'Which side?'

'The right,' she answered eagerly before heaving a sigh: 'But so many cars look the same these days.'

Wisting made no comment. It could be something to work on. At any rate, he was satisfied. Vera Kvålsvik had told him more than she realized she had seen. That had been his goal; that was always his goal. He asked a few supplementary and verification questions before ending the interview. He accompanied her to the door and stood watching as she left. The path through life from the time they had known each other had been long and twisting. Shaking off the thought, he disappeared back into his office.

13

The old timber house at Scheensveien 11 was one of the few residences spared when the motorway traffic was diverted to a bridge crossing the Farris river, the railway and the old road network.

The house was tucked between a chemical works engaged in the vulcanization of rubber and the exit road that led traffic from the E18 into Larvik. It had two storeys and was covered in ochre-coloured fibre-cement panels that had become grubby from exhaust fumes and road dust. The garden was overgrown with weeds and shrubs.

Parking in front of a primitively constructed carport, Wisting stepped out of the car and squinted at the house. Cato Dalen, pulling the curtain aside, looked back at him from the kitchen window. His head was shaved and he had a red goatee beard.

Each country for its own people was the slogan used by the far-right nationalist group of which the man in the window was the leader. The words were printed in red-and-black letters on his white T-shirt.

Wisting had no faith in this lead. The Patriotic Front had between twenty and thirty members countrywide. Admittedly, they needed publicity, but the idea that they were responsible for one of the most ruthless murders in the history of Norwegian crime was something that made no sense to him. But the coincidence of the timing, on the anniversary of Kristallnacht, was still reverberating through the investigation and the possibility of a racist motive was the first thing they had to check out.

Cato Dalen was known as a loner who was introverted and unwilling to communicate or cooperate with the authorities. However, Wisting had established some kind of trust with him: he was not judgemental but took time to listen to the man's thoughts and opinions. This was not special treatment he reserved for Cato Dalen. Wisting had listened with equal patience to young men spouting obvious lies as they tried to wriggle out of their guilt and tough men of violence who showed no regret for any of their brutal actions.

He had always maintained respect for individuals. This allowed him to put his own prejudices aside and place himself in other people's shoes, even if they were liars or killers. It helped him get closer to the mindset of a murderer and often resulted in a confession.

Opening the door to him, Cato Dalen greeted him with a nod and ushered him into a combined living room and workroom. As it faced west, the afternoon sun cast dancing shadows on the wall from a bare oak tree outside.

Cato Dalen took a seat behind a massive desk of dark wood and the glow from a computer screen lit up his pale face. The wall behind him was dominated by a two-metre-long floor-to-ceiling bookcase filled with a mixture of literature, biographies, history books, non-fiction titles and ring binders. It appeared to be a well-used selection of books, with some thrust in here and there with no obvious system. Many volumes lay out, open and with sections underlined and comments in the margins.

Wisting sat down in the chair opposite him. This was a strange feeling, sitting on the other side of the desk. When he took out his notepad, he immediately felt more at ease.

'I thought you would come,' Cato Dalen said. 'You could

have saved yourself the trip. We fight our battle and do what we can to prevent the growth of Islam in Norway, but that battle doesn't include the decapitation of Muslim girls. I know nothing about this.'

Wisting fixed his eyes on the man before him, who made no attempt to avoid his gaze.

'If nothing else, you must know a thing or two about Sharia laws and Muslim methods of punishment,' Wisting said, leaning forward to create an atmosphere of confidentiality and trust.

The man, who regarded himself as the country's foremost freedom fighter, smiled.

'It sounds as if you've turned your investigation on to the right track,' he said. 'The mass immigration of foreigners – including Muslims – is a threat to our country. They are Europe's most dangerous enemies.' He folded his hands on his lap. 'Islam is incompatible with our values, customs and cultural heritage. It's not a religion but a political ideology that has the express aim of gaining control of the world. All statistics show that we're only talking about a few generations before ethnic Norwegians will be the minority here in this country. But we don't kill children.'

Wisting had his own objections to and comments to make on Cato Dalen's view of immigration but said nothing. He merely nodded, almost imperceptibly, as if taking note of the other man's opinions. An interview was like building a bridge between two individuals.

'Do you know what night it was last night?' he asked instead.

Cato Dalen's eyes narrowed before he sat up straight and cleared his throat.

'Eighteen months ago, a bunch of teenagers in Vestland borrowed an old saloon rifle from one of their fathers, without asking,' he said. 'They shot a whole box of ammunition and then put the rifle back. Four of the bullets had gone through the undergrowth to a centre for asylum seekers on the other side. A Somalian man was shot in the leg. You must remember it; it was in all the news broadcasts at the time. The shots were fired on 20 April. I didn't think anything of it then, but that day was the 118th anniversary of Hitler's birth. It was blown up into an instance of dreadful hate crime against immigrants. Twelve days later, the police tracked down the boys. It turned out that they were from Syria and Iran.'

Cato Dalen smiled as he leaned back in his chair.

'You didn't answer my question,' Wisting challenged him.

'Of course I know what night we're talking about,' Dalen snorted. Getting to his feet, he crossed to the bookshelves behind him, took out a book and threw it down on the desk in front of Wisting. *Kristallnacht*, Wisting read. *By Ingrid Weckert*.

'You should read this,' he said. 'Kristallnacht was a Jewish-Communist black-flag operation. Jews are known for hating others for their own fate.' He sat down again. 'From 1926 to 1939, Poland was a fascist military dictatorship where Jews were persecuted. Many of them fled. One of them was a workshy, confused and bitter Jewish boy by the name of Herschel Grynszpan. He was taken in by relatives in Paris and became active in a Jewish action group that declared war on Germany in 1933. On 7 November 1938, Grynszpan entered the German embassy in Paris and shot the diplomat Ernst vom Rath five times. In the days that followed, Jewish provocateurs in disguise caused riots in a number of locations in Germany and Austria. They ransacked their own places and caused the situation to run completely out of control of the authorities. Kristallnacht was a Jewish operation with the aim of tarnishing Germany internationally, and the Jews

68

succeeded thanks to the control they exerted over the media. The same media control that keeps these Jewish lies alive to this day.'

Wisting looked at the man facing him. The racist hatred lay deep within him and overshadowed all rational thought and action.

'Where were you last night?' he asked instead of passing comment.

Cato Dalen stroked his chin and tugged at the point of his beard. 'Mona!' he shouted, canting his head a little.

No one answered and Dalen shouted again.

A young woman came stumbling out of the adjoining room, sweeping her tousled hair back from her face as she squinted at them with sleepy eyes. She was wearing a white T-shirt with a Donald Duck motif emblazoned on the chest and nothing else. The T-shirt reached only just below her hips.

'Tell the policeman where I was last night,' Cato said.

The girl looked at them in confusion. 'Were you some-where last night?' she asked, scratching her thigh.

Cato Dalen turned back to face Wisting. 'I was at home,' he said, glancing up at his girlfriend. 'Wasn't I?'

It looked as if it had finally occurred to the girl what this was all about. She nodded enthusiastically. 'He was lying beside me all night long,' she assured Wisting.

Cato Dalen stood up, moved towards her and put an arm around her shoulders.

'In the West, women are free and independent individuals,' he said, bundling her off to the bedroom again. 'That's not the case in Muslim countries. According to the Koran, women are the property of men. Honour killings, violence and the subjugation of women are everyday events and women become victims of extreme forms of punishment such as whipping, stoning and beheading.'

'We punished criminals in that same way only 150 years ago,' Wisting protested.

'Fortunately we managed to develop our society and move away from that stage,' Cato Dalen countered.

Wisting let his eyes dwell on him, wondering whether they really had moved on. Then he snapped his notepad shut to mark that his visit was over. At that very moment the living-room window exploded in a shower of broken glass.

14

Wisting dived to the floor. He took his hands from his face and looked up at the smashed window. Outside, a black bird wheeled around beneath the hazy clouds. The sound of car tyres gripping asphalt and spinning away reached him before silence fell, leaving only the rhythmic hum of motorway traffic in the background.

Cato Dalen lay on the floor on the opposite side of the desk. He sprang to his feet, ran his hand over his shaved head and moved across to the window. The shattered glass crunched under his feet.

The girl in the Donald Duck T-shirt popped her head round the bedroom door, an even more confused expression on her face than last time.

Wisting got up, brushing the dust of the living-room floor from his trousers. On the other side of the room, beneath the bookcase, he saw a red brick with a note tied to it with string. Wisting left it there and crossed to the window. Two black tyre tracks in the street below were the only traces to be seen of the perpetrators.

'Cowards,' Cato Dalen said, turning round. 'They don't dare to meet us to discuss our arguments and reasoning but launch pathetic attacks instead.'

'Do you know who it was?'

Cato Dalen answered with a shrug before moving towards the brick. Wisting warned him not to touch it, thinking of fingerprints, but he was too late. Cato tore off the string and grabbed the note. The girl picked her way across the room and, curious, leaned forward to take a look.

'Neimen,' she read out.

Cato Dalen threw the note down on the desk. Wisting came over and looked at it. The letters were big and clumsy, but the girl had misread it. *Nemein* was what it said.

He gave Cato Dalen a questioning look.

'It's Latin,' he explained. 'It means something like *give what's fitting*. It has some connection with Nemesis and Greek mythology.'

The vengeful goddess of reprisals and punishment, thought Wisting.

'This isn't the first time?'

Shaking his head, Cato Dalen lifted a Latin phrase book from the desk and pushed it back into a space on the bookshelf.

'There have been a few letters,' he explained, flopping down on the chair. 'It's a so-called anti-fascist action group that has chosen us as their opponents with the aim of fighting us both ideologically and physically. They describe themselves as a militant extra-parliamentary left-wing movement.'

'Do you have the letters?'

'They're archived,' Cato Dalen said, laughing.

Wisting gave him a stern look to prompt him to explain what was so funny.

'Your colleagues in the security service spend lots of man hours keeping our folk under surveillance, but I think this is the first time in years that anyone from the police has shown any interest whatsoever in the left-wing radical activist network.'

Wisting remained silent, reflecting that what had just happened was exactly what they had long feared. To a certain extent the police kept a watchful eye on right-wing extremists and did not regard them as a specific danger to national security. A confrontation with extremists on the left could, however, rapidly develop into a vicious cycle.

The radical camps had been smouldering for a long time. Extremist political forces on the right were blamed for systematically building, over a long period of years, a hostile image of asylum seekers, immigrants and refugees by over-dramatizing the criminality among these groups and stirring up an exaggerated fear of terrorism. This had created a climate that provided fertile soil for racist action and violence. It was far from surprising that a counter-attack should come and that the opposing forces would turn against each other. There were extremists in both camps and a more than likely racially motivated murder would scarcely be met with letters to the editor and torchlight processions.

'I'll send some of our people to take a look at this,' Wisting said, using his mobile to call in the incident report. He was promised that a local patrol car would drive over and take care of things. Just as he hung up, his phone rang. The display told him it was Line. This was a phone call he had known would come, but he was not looking forward to it. This case would drive a wedge between them. He could give her no information.

Answering, he listened for forty seconds to what his daughter had to tell him. Then he excused himself to Cato Dalen and dashed out to his car.

15

Wisting ducked under the tape that closed off the narrow entryway as the press corps bombarded him with questions. The place was buzzing with speculation and rumour that a body had been found and an arrest made.

At the far end of the backyard, a crime-scene technician in white overalls was perched on a stepladder. His camera lens was directed down into a rubbish bin.

A journalist had been given permission to wait inside the police cordon. He saw that it was Line, leaning against the wall of the building, out of sight of her colleagues, talking on a mobile phone. She ended her call and flashed him a quick smile. He nodded his head in response.

'Hi,' Wisting said with a smile. He felt uncomfortable with the situation and was not entirely sure how to tackle it. 'How's it going?' he asked.

'Fine, I've given Hammer my statement,' she said, motioning towards the broad-shouldered policeman in plain clothes who was standing with a folder tucked under his arm. 'I think I have permission to leave.'

'I'm sure you have,' Wisting replied. 'At least I know where I can get hold of you if necessary.'

'When will you be home?' she asked.

'Late,' he answered, feeling a lump settle in his chest. He had looked forward to a break from his solitary existence, spending a long evening with Line on the other side of the coffee table in the living room at home. 'What about you?'

'Probably the same, I think. I have a key.'

Her phone began ringing and she dug it out of her bag. Wisting moved across to Nils Hammer.

'Tell me about it,' he said.

'Well, there's not much more to say than what you already know,' Hammer said, moving towards the rubbish bin. 'Or what you can see for yourself.'

Wisting followed him and looked down into the bin.

'A white T-shirt, Manswear brand, size XL,' he said, using his pen to point at the neckband. 'Well used, dirty and stained with blood.'

'So it's not hers,' Wisting concluded.

'No, and it doesn't necessarily have anything to do with our case, but it may be linked to the observation made by the woman from the bookshop of a white car in Nansetgata.'

Wisting turned to face the man in the white overalls.

'Anything else?'

The crime-scene technician, who had come from one of the other police stations to assist, shook his head.

'I've examined the yard here for tyre tracks and footprints, but it's absolutely pointless,' he said. 'We'll take the T-shirt to Forensics, along with the head, sometime this evening. The DNA results should take no more than a day or two.'

Wisting thanked him and turned to Hammer again: 'How can *VG* manage to find a bloody T-shirt forty metres away from the scene before we do?'

Hammer took out his folder, pulled out a bundle of notes and riffled through them until he found what he was looking for.

'We did some door-knocking in this building at eleven thirty this morning. Only Mrs Larsen in apartment C and a young girl in E were at home,' he explained before glancing up again. 'Even if they'd all been at home when we called in, I can imagine that some of them wouldn't be particularly keen to talk to the police.'

Wisting's eyes narrowed. 'What do you mean?'

Hammer leafed through the papers again. Behind him, the crime-scene investigators began to empty the bins in their search for other evidence.

'It was Tommy Kvanter who found the T-shirt.'

'The Danish guy?' Wisting asked, opening his eyes wide.

It had been a few years since he had heard that name, when it had normally been mentioned in connection with cases concerning the import of substantial quantities of hash from Denmark.

'He lives on the ground floor,' Hammer said. 'The window facing the backyard.'

'What's he saying?'

'The same as he said to *VG*. A pretty solid statement, really.'

Wisting raised his head. The lowering grey sky looked almost threatening.

Line ended her phone call and gazed across at her father, watching how the other investigators listened when he spoke. He radiated a calm and authority that gave everyone around him a sense of security and assurance that he would see this investigation through to a satisfactory conclusion, as per usual. She felt proud of how he was always described as convivial, inclusive and compassionate.

The mobile in her hand signalled a new message. *Lovely to meet you. Have you time for a cup of coffee/snack?* she read. The sender was a number she had not yet stored in her contact list. Glancing up at the window, she spotted Tommy Kvanter standing there watching the activity in the backyard. He made eye contact and smiled.

She realized she was hungry. The story had already been written and published online. She would have to write a more comprehensive article for the paper edition, but she would have time to grab a bite to eat as well as that.

Kaffebryggeriet in 25 minutes was her response.

16

She found a table indoors, in the afternoon gloom of the café. There were very few customers here now and they were a different clientele. Young mothers with prams meeting up for lunch had been replaced by young men with half-litres of lager. None of her journalist colleagues had found their way here and she assumed most of them had installed themselves down in the hotel bar.

She had bought herself a triangular cornbread roll with chicken, garnished with red pepper and onion rings. She let it sit there while she waited, breathing in the sweet aroma of apple and cinnamon from the wide-brimmed teacup in front of her.

She was really a tea person. Variations of hot coffee had been a trendy habit she had acquired mostly because it was practical to take a paper cup with a lid when she was on the move. When she had time to sit down and relax, she always chose tea. She liked everything about it. The fragrance that filled the room, the dried leaves, the interaction between spices and herbs, pine needles and berries.

He turned up twenty minutes later.

Erik Thue stood in the doorway for a second or two, running his eyes over the interior and smiling when he caught sight of her. He walked towards her and his eyes lingered on her breasts as he sat down.

Line was about to object that she was waiting for someone when the misunderstanding dawned on her. It had been the young journalist from *Dagbladet* with the shark-fin hair who had invited her for coffee, not Danish Tommy. She felt foolish. She should have checked the number before answering. Now it was too late.

'Nice,' Erik Thue said, with a smile on his face. 'We only had time for a hello in passing this morning.'

Line merely nodded and began to eat.

'Great piece you had on the blood-stained rag,' he went on, shrugging off his jacket. 'Probably the only news to come out since the press conference.'

Line nodded as she chewed.

Erik Thue dug out some banknotes from his wallet and glanced across at the selection displayed at the counter.

'Do the police think it has a connection to the murder?' he continued.

'They're keeping that possibility open,' Line replied, in the same words she had used in her article.

Erik Thue sprang to his feet, vanished across to the counter and returned with a large baguette, a cola and a coffee.

Line was sipping her tea.

'Do you drink tea?' Erik Thue asked, laughing and shaking his head. 'Tea must be the culinary anticlimax of our times. It hardly tastes of anything; it's almost like drinking a scent, like swallowing an aroma. It's nothing but hot water with an indefinable dash of flavour.'

'I like it,' Line answered, putting down her cup. She made up her mind that this meeting was going to be brief.

Erik Thue took a bite of his food and went on talking, his mouth now full: 'I suppose it's true that the fragrance gives you some expectation of what it's going to taste like when you get it in your mouth.' Putting down his baguette, he drew her teacup towards him and lifted it up to his face. 'But tea is just a con. When you raise it to your mouth, the scent grows more intense, with the promise that you'll soon experience

79

something you had never imagined in your wildest dreams. It's a perfect fragrance, but as soon as the tea hits your tongue you realize you've been tricked. A taste sensation turns to disappointment.' He put down her cup, fortunately without drinking from it. 'Drinking tea is like hearing a touch, like seeing a sound or like drinking a smell,' he concluded smugly and took a swig of cola.

He had the gift of the gab, she thought. But he was almost unbearably conceited.

'Was it tea you wanted to talk about?' she asked.

'No, we can talk about you.'

'I don't think so,' she said dismissively, indulging in a smile.

'We can talk about coffee, then,' he suggested. 'Not mocha, latte, arty-farty, or any of that nancy nonsense, but real coffee.' He lifted his cup. 'Aromatic, rich, well-rounded, freshly ground and newly pressed coffee. Black as an oil slick. I love it.'

'We can talk about *Dagbladet*,' Line said.

'Oh, what about it?'

'I used to read *Dagbladet*,' she told him. 'At the time when the people who worked there manned the barricades and highlighted injustices in society. Now the headlines scream mostly of sex.'

Erik Thue put his coffee cup to his mouth again, drinking slowly before setting it down, all the while gazing at her with a serious expression. Then he leaned forward, winked and smiled.

'Don't you like sex?'

She ignored him. 'The culture stuff is good,' she said with a grudging admission. 'And their debate and commentary pages.'

Erik Thue did not appear interested in those sections of his newspaper.

'We can talk about the murder,' he suggested. 'Have you spoken to your father?'

Line twirled her cup before raising it to her lips and drinking and then put it down again decisively.

'I think we're finished talking,' she replied as she rose from her seat.

17

It was just gone half past ten that night when William Wisting swung his car into the driveway of his home in Herman Wildenveys gate. The birch tree, small and spindly when he and Ingrid had built this house almost thirty years ago, now cast long shadows across the deserted courtyard. He snatched up the folder from the passenger seat, noticing that Line was still not back. That gave him time to go through some of the reports again.

He carried in some groceries he had bought at the Statoil petrol station and looked around for the cat before he let himself in. Usually Buster ran to greet him and rubbed his head against his owner's legs all the way through to the kitchen, but tonight he was nowhere to be seen, even though Wisting called out his name.

Placing the food on the worktop, he glanced at the thermometer outside the window. Six degrees Celsius. It was also cold inside the house. Shivering, he decided to lay a fire in the hearth. He crumpled up some advertising leaflets, put a match to them and added a couple of dry logs. Then he sat down with the crime-scene report as the flames took hold.

The case was scarcely sixteen hours old. They had begun to gain an overview of everyone who had been on the move outdoors last night, but it was nowhere near giving them any understanding of what had happened. He reread the report, aware that every single detail could be important. The answer always lay in the detail. What seemed unimportant now could become of major significance later.

But he found nothing that had not already churned around in his head. No hidden meanings, no discoveries that could be interpreted in different ways, sightings that could be compared to others or information that might have been overlooked. He sat holding a sheet of paper in each hand, like pieces of a jigsaw that did not fit together. Finally laying them aside, he got to his feet and went out to look for the cat again.

The yard outside was bright with car headlights when he opened the door. The engine stopped and Line stepped out.

'Are you standing there waiting for me?' she asked, smiling.

'I'm looking for Buster,' Wisting replied, returning her smile.

'Has he gone walkabout?'

'I'm sure he'll turn up.' He took her travel bag from her. 'Let's go in. It's freezing out here.'

She followed him into the kitchen.

'Hungry?' he asked. 'I was thinking of frying some hamburgers with a couple of eggs.'

'That sounds good.'

She sat down at the kitchen table while he took out the frying pan.

'Have you finished for the day?' he asked.

'If nothing else turns up,' she replied with a questioning look. 'The deadline's not until 4 a.m. I don't think we have anything that the others don't have.'

Wisting took some butter out of the fridge. 'Or the police have, for that matter,' he said.

'There's a lot to indicate it's an honour killing,' Line suggested.

'Such as what?'

'In the first place, the victim is a young, minority ethnic girl; secondly, it seems as if there's something ritualistic about the actual killing. It's obvious that the murder was planned in advance. That the perpetrator has taken some kind of "rational" decision.' Line paused before adding: 'Because of this, I think the killer considers himself to be a victim. The murdered girl has angered him somehow, perhaps brought shame upon him. She's deprived him of his honour and now he wants to show the whole world that honour has been restored.'

Wisting used a spatula to stir the butter around in the hot pan before adding the hamburgers.

'The trouble is that loss of honour comes about only when the shame is public,' he objected. 'The restoration of honour assumes that other people know both who the victim is and who the killer is. Honour killing is normally easy to clear up because the killer stands by what he has done.'

'This could be some kind of Western version of honour killing, though,' Line suggested. 'Or else it could be known in circles we have no access to. Among people where honour has to be restored.' She shifted in her seat. 'Do you have any experience of investigating honour killings?'

'Lengthy, copious experience,' Wisting told her, cracking the first egg into the frying pan. 'It's just that we call them family tragedies.'

Line looked at him inquisitively.

'When a Norwegian man murders his wife and children, and himself if he has the courage to do that, it's usually down to lack of self-respect, injured pride, jealousy or feelings of shame. It's normally to do with getting the last word or, looking at it another way, honour. Over the last ten years, more than fifty Norwegian women have been killed by their Norwegian husbands or ex-husbands. Even though we don't have a patriarchal culture or tradition here in Norway, the principle remains the same. An old-fashioned view of women lies behind it.'

Wisting broke the yolks of the eggs intended for Line. Then he took out a loaf of bread and cut some slices.

'Does that mean you're working on the basis of a racism theory?' Line asked. 'Don't you believe the bloody T-shirt and the two men Tommy Kvanter saw in the backyard have anything to do with the case?'

Wisting smiled. Line analysed everything he said.

'Racism is also probably a kind of honour,' he replied as he served up the food. 'A defence of national sentiments, culture and tradition, but I don't think the organized right-wing nationalists have the ability to carry out such an attack.'

'The security services believe they're behind a number of thefts of firearms; surely that demands both planning and structure?'

'But what would the reason for that be? I can understand that a gang of extremists think it's great fun to possess weapons, but this is something else entirely.'

'What are you left with, then?' Line ploughed on. 'That we're dealing with a sick madman?'

Wisting sat down at the table and stabbed his fork into the food. 'Let's eat now,' he said, as if to put an end to the discussion.

'Do you remember Tommy Kvanter?' Line asked. 'He was in my class at school.'

'I remember your mother and I being a bit concerned about him,' Wisting said, nodding.

'Why was that?'

'The other parents were too.' Wisting was chewing. 'You were a lovely little class with great team spirit. Tommy was a disturbing element and caused some friction when he arrived.

Your mum was afraid you'd hook up with him. But then we also knew something the other parents didn't.'

Line sat still with her fork in the air. 'What was that?'

Wisting frowned. 'I thought you children had also found out about it, at least once you'd grown up. It came up at a parents' meeting when you were in Year 8.'

'What was that?' Line repeated.

Putting down his fork, Wisting weighed up whether or not he had already said more than he should and whether it would be better to drop it but decided to spill the beans.

'Tommy's father is Claus Kvanter, a kingpin in the Hells Angels in Aalborg. He controls a lot of the organized crime in that locality. Narcotics, prostitution, blackmail, credit-card fraud and money laundering. In the mid-nineties, the war in the Nordic countries between the Hells Angels and the Bandidos was at its height. It was ferocious, with bombs, machine guns and anti-tank missiles. Attacks and counter-attacks in revenge. Tommy's father was involved in most of it and was arrested for shooting and killing a Bandidos member in Kastrup in 1994. The day he was arrested, Tommy's mother took him in a car and drove north. They boarded the ferry from Fredrikshavn and landed here. Claus was sentenced to sixteen years in jail, served ten of them and is now back in business.'

Line sat, her head spinning with questions.

'Does Tommy have any contact with his father these days?'

'Other people know more about that than I do,' Wisting replied evasively. 'He did move back there to live when his father was released.'

'Is he involved in his father's business?' Line went on to ask.

Wisting rose from the table, moved across to the fridge and took out a carton of apple juice without answering.

'Why did he move back to Norway?' she pressed him.

'You're asking me more than I can answer.'

Line was on the verge of a new question but was interrupted by her mobile phone alerting her to a new text message. She took it out and saw the name Suzanne on the display before she located the message: *Must talk to you. Do you have time tomorrow? Think it's important.*

It had to do with the suitcase story. She had not given a thought to the blue suitcase or the woman who thought she might have information about it since this morning. She wondered whether she should refrain from answering but instead keyed in a message that she was still busy but would give her a call.

18

It was a perfect night, dry and fine. The moon lay hidden behind wisps of cloud and there was almost no wind.

Karl Henry Steinsnes pushed out the flat-bottomed rowing boat and jumped aboard. He made substantial progress with each stroke of the oars on the calm, black waters of the Lågen river. It would be one of the last trips of the year. The spawning season was almost over but the low level of the water had prevented many of the salmon from moving upriver, so it was still possible to find one or two stray fish. The advantage of fishing as late as this was that the inspectors had given up and gone home.

The salmon's fantastic ability to force its way through waterfalls and rapids and its incredible double life in rivers and seas had never ceased to fascinate him. One of the great mysteries of life was how the salmon could leave behind the narrow rivers of Norway, follow the coastal currents out into the North Sea, the Barents Sea and all the way to Western Greenland before turning with razor-sharp precision and finding their way back to their birthplace in the river. Some of these fish had travelled unbelievable distances before ending up in his nets.

He had three lines out and on a good night he could haul in more than seventy kilos and make some dosh. A welcome addition to the paltry amount he received in benefits, but it was not the money that motivated him. It was the thrill and the tradition. His family had operated gill-net fishing for generations. He knew the river and the salmon. Understood everything about them, and a couple of sentences that the politicians in Oslo had concealed within a legal paragraph were not going to stop him from harvesting food from nature's larder.

Drawing the boat up beside the deep pool, he peered into the river, black as night, until his eyes caught sight of the small piece of driftwood that marked where his net had been sunk. He made some effort with the oars and manoeuvred back into place before grabbing the line, pulling the stone weight on board and starting to haul.

The owl that lived in the treetops at Yttersøgården loudly announced its presence. He felt an affinity with the wise bird. They both moved around in the darkness, using their sharp eyes and keen hunting instincts.

A sharp gust of wind rippled the surface of the river. The water was cold and would make his fingers numb. He had already rolled three cigarettes that now lay in his tobacco pouch and he was looking forward to lighting up the first of these.

He worked swiftly while the boat drifted on the current towards the bracket on one of the posts from the old log boom, hauling metre upon metre of the sunken net on board, folding it on the floorboards of the boat so that it would be easy to clean later. He smiled broadly when he saw something white and glistening move towards him through the darkness. The first salmon flipped over the gunwale, squirming in protest until it was left there gasping. Three kilos, he reckoned, and he could feel from the net that there was a larger catch on the way.

The moon slid out through a crack in the clouds. He automatically hunched further down in the boat, scanning the riverbank with his eyes as he went on tugging. He ran his tongue quickly over his cracked lips. Something gleamed pale and bright down in the net. The fine threads of the stitches dug deep into his fingers as the weight of the catch grew heavier the further up through the water it progressed. Then he came to a sudden halt and just sat staring while the boat drifted on the current. Fear and dread crept up his spine as he realized what he was looking at.

A naked human foot was tangled in the nylon threads, the pale sole wrinkled and swollen with the water. Flakes of epidermis were loosening and a black trouser leg had slid up to mid-calf. Further down in the water, the other leg was rocking in the current and he could make out the dark contours of the rest of the body.

The hand holding the net began to tremble. As he let go, he allowed the corpse to slide back into the water before he took hold of the remaining coil of net and flung it back in, along with the three-kilo salmon and the sinker stone. He let the boat drift on the current until the spot where the net was situated disappeared into dark shadows. Various options raced through his head but there was only one thing he could and should do. His hand groped for his inside pocket and he took out his phone.

The mobile phone vibrated on the bedside table, waking William Wisting out of a heavy sleep. He stretched out his hand, fumbling for it, and focused his eyes on the bright display. Registering that it was 3.07 a.m., he answered as he always did when he failed to recognize the number, in a gruff and dismissive voice.

The man at the other end, jittery and nervous, apologized three times for calling in the middle of the night.

'I didn't want to wake you, but I didn't know who else to phone.'

'Who am I speaking to?' Wisting asked abruptly.

'Sorry,' the man replied. 'It's Karl Henry Steinsnes.'

A vague connection surfaced far back somewhere in Wisting's memory. A picture emerged of a small man in his fifties, his reddish-blond hair streaked with grey and the cheeks on his puffy face mottled with broken veins. He was a poacher who caught salmon and sea trout on the sly, using gill nets at the mouth of the Lågen river. The last time Wisting had spoken to him, someone had stolen his boat. As luck would have it, it was found an hour later with two drunk teenagers on board. The next day, Ingrid had served fresh salmon for dinner when he got home. A man had come to the door and dropped it off, she said, and asked her to pass on his best wishes and say thanks for his help.

'What's this about?' Wisting asked, struggling to sit up in bed.

'I think you should come,' Steinsnes said.

Line had woken when she heard the phone ringing in her father's bedroom. She lay listening to him talking in a firm voice, but she was unable to catch what he was saying. She heard him ask questions, wait for answers and then pose more questions. After that she heard his footsteps. Rapid steps across the floor, down the stairs and into the bathroom. Something had happened.

Throwing aside her quilt, she planted her feet on the cold floor. Once up, she pulled on a sweater and headed downstairs. Her father was talking on the phone again. Staccato commands this time. He rang off and turned towards the door when she came into the bathroom.

'I didn't mean to wake you,' he apologized as he went past her.

'What's going on?' she asked, following him out.

'I have to go to work,' he replied, pulling on a shirt.

'Why's that?'

Heaving a sigh of exasperation, he dropped his arms to his sides and stood studying her. She could see that he found the situation difficult, that he did not enjoy this dual role of investigation leader and father to a journalist daughter.

'A body's been found,' he said finally, continuing to put on his clothes.

Line glanced at the clock. Three quarters of an hour to deadline.

19

Wisting parked his car at the rear of the desolate industrial area on the west bank of the Lågen. A couple of old caravans, stacks of wooden pallets and a heap of twisted metal were all piled up on the riverbank.

A police patrol car was already on the scene. Two uniformed officers were setting up a generator and floodlights.

Karl Henry Steinsnes stood holding a cigarette between two yellow fingers, but he pinched off the glowing tip and stuffed the butt into his matchbox when he caught sight of Wisting. Wisting let him tell the whole story all over again as he stared at the black river flowing past.

'You'll have to row me out there,' he said when the man had finished his account.

Steinsnes stared at him in disbelief. His eyes looked big and round in his face.

'I'd hope to avoid . . .' he began, but got no further before Wisting jumped aboard the boat and sat down on the thwart at the stern.

Shaking his head, Karl Henry Steinsnes clambered aboard, pushed off and took his place at the oars. The police officers fired up the generator and a dazzling light spilled over the water.

They rowed in silence. The boat glided under the railway bridge towards the spot where the river widened out a little before the old poacher pulled up his oars.

'There,' he said, pointing.

Wisting saw an old piece of wood floating on the surface

of the water. Leaning forward over the gunwale, he grabbed the wood and pulled it up. The net rose through the water and he hauled it aboard, gathering it into a heap on the base boards of the boat. A salmon measuring half a metre was heaved up with it before he felt that something heavier was on the way up. He knew what he was about to see, but his heart skipped a beat all the same when the pale left foot came into view.

Staring down into the water, he saw the other leg swaying in the weak current. It was not a large body, but it would be too heavy to lug aboard. He turned to face Steinsnes.

'The rope,' he requested, indicating the coil at the front of the boat.

Once it was tossed back to him, he tied a simple loop and slipped it around the leg protruding from the water to ensure that the cadaver would not come adrift from the net and disappear into the river. Then he fastened the rope to the gunwale and went on hauling in the net. Two more salmon and a sea trout came with it before he was able to detach the line and give Karl Henry the green light to row back.

Espen Mortensen was waiting ashore with the crime-scene van. Another police patrol vehicle had also arrived and taken up post in the middle of the illuminated stretch of land beside the workshops. Behind it, he recognized Line's car. She was standing beside it with two men, one with a camera lens directed straight at them.

Wisting turned his gaze to the foot sticking out of the water. It juddered, as if the owner were kicking out, when the rest of the body came to rest on the riverbed.

Line glanced at her watch as her father moored the boat. It was seven minutes to four. She had let the news editor in Akersgata know and he had cleared some space for the headline *ANOTHER BODY FOUND TONIGHT* or possibly *MORE BODY PARTS FOUND TONIGHT*, but she was forced to realize she would not manage to deliver a story before the first edition went to print.

'They're towing something along behind the boat,' the photographer said.

Line heard the shutter mechanism working away. Several photos were taken in quick succession before the photographer tilted the camera to one side, took a swift look at the large display and zoomed in on something before showing the image to his colleagues.

'Christ, it looks like a leg!' Morten P. exclaimed. He had still not managed to clear the sleep out of his eyes.

The photographer did not allow them time to study the picture more closely before raising the lens to the river again.

Morten P. disappeared, heading for the car, and returned with a small pair of binoculars.

'Who's the man rowing?' he asked, handing the binoculars to Line.

Adjusting the focus, she saw her father release a blue nylon rope from the gunwale and step ashore. In the middle of the boat she saw a small, red-faced man resting his arms on the oars.

'No idea,' Line replied, handing back the binoculars. 'He's not a policeman, at any rate.'

'A civilian, then,' Morten P. mumbled. 'He must be the one who found the body.' He placed his hand on her shoulder. 'Then we have our story. You latch on to him and I'll quiz the police.'

Wisting handed the rope to one of the uniformed officers waiting ashore and helped Karl Henry to haul in the boat. Espen Mortensen waded out to the body, took out a knife and cut it free of the net. The other policemen joined him and, taking a leg each, they carefully dragged the cadaver to the riverbank.

Wisting had worked so long in the police force that he was rarely surprised by anything. However, he was completely floored when he saw the body.

He had expected this discovery to move the case forward, that they would now find out who the severed head in the square belonged to, but when the corpse was dragged on to dry land he was left standing with his jaw dropping. At the end of the slender body there was a head with short, curly hair.

20

Espen Mortensen recorded the find in a couple of photographs before the two uniformed policemen lifted the corpse across to a white body bag that was ready and waiting.

It was a man. Slim and short, his age was difficult to place with any accuracy, but he must be somewhere between thirty and forty. Probably nearer forty. His arms were extended stiffly from his torso as if to defend himself from something. He was dressed in dark blue denim jeans and a white sweater. Brown river sludge was clinging to his clothes and skin and rotted leaves and other fragments of vegetation were entangled in his black curls.

He had similar features to those of the young girl found in the town square. There was a distinct tear at the left corner of his mouth and above his eye on the opposite side there was a deep gash in his skin. Clear signs of injury from repeated blows to the face.

Wisting found it impossible to believe that there was no connection between the discoveries of these two bodies. The two could be linked in more ways than just their ethnic origin. Could they even be members of the same family?

Mortensen took a few photos before pulling on a pair of latex gloves, crouching down beside the body and taking hold of the chin. As he straightened the head, a large, bloody wound at the top of the throat became visible. Wisting wondered whether someone had also tried to cut this man's head off, but it seemed unlikely. The gash looked like a star-shaped crater with big flaps of skin torn loose. He had seen this before and his suspicions were confirmed when Mortensen turned the body over. At the hairline on his neck, the man had an open, circular wound.

The young crime-scene technician stood up again. Taking a couple of steps back, he studied the dead body from a short distance.

'Shot through the back of the head,' he said finally. 'The exit wound is ten centimetres lower than the entry wound. The killer stood behind him while the victim was on his knees.'

Wisting had drawn the same conclusion. 'An out-and-out execution,' he said.

Hunkering down again, Mortensen pushed the victim's hair aside and examined the wound.

'Two shots,' he said, turning the body over again. He studied the wound in the throat before pulling up the sweater and checking the stomach and chest. Black leeches were sucking at the pale skin but it was otherwise unscathed. 'One bullet path has penetrated deeper than the other,' he said. 'That means one projectile may still be in his body.'

Raking his hand through his hair, Wisting nodded in satisfaction. The little lump of lead left behind by the gun could be of crucial significance in the forthcoming investigation. Every bullet had a history that could be traced.

Mortensen continued his examination of the body under the harsh yellow beams of the floodlights. He turned out the left-hand trouser pocket, took out some coins and screwed up his nose, as if he did not like what he was seeing. He spread them out on his palm, holding them up so that Wisting could see. The profile of Queen Margrethe and the Danish national coat of arms were embossed on the coins, a total of fourteen Danish kroner.

'That doesn't simplify things,' Wisting said with a sigh, as it crossed his mind how much more difficult the investigation would become if the murder victim was not Norwegian and had no fixed address in the country.

Mortensen let the coins slide down into a transparent evidence bag, labelled it and plunged his hand into the other pocket. They could hear metal clinking as he drew something out – three keys hanging from a keyring. One of them obviously belonged to the front door of a house, another to a vehicle, while the third could be for a padlock or a cupboard door.

The keys were dropped into another evidence bag. The back pockets were searched and found to be empty. Mortensen located a label inside the waistband and took a close-up of it. He did the same with the neckband of the sweater.

'European,' he commented tersely before returning his photographic equipment to his bag and zipping up the body bag.

Wisting had been about to say something but shut his mouth. In the distance he could hear the sound of sirens approaching and see the blue lights of an emergency vehicle travelling along Elveveien. He caught a glimpse of two fire engines before they turned off and drove towards the town.

He gave one of the uniformed policemen a questioning look. He was pressing his finger on his earplug, listening to a message.

'House fire,' he relayed the message. 'Scheensveien 11.'

Cursing, Wisting strode quickly across to his car. He knew that address.

21

Plumes of flame soared from the old timber house into the night sky, colouring it with a yellowish sheen. Thick, dark grey clouds of smoke belched out through the windows and up through the roof. The firefighters were running to and fro, rolling out bulky water hoses. Wisting parked some distance off to avoid getting in the way. Stepping out of the car, he approached the burning house. Long ice-blue flames suddenly shot out through the shattered windowpanes. As he came closer, the flames changed in colour and character, turning to orange and eagerly licking the walls. He used his hand to shade his eyes from the intense light. The smell of burning wood stung his eyes and nose, giving him a headache, and he knew that his hair and clothes would soon be stinking.

Two masked firefighters entered the blazing building. The water thundered through the hose they carried but the strength of the flames seemed to increase, as if they were being fed continuously, and the men had to turn back.

Wisting looked around and saw that cars had stopped along the crash barriers up on the motorway with rubberneckers huddling together to stare at the fire as it greedily consumed the house.

His eyes found what they were searching for. Cato Dalen stood with his girlfriend, partly hidden behind one of the fire tenders. He was wearing clogs, jeans and a white T-shirt printed with a half-moon and stars beside a red cross and the text *Keep Norway Norwegian*. His girlfriend had a quilt draped around her shoulders and her tousled hair hung limply around her distressed face.

Wisting moved across to them and Cato Dalen gave him a nod. The corners of his mouth were trembling and his eyes were flitting in every direction like those of a startled animal.

'What happened?' Wisting asked.

Cato Dalen shrugged and ran his hand over his shaved head.

'It all happened so quickly,' he replied. His eyes were red-rimmed. 'Something exploded.'

'An explosion?' Wisting repeated, to encourage Dalen to elaborate.

'We were in bed, fast asleep,' Cato Dalen explained, pointing to a window on the north side of the house. Tentacles of orange-and-red flames twisted and turned their way up along the first floor of the building. 'I woke when I heard a sudden loud noise. I thought at first someone had thrown a stone through the window again, but when I went into the living room it was all on fire.'

'Did you see anything or anyone?'

Cato Dalen shook his head. 'I only just managed to pull on my trousers and get out.'

His girlfriend stepped forward. Tiny flakes of ash had begun to settle on the quilt she had wrapped around herself. She took Cato Dalen tentatively by the arm and opened her mouth, as if about to say something, but she was interrupted by a series of small explosions from inside the blazing house. The firefighters crouched down and moved back. A fire officer came running over to them.

'Do you have anything explosive in the house?' he demanded.

Cato Dalen seemed unsure.

'Propane, gas or anything like that?' the firefighter added.

'I've got some ammunition,' Cato Dalen answered cautiously.

'What kind?'

'Different types – 9 and 6.5 millimetre.'

'How much?'

'A few hundred cartridges, stored in a cupboard in the living room.'

'OK, but no gas under pressure?'

Cato Dalen shook his head.

An ambulance swung up behind the fire engine where Wisting was standing. Two paramedics in red-and-yellow suits approached them. Cato Dalen accepted the woollen blanket they offered and draped it around his shoulders. Wisting withdrew along with the fire officer, who issued commands into a microphone dangling on his chest and then turned to face Wisting.

'It was well ablaze when we got here,' he explained. 'It had developed most down at the south end of the building.' He pointed at what had been the living room. 'But it has a good hold and is spreading really fast.'

'What started it?'

The fire officer shrugged. At that moment, parts of the roof caved in and a flurry of sparks surged out. The south-facing wall collapsed entirely. The firemen poured water on the blaze but had not yet gained control of the fire. The house would burn to the ground and there would be little or nothing left by way of evidence to explain how the fire had started or what other secrets had been concealed within its four walls.

Wisting moved to his car to drive to the office. It was going to be a long day.

2 2

Line sat in the hotel's breakfast room, browsing through the pile of the day's newspapers while Morten P. helped himself to seconds. She skipped past the political comment that *Police lack resources* and *Integration policy set back decades* and simply skimmed through the various papers' crime coverage. None of them could be said to have won the battle for headlines. All the front pages were similar and told the same story about yesterday's developments in this case. However, there was no doubt who was leading the pack in the hunt for the latest news. She smiled at the thought of Erik Thue from *Dagbladet* and her other competitors waking to the broadcast news channels quoting *VG*'s online coverage of the overnight discovery of a new murder victim.

The old poacher had been persuaded to give his name and have a photo taken, but she had bagged his whole story and, anyway, the picture of the police dragging the corpse out of the river in the glare of the floodlights was far more dramatic. It had been taken from an angle that ensured readers could only guess at the contours of the dead body, while the serious expressions on the surrounding faces left no doubt whatsoever as to what this was all about. If the discovery had been made an hour or two earlier, it would have been splashed on the front page.

Morten P. had received confirmation that the body was of a man from a minority ethnic background and that he had been shot. He had not been identified and so far the police had no information about who he might be. The police had no grounds to say that the murder had any connection with the previous day's finding of the severed head but did go so far as to suggest that this was an obvious line of inquiry.

The duty editor at the online news desk had printed a black ribbon across the photograph, emblazoned with white lettering: *EXTRA*. The story was still the lead item but there was now competition from another piece of news – *Explosive fire at house of anti-immigration Patriotic Front leader.*

Morten P. had returned after piling his plate with more bacon and eggs, his mobile phone gripped between his chin and his shoulder. He rounded off his conversation, sat down and gave Line a broad smile.

'The editor says hi,' he said, tucking into his food. 'They're sending down another team, who'll be responsible for covering the body in the river.' He chewed as he went on: 'The local office will take care of the fire, and we'll follow up on yesterday's story. Have you got any bright ideas?'

Line laid aside the newspapers and picked up her teacup.

'I thought I'd speak to Tommy Kvanter again,' she said.

'The Danish guy who found the blood-soaked T-shirt?' Morten P. wrinkled his nose. 'Why on earth? It was a good story, but surely there's no potential for anything further there?'

Line shrugged, struggling to come up with an answer, but all she knew was that she was really keen to talk to him again. She drank her tea and told her colleague what she had learned about Tommy's father's involvement with crime in the motorbike fraternity.

'Interesting, but does it link up with our story?' Morten P. folded a slice of bacon and popped it into his mouth, swallowing it down with a swig of coffee. 'This surely has nothing to do with a narcotics showdown?'

Taking out her notebook, Line read out a name: Dhuhulow.

'He's an imam in an Islamic community. I thought I might speak to him or someone in the Islamic Cultural Association for some background to the story.'

'Why?' Morten P. asked.

'If the victim is from this town, then someone in those circles might know her or have some idea of what might have happened.'

'You're going to do some digging, then?' Morten P. smiled again. 'I like that.'

Line returned his smile. She had another name in her notebook: Suzanne Bjerke. It was linked with the inquiry into the blue suitcase. She did not want to tell Morten P. that she would also be working on another story, but something told her that there could be a connection somewhere.

23

In the crowded conference room at the police station, the atmosphere around the table betrayed signs of lack of sleep. Many of the investigators were already overworked and had been compelled to shelve other important cases. Their participation in the homicide investigation would impact on case-handling time and the general clear-up rate and statistics.

Wisting sat studying the worn surface of the table in an effort to collect his thoughts. More than twenty-four hours had now passed and the information they had amassed was extremely limited. The way forward appeared long and arduous but, as the officer in charge, it was his task to motivate his colleagues and keep them going. He had to find ways to inspire and stimulate the others.

Wisting let his chair scrape across the floor as he got to his feet and stood with his hands on the headrest, as if steering a ship through calm waters. He gazed at the familiar faces around the table and nodded to Espen Mortensen. In response, the crime-scene technician switched on the projector suspended from the ceiling and one of the pictures he had taken on the riverbank in the early hours of that morning immediately filled the screen.

The image required no further explanation. Everyone in the room was well aware of what had been found. Some had been called in several hours earlier while others had woken to the news on the radio or breakfast TV.

'Who is this?' Wisting asked, his fists clenching on the back of the chair.

Silence filled the room. Nils Hammer reached into his trouser pocket for his snuff tin and cocked his head as he studied the series of pictures shown one after the other on the screen.

'I think he resembles the girl in the town square,' he said, jiggling the tin out. 'Could he be her father?'

Wisting spread his arms wide, as if returning the question to the others.

'Well, there really has to be some connection,' said Jan Osther, who had instigated the racism theory at the previous meeting, 'to both the head found in the square and the fire in Scheensveien, as well as the body in the water. The cases must be related somehow.'

Espen Mortensen hunched over his computer and showed them photos from the fire before projecting pictures of the two victims side by side. There was little doubt that they belonged to the same minority ethnic group, but whether they had any familial link was something Wisting found difficult to judge. But the man on the right was about twenty years older than the girl, so in theory he could be her father.

The young crime-scene examiner gave an account of how the unknown man had been killed and showed close-ups of the bullet wounds. The spot where the muzzle of the gun had been pressed against the man's neck was clearly outlined on the torn skin.

'Do we know when he died?' Nils Hammer asked, pointing to the picture.

Espen Mortensen replied: 'I don't think he was in the water for more than twenty-four hours. That suggests he was killed around the same time as the girl, that is, the night before last.'

'Kristallnacht,' Jan Osther pointed out.

'If they were murdered at the same time . . .' Torunn Borg began. She had been listening to the others, making notes. '. . . there's probably reason to believe the killer tried to get

107

rid of the bodies at the same time too. In that case, we should search in the river for the rest of the girl's body.'

Her suggestion received a positive response and she was rewarded with being assigned to organize the search.

Releasing his grip on the chair back, Wisting took a few steps towards the window and stood there, gazing out.

'Until the night before last, they were members of our community,' he said, clenching his fist. 'It shouldn't be possible in an open, transparent society for two people to simply disappear without anyone raising the alarm. Not even now, when they've been found murdered, has anyone taken the time to get involved and come forward to let us know who they might be.'

'That surely suggests they weren't members of our community,' Hammer commented as he finally managed to push some snuff under his lip. 'They must have been living as outsiders, as illegal immigrants, opportunists or roving criminals.'

'If that turns out to be the case, then we could actually move a step forward,' Mortensen said. 'I've taken fingerprints from the man we found last night and am about to send out a query on them. If he's registered in any country in Europe, we'll have an answer by lunchtime.'

'Well, that's one thing we can be pleased about,' Hammer commented. 'This means there's no crazy bastard running around chopping the heads off random immigrant girls and displaying them for all to see.' He pointed at the man on the screen. 'He was liquidated with a bullet to the back of the neck. Someone must have some kind of motive. We just have to find out what that is.'

Wisting did not know whether he agreed with that assessment. Madmen usually made lots of mistakes and left clues behind. A cold, calculating killer was far more difficult to find.

24

Einar Brodtkorp dropped his head back and gazed up at the sky. Several layers of low stratocumulus clouds had piled up, completely covering the heavens. The high level of humidity gave them a greyish-blue colour. The weather front was travelling eastwards but strong winds were driving the clouds higher into the air. It was likely that the condensation of water vapour would turn into droplets, so there would be rain. He glanced at his watch. Three minutes past nine. He would bet that the first drops of rain would start to fall about half past nine. By then he would be back at his kitchen table with the newspaper open in front of him.

The dog was walking off the leash by his side. Brodtkorp always let him do that when he was strolling to and from the shop except in the period when using a leash was compulsory. The dog was not made to wear a collar around his neck. Anyway, he was absolutely harmless. A slightly overweight, ageing golden retriever that dragged one of its hind legs. Brodtkorp let him run and play at will when there was no one else along the route. The dog pounced on some seagulls and disappeared in between a couple of boats laid up down by the harbour.

'Kelvin!' he shouted, causing the dog to turn quickly and come back.

He had bought milk, bread, some cold meat and cheese, a tin of dog food and a Danish pastry. The newspaper was tucked under his arm, as if he wanted to be certain of where it was. Taking it out, he saw on the back page that he was right. Widespread downpours were forecast in the course of the afternoon. Towards evening the amount of precipitation would increase and the wind would pick up. The outlook was unchanged for the next three days.

He turned to the front page and looked at it again. *POLICE FEAR MAD KILLER* was the headline. It had been taken from a statement made by Police Superintendent Audun Vetti, who stared gloomily at him from a small inset photograph. One of the theories the police had come up with was that it must be a disturbed person who had separated the head from the rest of the young girl's body and placed it on a stake in the middle of the town square. The words *MAD KILLER* were larger than all the others on the front page. *VG*'s coverage of the story ran to six pages but there was nothing about the second body they had talked about on the radio. Probably they had found it after the paper had gone to press. He could read about it online if he could manage to start up his old computer.

Shaking his head, Einar Brodtkorp folded the newspaper and pushed it back under his arm. One of the reasons he had moved from the capital city when he retired from his job as a state-employed meteorologist was that he had wanted to leave behind the brutality, violence and serious crime the newspapers reported every day and that had become a feature of life in the big city. They lived in a time of greed and temptation and crimes were becoming more numerous and callous. Concepts such as customs and morals were being wiped out and it was becoming increasingly easy to cross the boundaries. Now he felt that what he had fled from had caught up with him. Vicious reality had arrived here in Stavern.

Glancing again at his watch, he reassured himself that he would have time for a cup of coffee while he read the newspaper story before the radio station phoned him. Every

Tuesday morning, *NRK* called to get his take on weather events for use in an item a few hours later in the day. He had done this ever since he had stopped working. They had never offered him any kind of payment but that was never his motivation for agreeing to do it anyway. He appreciated being useful to them and liked talking about the weather. Today he had decided to talk about advection fog. For many people, fog was just fog. Very few knew that there were ten different kinds of fog, depending on how the cooling of the air led to the condensation.

The dense fog they had wakened to yesterday morning was a complex phenomenon. A rare layer of warm air had met cold air from the mainland all along the coastal strip and been quickly cooled down from above. The onshore wind had ceased suddenly and the thick fog had come rolling in across the land, where it had settled. Thicker than he had ever seen before.

Shifting his shopping bag to his other hand, he pulled his jacket more snugly around himself. The temperature had dropped – perhaps the rain would arrive sooner than he had initially expected. The wind was rippling through the leaves on the trees and stirring the pennants on the boats in the harbour. Four or five knots, he thought. Moderate to fresh breeze on the scale devised by Francis Beaufort.

Usually he took a stroll down to the marina to extend the walk a bit for Kelvin, going to the very far end of the break-water, gazing out at the mouth of the fjord and revelling in the salt sea spray on his face. Now he was keen to get home as fast as possible and sit down with his newspaper.

From habit, the dog ran across the gravel yard and down to the quayside. Brodtkorp called out but this time the dog did not turn around. He walked on, trying to whistle, but failing miserably.

A woman with a pram came striding towards him. Brodt-korp stopped and stood watching the dog. He liked to keep him under control when there were children around. Not that he was dangerous, but he could be boisterous and seem scary.

Kelvin barked a couple of times down at the quayside. The dog was jumping up and down, lunging at something in the water below and barking again.

'Kelvin!'

The dog came panting towards him, but turned and ran back again.

With a heavy sigh, Einar Brodtkorp changed the bag to the other hand again and headed down to the harbour. The dog's tail was wagging, its tongue lolling, and its dark eyes were staring expectantly up at him.

'What is it, boy?' he asked, using his free hand to scratch behind the dog's ear. He took a few steps closer to the edge of the quay and stared down into the greenish water to see what was so exciting.

He realized at once what it was. Before he had managed to take in the sight of it, he became rooted to the spot. He dropped the shopping bag and collapsed on the ground.

The first drop of rain from the grey clouds above him was so enormous that he managed to focus his eyes on it before it struck his forehead.

25

The chubby retriever clung to his master's legs and pushed his wet snout into his hand, almost as if he expected to find a treat there. When there was none to be had, he lay down, thumping his tail on the ground a few times and staring apathetically up at him.

Wisting strode around it and walked all the way up to the edge of the quay. He put his hands in his pockets and gazed down at the water, almost still in the harbour basin, except for the small rings made by the rain, as if the surface of the sea were trembling.

The body, small and slender, was floating between driftwood and marine debris. Only the back was visible above the surface and at first glance it looked as if the dead girl lay with her head dipped down into the dark water. A number of tiny fish were nibbling at the open wound where her head had been cut off.

Entering the water, the divers from the salvage vessel dragged the corpse over to a net that they hooked on to the loop suspended from the crane aboard the boat. They signalled for the body to be raised on to land, where a couple of uniformed police officers hauled it on to the quay and down on to a white tarpaulin.

The gulls sailed low above the harbour. Wisting tugged at the lapels of his jacket as he breathed in the salt tang of the sea. The man who had phoned in the report sat sheltering from the rain beside the open doors of the ambulance. He had a woollen blanket wrapped around his shoulders and someone had brought him a hot drink. Wisting had seen him many times before. For years he had filled TV screens, giving the next day's weather forecast. Now his cheerful face was pale and his lips were quivering.

The wind tugged at a newspaper on the ground and swept it away across the gravel. Wisting rubbed his face, wet with rain, and moved to the tarpaulin that held the headless body. Seaweed was twisted around the slight torso, with shrimp larvae and other tiny sea creatures scrambling around in the large open wound between the narrow shoulders.

Espen Mortensen, looking tired and frazzled, was setting up his photo equipment. Across at the barriers, pedestrians had gathered, craning their necks to see what was going on.

A mixture of salt and rot wafted from the cadaver. Her patterned blouse was plastered to her body and he could see the outline of her bra under the sodden fabric. The buttons were intact and the material was not torn. His gaze moved on down to her narrow legs, her blue jeans and bright socks. The jeans were done up with a zip and a button. The body was swollen after its immersion in the water and was bulging over a white belt. Wisting crouched down to take a closer look and noticed that the hole where the buckle was fastened showed signs of wear.

Wisting lifted his eyes to the sea where the body had washed up. The surf was breaking over the bare coastal rocks. Further out, a cargo ship was steering in an easterly direction.

There was nothing to suggest that the murder had been sexually motivated or committed in order to hide a sexual violation, but the socks piqued his curiosity. The waves and currents could have pulled off her shoes if they were low cut and had not been properly fastened but they could also indicate that she was in her stocking feet when she was killed. That would suggest that the actual crime scene was probably somewhere indoors. A place where she had felt at home and thought she was safe. The man they had hauled in with the net had also worn no shoes.

Espen Mortensen raised one of her arms. The epidermis was about to loosen but not so much that it would be impossible to secure the girl's fingerprints. Two of her nails were broken: maybe she had fought against her killer.

There was a bracelet round her wrist. Wisting hunkered down and joined Mortensen in studying it. It was half of a stone attached to a brown leather strap. The stone was polished and marbled with orange stripes on a grey-black background. No engraving or inscription.

Putting the girl's arm down again, Mortensen enclosed her hand in a plastic bag with elastic around it to make sure that no skin scrapings or anything under her nails would be lost during transportation. Then he began to examine her pockets. From the front on the left-hand side, he took out a small tube of lip salve.

'Perfect Lip Honey,' he read out, squinting to make out the small print: 'The small print is in Swedish: "Multipurpose lip balsam to moisturize your lips and make them soft and supple."'

'From Sweden, then?' Wisting asked.

'It could still have been bought in Norway.' Mortensen put the tube into an evidence bag. 'We can try to trace it.'

From the other pocket he pulled out a folded piece of paper. He smoothed it out carefully as Wisting watched. It contained a number of simple handwritten notes. The ink had run, making the text illegible, but it looked like a name and a phone number. Mortensen fastidiously inserted it into another evidence bag to take with him and begin the drying process so that the text could hopefully be retrieved.

The other pockets were empty.

Wisting drew his thumb and index finger repeatedly over the bristles on his chin as the dead girl was being wrapped up. They had found two bodies in less than seven hours. They still knew nothing about the identities of either victim. The clouds in the sky above had grown even murkier and he envisaged that the investigation would be groping in the dark for weeks and months to come.

26

The windscreen wipers scraped across the glass. The rain had stopped at last. Wisting turned them off, swung into the backyard at the police station and parked his car.

A man in blue trousers with braces and a woollen sweater, parked two spaces away from him, untied something that had been firmly fastened to the cargo bed of a pickup. He lifted out a wooden stave, hoisted it over his right shoulder and came towards him.

Wisting stepped out. The man greeted him with a nod as he put the stave down and stood leaning against it.

'There you are,' he said, as if they knew each other. Wisting returned the nod. It was well known through the media coverage that he was in charge of the current investigation.

'I think the wooden post that the head was put on belongs to me,' he added.

Wisting looked at the wooden stave the man was leaning on. It was slightly taller than the man himself, about six to seven centimetres thick, pointed at both ends and looked identical to the one that lay up in the examination room.

'For making a hay-drying rack?' he asked.

The man nodded. 'Anyway, two men stole one like it from me on Sunday,' he explained. 'I brought this one for comparison.'

Wisting blinked, aware that lack of sleep was having a detrimental effect on him.

'Come with me,' he said, walking towards the door. 'We can go up to my office.'

He escorted the man up the stairwell, through the corridor and into his office. The bundle of messages on his desk had multiplied and the light on the phone was flashing to tell him that the switchboard also had information for him.

Showing the man to a vacant chair, he introduced himself.

'Johan Eskedal,' the man reciprocated, handing the stave to Wisting before he sat down.

Wisting propped it up in the corner behind the door and cleared some space on the desk.

'Tell me all about it,' he said.

Eskedal cleared his throat and massaged the palm of his right hand with his other thumb.

'I run a small pig farm in Hagtvedt,' he began. 'In actual fact, it's mostly a hobby. I work as a carpenter, building staircases in my brother's workshop, but I have thirty animals. Also, my young daughter has a pony.'

Wisting nodded to let him know he was following his story with interest.

'I don't really cultivate grass,' the man went on, 'but I have a few hay racks for horse fodder, mainly to keep the old tradition going. The staves are stacked up behind the old loading platform for milk cans down by the main road once we've finished with them for the season.'

Eskedal shifted in his seat and stopped for a moment as he surveyed the room. His eyes came to rest on the pictures of Ingrid and the children before they moved on to the faded children's drawings and class photographs from police college. Wisting waited with his fingertip on his lips, giving the man time to provide inconsequential details in order to create an atmosphere in which he felt relaxed. In that way, details of important points would also emerge.

'On Sunday we had an early dinner with my parents-in-law

in Holtebygda,' the man went on. 'They always eat around one o'clock on Sundays and we were home by about four. The others went inside while I got changed and went to the barn to see to the tractor. It's an old Valmet 605 that's done 10,000 hours. I had drained out the engine oil that morning and went in to change the filter and put in new oil. I changed the oil on the front wheel hubs and tightened and greased the kingpins as well. It must have been half past five by the time I was finished. The sun had gone down and it was getting dark but I saw a white estate car down by the road.'

Wisting reached out across the desk for his pen and note-pad. Questions would only break the man's concentration and information could be lost. Instead he remained silent and jotted down some notes as the man carried on.

'It might have been a Toyota,' Eskedal continued, glancing at the key words Wisting was writing down. 'It was parked with its engine running and the back door open. There were two men beside it. One stayed by the car while the other was busy doing something over at the pile of staves. I went down towards them. They were foreigners and I reckoned they didn't have honest intentions, so I thought I'd ask whether they needed help, just so that I could make my presence known. But when the man yanked one of the staves out and walked off with it, I yelled down to them. They were sud-denly scurrying about and the man with the stave tripped up twice beside the ditch, but he regained his footing, tossed the stave into the car and they sped off.'

'Can you give me a description of these two men?' Wist-ing asked, suggesting a few possibilities: 'Height, weight, age, clothing?'

'Never seen them before,' the man said firmly. 'There are a lot of Poles and Lithuanians working on the farms around here, but these weren't Eastern Europeans. They looked out of place here, from the Middle East or somewhere. Normal build, and they both had beards. They looked a bit odd.'

'Why is that?'

'Because they were really too young to have full beards, but I suppose that's what they look like.'

'Who do you mean?'

Eskedal leaned forward and lowered his voice: 'Religious fundamentalists.' Then he broke off as if something had just struck him. 'They were wearing odd clothes as well, at least clothes that aren't suitable for out here in the countryside. White shirts and jackets, black trousers and dress shoes.'

'What about their vehicle?'

'Most likely a Toyota Carina. White, as I said. An old model from the mid-nineties, I'd say. It's nearly sixty metres down to the road, so I didn't manage to catch sight of the number plate. Not that I thought about it in the heat of the moment either.' The man's eyes grew distant as he conjured up an image in his memory. 'And it had some damage on the right side at the front,' he added. 'The wing mirror was hanging off.'

Wisting completed his notes with a thick underline as a familiar, longed-for feeling washed over him: at last, some things were coming together. The car from the Hagtvedt farm must be the same one that Vera Kvålsvik had seen on her way to work and that Tommy Kvanter had spotted in his backyard near where the severed head was discovered in the town square. The descriptions were sufficiently specific for them to issue a wanted notice that could take the case a good distance forward.

27

Line rushed out of the stone building, settled into the driver's seat of her car and gave a sigh of relief. She had found the imam's statements very provocative. His strong conviction, based on religious belief, was that women should submit to male authority. As an unmarried woman, she was subject to her father and brother; in marriage she would be subject to her husband. Since God regarded women as a destructive element in the social order, in that she took man's attention away from God and God's admonitions, she should live separately from men and be denied the opportunity to take part in activities outside the home. In this way, the danger was reduced that she might distract men from their most important task in life: devotion to God.

Imam Dhuhulow had concluded that men have higher status than women – the sexes had different roles that should complement each other. The man had the responsibility to ensure that his daughters and wife were mindful of his reputation. If the family's women did not obey him, he was made a fool of in the eyes of his peers. He would be a man without honour, and shame would be brought down upon the whole family.

What had infuriated her most, however, was his macabre lack of principle. She had challenged him with questions about the physical punishment of women and the restoration of lost honour. He had wriggled out of it by saying that these were theological questions he could not answer and asked for her respect and understanding. When direct questions were posed about Islam's fundamental texts in support of the subordination of women in more or less every area of life, he had spoken about Sharia law in an attempt to appease both his own flock and his critics. As a *Norwegian* Muslim, he distanced himself from all kinds of violence against women. However, she thought she understood what he really meant but would not be able to include that in her article.

She tossed her notebook on to the passenger seat and fired up the engine. There was enough material to compose an ancillary story highlighting the imam's assurances that honour killings had nothing to do with Islam, though he was aware that some people had directed their suspicions at the Muslim community, but it would be too simple and superficial. If she wanted to build a story on this, she would have to dig deeper and throw light on the values, culture, traditions, customs and convictions in a more exhaustive fashion.

She had manoeuvred the car through the streets of the town centre and ended up outside Tommy Kvanter's apartment. Although she was reluctant to admit the real reason to herself, she had made up her mind to drop in on him with a copy of that day's newspaper, to thank him for what he had done yesterday and ask if he had come up with anything new. Also, she was keen to find out what the police were focusing on and how much attention they had paid to his observations.

The phone rang, interrupting her. The display told her it was Morten P.

'They've found her,' he said. 'A headless body has washed up in the Stavern marina.'

Line put the car back into gear.

'You don't need to come here,' Morten P. added, as if he had heard her accelerate. 'They've already packed up the body and driven it away, but we could really do with something from the police. To see if they have any idea about who she could be.'

'What are you going to do?'

'I'll pick up any loose ends here. There are only crumbs left for us. Your pal from *Dagbladet* is sitting talking to Einar Brodtkorp right now.'

'The meteorologist?'

'He was the one who found her. They have it out on the net already. The interview will probably be a hell of a spread. It's not every day a TV personality finds a dead body. The only thing we can hit back with is if we can start giving our readers some answers rather than just asking fresh questions.'

Morten P. wrapped up the conversation by asking for a meet-up and run-through at twelve o'clock. Line glanced at the dashboard clock. Just over an hour till then and she knew what she had to do. She shrank from talking to her father about the case but felt compelled to key in his number. She jumped when the phone rang just as she was about to press the button.

Suzanne Bjerke appeared on the display. That had to do with the suitcase inquiry that she kept pushing aside. In her text message the previous evening the woman had written that what she had to say was important. Line had promised to make contact, but she knew from experience that what was important to one person was a highly individual matter. She really had no time to speak to Suzanne but realized it gave her a reason to postpone her phone call to her father.

'I'm sorry to be hassling you like this,' the woman at the other end said in an undertone. 'But I think I know who the beheaded girl might be.'

28

Someone had left a bundle of that day's newspapers in the conference room. All the front pages were splashed with the *Beheading Murder*. The attention of the entire country was focused on it. It crossed Wisting's mind that the media interest could not even be compared to when he started out as an investigator, or when the city of Ålesund had burned down, and he smiled at the recollection of a lecturer on a media course in which he had participated a number of years ago.

The catastrophic fire of 1904 had claimed two lives and rendered 12,000 inhabitants homeless. The first news report had been published in *Aftenposten* the next day in the form of a telegram sent from Trondheim. The following day, *Aftenposten* had based their coverage on a special telegram from Molde. On the fourth day, *Aftenposten*'s own reporter had arrived in nearby Kristiansund and had to fight for space on a solitary, sluggish telegraph line. Not until the fifth day did the journalist who had been dispatched arrive in Ålesund itself and only then was he able to describe the burnt-out town and ongoing rescue work from personal experience.

Wisting shook his head at the thought of how the mass media had developed as he leafed through the pages. Maybe whoever was behind these two bestial killings was also leafing through the very same newspaper, reading about the leads the police had and how far they had come in their pursuit of the killer.

At its worst, the media presented Norway as a society that was more dangerous and more threatening than it was in reality. Their intense focus on crime had a resultant impact on people's behaviour. They became more anxious, stayed at home more and took precautions against a violence that they in all likelihood would never encounter.

Around forty people were murdered in Norway every year. The number was so low in an international context that this was in itself a sign that Norway was a safe country to live in. In the majority of murder cases, there was a close relationship between the victim and the killer, mainly crimes of passion or drunkenness perpetrated on relatives or friends within the domestic sphere. They were not over matters of principle, they did not reveal significant trends and usually said little about developments in society and politics. There was nothing about them to suggest that the whole of Norway should be told all the details, but they did of course whet the fundamental human appetite for the melodramatic. He shared this inclination himself and sometimes wondered if that was what had drawn him to be a policeman.

Line's name was printed under two of the articles in *VG* and that made him proud. He pulled the newspaper towards him and skimmed through what she had written. The story about Vera Kvålsvik was the more substantial of the two. She had been pictured among the bookshelves at her work. The photo did not really do her justice – her face looked serious and mournful.

It seemed that Line had asked virtually the same questions as he had. Vera's input had been described in words that were slightly more dramatic and subjective, but the content was more or less the same as her statement to the police.

Tommy Kvanter had been anonymized in the article on the opposite page, but he gave a good account of his discovery of the bloodstained T-shirt in the backyard. Of course, the point was made that it had been the newspaper and not the police that had tracked down this lead, but the words *police blunder* had been omitted. Instead it was emphasized that both Vera Kvålsvik and Tommy Kvanter had spotted a white estate car in the course of those dramatic early-morning hours.

Wisting continued browsing. An aerial photo of Larvik town centre was printed across almost two whole pages under the headline *MENACE SPREADS*.

Wisting hunched over the table, studying the image. It must have been taken at midday. Several vehicles were parked in a protective ring around the closed-off area in the middle of the town square. Outside the barriers he could see a group of people. The streets extended like the threads of a spider's web out from the square, which lay like a spindle in the middle of the townscape. They wound their way into entrances and backyards, along past office buildings and apartment blocks. The roofs looked like flimsy shields against the threat from above.

He stared at the picture for a long time, thinking about what must really have happened. What secrets were hidden along these narrow streets and within the walls of the numerous buildings? What thoughts and feelings were people left with? Did they have confidence that the police would solve the case? Did he himself believe that?

Enthusiastic voices in the corridor made him sit upright and fold up the newspaper just as Espen Mortensen and Nils Hammer appeared at the door. Gazing at them, he could see from their excited faces that there had been a development. Some of the technical examinations Mortensen had set in train must have yielded results. His eye fell on a printout from the tele-fax machine that the crime-scene examiner was holding in his hand. He recognized the Kripos logo and the standard form of the lab reports from the fingerprint section.

'We have a match,' Mortensen said, waving the piece of paper.

'The man from the river?' Wisting asked hopefully.

Mortensen shook his head.

'For her.'

'The young girl?'

'The man's not listed,' Mortensen told him, 'but we got a match for the girl in the trace records.'

Wisting knitted his brows. The fingerprint register consisted of two lists: the main part contained prints from more than 120,000 convicted criminals but the trace register contained around 40,000 unidentified prints from various crime scenes and cases that had not been cleared up.

'In connection with what?'

'The suitcase inquiry,' Mortensen replied. 'Fingerprints from the beheaded girl were found on the handle and the surface. The blue suitcase must belong to her.'

29

Wisting flopped down in his office chair, swivelling round to take out the green folder that held the documents about the blue-suitcase investigation from the shelf behind him.

He looked out the illustrations and sat staring at the pictures of the blue suitcase with the Mickey Mouse stickers on the side. Deep furrows formed in his forehead above his attentive eyes.

The file was dated 23 October. Nineteen days had now elapsed since the suitcase had been handed in at the lost-property office on the ground floor. It had been found by a traffic controller from the National Rail Administration after someone had left it on the platform when the train departed.

Wisting withdrew the statement, running to five pages, given by Kyrre Anker Fredriksen. He had not been able to say which train the passenger had been likely to leave on or how long the suitcase had sat unattended by the time he found it. He had worked at the station for nine years and was well aware of how absent-minded people on the move could be. He had carried the suitcase into the freight office, fully expecting someone to phone and ask about it. If the person in question were lucky, he could have the suitcase sent on aboard the next train.

No one called to inquire about the case, but Fredriksen had received a phone call from the school where his eleven-year-old son was a pupil. The boy had fallen and knocked a lump out of his head and was en route to the hospital in a teacher's car. His wife was out of town and he had got hold of a colleague to take over his duties at the station before he dashed off. He had not given the suitcase another thought until an employee in the freight office came wheeling it along a couple of days later, wondering whether he knew anything about it.

Apart from the Mickey Mouse stickers, the case had no markings of any kind. It had been locked with a four-digit code and there was nothing to set them on the trail of an owner. The suitcase was left there for a day or two before a new recruit pointed out that they actually had rules and regulations for dealing with luggage that was unattended or left behind. If they had been working in an international airport, the terminal would have been evacuated and a call sent out for a robot to blow up or neutralize the unclaimed baggage. Fredriksen contented himself with driving it up to the police station during his break and delivering it to the lost-property office.

The suitcase sat there for another day or so before the person in charge decided to break the lock open and go through the contents in an attempt to locate the owner. She was reluctant to take this action on her own and the next day she enlisted the help of a police officer to open it.

Wisting returned to the photographs and leafed through to the last few pages, where the contents of the suitcase were documented as they had first been found and later as they were stored at the Kripos laboratories.

The suitcase had contained 14.3 kilos of heroin. The degree of purity had been analysed at as much as eighty-seven per cent, so that it could be mixed with other chemicals and the quantity increased by three times before being sent out to the market. Depending on the final purity, each gram of the drug could produce up to ten user doses and that would bring a street value of almost one hundred million kroner.

All the same, the quantity of narcotics in the suitcase was sufficient only to cover just under a week's demand on the illegal market. It was estimated that around 15,000 people were dependent on a daily dose of heroin to avoid withdrawal symptoms. Through his years in the police, Wisting had seen far too often what the drug did to addicts. What began as a euphoric experience with an intense sensation of wellbeing and nonchalance quickly moved on to a flight from reality in which hunger, pain and everyday needs no longer played a role. The intoxicating feeling of happiness was replaced by restlessness, stress and anxiety. Users underwent a physical and psychological change. They were affected by a lack of initiative and ended up in emotional imbalance. Addiction to narcotics often led them into crime and prostitution and a lethal way of life characterized by pain and humiliation. And for each of these drug addicts there were family and friends who struggled with despair, fear, feelings of guilt, shame and desperation in their efforts to help their son, daughter, grandchild, brother or sister.

Wisting collected the documents together again and leaned back in his chair. He thought he could make out the contours of something. A fragile framework of a theory began to take shape. It went further than the evidence to hand, but he felt that the investigation was beginning to take a serious turn. Several pieces of the puzzle would fall into place if this all had to do with the drugs trade. Some kind of business deal that had somehow gone wrong? Someone had to pay for the loss? The two murder cases they were faced with could be part of a narcotics showdown in circles where the drug barons would stop at nothing to point the finger and make an example.

The ethnic origins of the victims also fitted with this theory. The largest opium fields were to be found in Central

Asia. He had read somewhere that the previous year's harvest in the borderlands between Pakistan, Afghanistan and Iran was estimated to value around three billion US dollars.

He rubbed his chin as he contemplated this. The narcotics theory was logical. However, what he did not understand was what the suitcase with the valuable, dangerous contents had been doing in the hands of a young teenage girl.

30

The streets situated on the slopes under the Bøkeskogen forest were right-angled and steep. The old buildings were in a bright, airy location overlooking the rest of the town and the fjord.

Line studied the house numbers and found her way to a box-shaped brick construction at the end of Nedre Bøkeligate. The building had two complete storeys and a decorative band of tiling set into the grey cement render.

Brown, withered autumn leaves were whirling in the wind and gathering in the recess in front of the wide entrance door. Someone had tried to set fire to the doorbell with a cigarette lighter. The plastic had melted and streaks of soot were smeared on the wall. She tried the button all the same and heard a shrill chime from inside the building. Immediately afterwards, the door was opened by a tall boy of about fourteen with dark hair.

'Hi,' Line said with a smile. 'I'd like to talk to Suzanne Bjerke.'

The boy in the doorway nodded and waved her in. The floor in the spacious hallway was crammed with shoes of various shapes and sizes and colourful jackets and an assortment of headgear were hanging on a row of pegs. A framed placard proclaimed the house rules.

'She's in the office,' the boy told her, and then stood waiting.

Line hesitated for a moment before untying her shoes and placing them neatly side by side. The floor was cold and her toes curled up.

The boy ushered her through a narrow corridor. Inside, the old building had a modern feel with bright colours and new furnishings. They passed the opening into the kitchen, where a young girl with dreadlocks sat on a tall stool beside the worktop, stealing a glance at them from her book.

The boy stopped at a closed door at the end of the passageway. He knocked twice before pushing down the handle and opening the door wide.

'Visitor!' he called out, and then turned to leave.

A woman in her forties rose from a desk inside. She was tall, with slim hips and coal-black, silky hair tied back in a ponytail. Her face was fresh and open and she used no make-up.

Suzanne Bjerke held out her hand with a smile. Line smiled back and saw that the eyes behind the woman's thin glasses radiated a warmth that instilled immediate confidence.

Line had made some inquiries in advance. Suzanne Bjerke had been born in Kabul, Afghanistan, in 1960. Her father had been a diplomat posted to Paris during the communist coup in his homeland in 1979 and Suzanne had studied social sciences at the Sorbonne. There she had met the Norwegian student Hans Bjerke and they had travelled to Norway together when her parents fled to America after the Soviet invasion.

She had married at the age of nineteen and trained as a child welfare officer in Norway. According to the information gleaned from local authority webpages, she had obtained further qualifications in family therapy and acquired expert knowledge of the treatment of trauma and understanding of multicultural issues. She was registered as a widow in 1984 and had no children. The employment records showed that she had worked in a number of different youth institutions. Nowadays she was in charge of the Child Welfare Service's residential unit for minority-language young people.

The room they sat in was small but functional, with two bookcases full of ring binders and various reference works, a filing cabinet on which the top drawer did not shut and a tidy desk with a compact computer. Pictures and children's drawings hung on the cream-coloured walls.

Suzanne had shown her to a small seating area in front of a circular table beside the window. A glass bowl on the table was filled with water, colourful pebbles and floating tea lights that gave off a sweet scent of spices.

'Sorry about the postponements,' Line apologized, rooting around in her bag for her notebook.

'You're here now.' Suzanne Bjerke smiled warmly, but it was easy to see that concern lay behind her friendly expression. 'Would you like something to drink? A cup of tea, perhaps?'

Leaning back against the soft cushions, Line accepted the offer. Suzanne disappeared out of the room and soon returned with two cups.

'Hanan is bringing the pot,' she explained.

Line nodded, waiting for the woman facing her to start talking.

'Hanan is from Somalia,' she said. 'There are seven youngsters from five different nations living here.'

Line sat up straight. Muddled thoughts began to take shape. Feelings and assumptions were being transformed into a theory. She understood that she might be coming close to something crucial, but she kept her questions to herself.

'They all came to Norway as young, single asylum-seekers,' Suzanne added. 'The ones living here have been granted leave to stay, but they're alone in the world and live here until they can stand on their own two feet. Many come from unendurable life situations and have experienced poverty, war, revolution, catastrophe and assault. They've come here in the hope of a safe life far from hunger and want. They require all the care, security and protection we can give them, so that they can make use of their own talents and resources.'

Line could see the commitment that burned within the woman on the opposite side of the low table and let her continue without breaking in with questions.

'Very few of these teenagers really want to be here. None of them has chosen to flee to this country. The decision is usually taken by the family or some other relative who has spent every last penny of what they own in an attempt to let some of the youngest generation have an opportunity to live a different life. They have placed a big responsibility on their young shoulders and many of them are refugees from war-torn places. Some suffer from deep-seated trauma that will affect them for a long time.'

There was a light knock at the door and the young girl from the kitchen entered carrying a pot of tea and poured it for them. Line smiled in thanks and picked up the cup.

'But there are also children and young people here with us who want to play and learn,' Suzanne said with a smile when they were alone again. 'Young people who are curious about life and who have their own hopes and dreams.'

Line sipped from the warm cup and nodded thoughtfully.

'Hanan fled from the perpetual war in Somalia,' Suzanne went on. 'For children who arrive here on their own, it is extra difficult to find their feet. They have no one to share their experiences with. If they don't receive help, the trauma can affect them for the rest of their lives.'

Exchanging her teacup for her notebook, Line felt it was time to get to the point.

'You said you thought you knew who the murdered girl might be,' she said, glancing at the bundle of that day's newspapers on the desk.

Suzanne nodded.

'Layla Azimi,' she said, clearing her throat. 'Not all of the teenagers who come here manage to adjust. Layla is a Pashtun from the eastern part of Afghanistan. She came to Norway eight years ago after her father was arrested when the Taliban seized power in the village where the family lived. She fled through Europe along with an uncle and two cousins. When they arrived in Norway, she was suddenly alone. She doesn't know why her uncle abandoned her, but probably he realized she had a better chance of being allowed to stay if she was on her own.'

Line made some notes.

'We don't know what age Layla is. She doesn't know herself, but the medical examination showed she is most likely fourteen. In her official papers she has a date of birth of 27 February 1994. That's her name day. Layla is an Arabic name that means night darkness and Laylatul Qadr is a holy night in Ramadan.'

Suzanne got to her feet, crossed to the bookshelf and pulled out a ring binder.

'Layla has lived with us for three years,' she explained, resuming her seat. She opened the binder and sat with a photograph of a serious-looking girl in front of her. The face was beautiful with a pair of green, intense eyes.

As silence filled the room, they heard the volume being turned up on a stereo system on the floor above.

Suzanne Bjerke kept leafing through the binder. Her voice became more formal when she continued: 'Layla has shown an extremely varying degree of adjustment. At times she has attended school, followed the rules and been fairly happy, but then she suddenly takes off, truants and becomes challenging and insolent. She changes friends frequently and it's difficult to keep tabs on her social network, but she mainly hangs out with older teenagers.'

She stopped, staring down at the papers, and it seemed as if she was weighing up what and how much she could say. Then she took a deep breath and it was as if she was getting ready to take a giant leap: 'The staff here describe her as very independent and difficult to get close to. She does not appreciate intervention and can react aggressively and use hurtful words. They experience her as being dismissive and withdrawn.'

Line turned to a blank page and nibbled at the end of her pen before asking the necessary question: 'Where is Layla now?'

Suzanne's eyes filled with despair.

'We don't know,' she answered, shaking her head. 'As I said, she often disappears, up to half a dozen times a month, and she can be gone for four or five days at a time before she comes home again. Sometimes she answers her phone when we call and she's usually to be found in Oslo. Now it's been four days since we heard from her.'

'Haven't you reported her missing?'

'She's gone off the radar so often that we've stopped doing that. She always comes back, you see, and we're usually able to get in touch with her by phone. We feel we're just a nuisance to the police. They don't do anything about it anyway. Teenagers run off and just end up as names on a list. They haven't the resources to drive around looking for kids who've run away from home.'

'Yes, but this is different, surely,' Line objected.

'But we don't know if it's Layla they've found,' Suzanne ventured. Her eyes flitted around the room, searching for something to fix on. Line could see that it was fear of having her worst suspicions confirmed that had held her back from contacting the police.

'Anyway, there's more to it,' Suzanne went on. 'I'm afraid

Layla and some of the other teenagers here may have become entangled in something dangerous. That was really why I got in touch with you.'

'What do you mean?'

'You were writing about the blue suitcase, weren't you? I wanted to talk to you since you have some knowledge of that and maybe know more than what the newspapers are saying.'

Line changed position and nodded warily as a sign for Suzanne to continue.

'I knew your mother,' she said. 'We worked together on a few school projects for children with behaviour problems.'

'Then you could have spoken to my father, couldn't you?' Line suggested.

Suzanne Bjerke nodded.

'I know he's a trustworthy policeman, but I'm sceptical about the police. I know I shouldn't think like that as a professional person, but I just can't help it. The police have a difficult job and it's their task to exercise power and make decisions in ways that upset me and conflict with all my beliefs.' She shook her head as if to underline the point. 'Children have the right to be reunited with their parents, but no automatic right to being reunited in a different country. We had a boy here with us called Khaled Athari. Last winter someone in the Immigration Directorate managed to trace his grandparents to an Afghan village on the border with Turkmenistan. Khaled had been given permission to stay in Norway but when his father's parents, now elderly, were found in his homeland the grounds for him staying lapsed. The Directorate are of the general opinion that it is not necessarily in the child's best interests for a family reunion to take place in Norway. They decided that Khaled should be deported back to Afghanistan and that his care should be transferred to his grandparents. The day Khaled was to begin in Class 8, officers from the Police Immigration Service came and picked him up. All he owned and was allowed to take with him filled two small suitcases.'

Line remained silent, giving Suzanne time to compose herself. Outside, it had started raining again and little beads of water settled on the windowpane.

'The youngsters here don't like to talk about the terrible things they've experienced,' she went on. 'That can be because they want to shield us or because they're trying to repress what happened. Just like Layla, Khaled was uncommunicative and dismissive and at times he didn't function well, but the evening before he was due to leave, he told a dreadful story. I don't know whether he wanted to explain himself or excuse himself. Maybe he thought that his behaviour and constant running away was the reason he was being deported, but it was as if he wanted to give me some insight into a story, a secret that would help me to understand.'

Line hunched forward, letting her pen and notebook rest in her hands.

'One evening at the end of May, a car with three men stopped beside him in the street. One of them spoke to him in Dari, asking the way to somewhere they could buy kebabs. Khaled gave them directions, but they didn't understand and he got into the car to show them the way. But the driver didn't stop at the takeaway café. The man who had been sitting in the front passenger seat moved into the back so that Khaled was wedged between them. They drove up the E18 to Oslo and then on through Østfold and over the border to Sweden. Not until they'd been driving for six hours did they stop, outside an apartment block in Gothenburg. Khaled was held captive in an apartment for two days before he was given a large suitcase and a train ticket back to Larvik.'

Line drew a long line at the foot of the page in her notebook. It felt as if she now had an almost completed crossword in front of her. Most of the squares had suddenly been filled in and only a few of them remained blank or incomprehensible. She wondered if this was how her father felt when an important witness came forward to put some crucial information on the table.

The story Suzanne had told dealt with coercion and cynical human trafficking in which children in a vulnerable situation were used to smuggle narcotics.

'What do you think about it all?' Suzanne Bjerke asked, meeting her eye over the rim of her teacup.

Line stared back and saw that Suzanne's face bore telltale signs of helplessness and worry. Her skin was taut across her cheekbones and she had blue circles under her eyes. Line let her eyes move to the clock hanging on the wall behind her. It had just gone twelve. Instinctively she calculated that there were just under sixteen hours to deadline. Words and sentences had already begun to take shape in the back of her mind. Then she leaned back, feeling almost faint from all the information she had just been given.

'I think I need to make a phone call,' she said.

31

When the phone on Wisting's desk rang, he automatically checked the number on the display against the list on the yellow Post-it note beside the phone. Increasing numbers of journalists had discovered his direct line and he always avoided answering. Anyway, he had nothing to tell them and considered himself fortunate that it was not his job to keep the media and the outside world up to date.

Seeing that it was a local number, he lifted the receiver. The male caller introduced himself with a name Wisting thought familiar, somewhere far back in his memory. However, it took him a while to realize he was speaking to the farmer who had left a hay stave in his office just a couple of hours ago.

'They're here again,' Johan Eskedal told him.

Wisting's grip on the phone receiver tightened.

'The men who stole the wooden stave. I'm standing here watching them now. They've parked their white estate car down at the old milk platform. It looks as if they're walking around searching for something.'

'Hold the line,' Wisting said. Swallowing audibly, he kept the Hagtvedt farmer waiting while he dialled the direct number of the top brass.

His eagerness to show his pal what he had found made Marvin Eskedal's heart beat faster than usual. He pushed open the door of his father's tool store and waved Erlend over. Picking their way through the messy room that stank of tar and sawdust, they moved on down the dim passageway and up the ladder to the hayloft.

His whole body was tingling with excitement.

Balancing on the thick beams, they crept up into the open loft. The walls had gaps where some of the scant daylight seeped in and sliced through the dust as it whirled up.

Under the small west-facing window eleven notches were carved, one for each day at the end of April 1945. His grandfather had told him the story of the American bomber that had crash-landed in Brunlanes. Ten men had jumped out with parachutes before the plane hit the ground. His grandfather had found two of them before the Germans did and he had kept them hidden up here until Milorg, the Norwegian resistance movement, had arranged transport for them to Sweden.

Marvin ran his fingers over the rough marks, as he always did. This little concealed spot had become a den for him and Erlend. No one else came here or even knew about it. They had spent hours up here. If they added all those hours together, they would almost certainly add up to weeks, maybe even months. They could lie here discussing all sorts of things, share their secrets, thoughts and emotions, or simply lie side by side, completely still, and read magazines or books.

'Where is it?' Erlend demanded impatiently.

Marvin smiled. The rain was drumming on the corrugated roof above their heads. He removed the loose plank, took out the bundle of porn magazines, the snuff tin that his uncle had lost the last time he had paid a visit, and four miniature bottles of whisky and cognac he had stolen from the tax-free shop on the Danish ferry last summer.

There it lay. A real pistol.

He lifted it up, revelling in the weight in his hands. The cold steel glistened. *Colt 1911. Hartford.ct USA* was engraved along the gun barrel.

'It's the same one as the Americans used during the war,' he said, holding out the gun.

Although he hesitated at first, Erlend took the weapon. He moved it from one hand to the other before turning the barrel around to face him and peering into the muzzle.

'Did you just find it?'

Marvin nodded, scratching his nose. The dust from the dry hay made it tickle and itch.

'In the ditch, beside the milk platform.'

'It's really heavy.'

Marvin took the gun back, weighing it in his hand again, and agreed. Then he held it out in front of him with his arm outstretched. Shutting one eye, he aimed for a knothole at the other side of the loft. His finger curled around the trigger and squeezed. The first few millimetres felt easy, and then the resistance grew greater until he had to stop.

Through the wooden planks of the walls, they heard a car drive up the farm track. They could hear from the sound that it was travelling faster than vehicles usually did on the potholed surface. Marvin opened the window a crack and peered out through the gap. A grey Volvo turned into the farmyard and stopped. A tall man in dark trousers, a shirt and suit jacket stepped out. He was talking into a mobile phone as he looked around and walked up to the farmhouse. Marvin's father came to the door to meet him. The man took his mobile from his ear and spoke to him, and he answered and pointed down to the main road as if he were explaining something.

'Shouldn't we tell some grown-ups?' Erlend asked cautiously.

'No, why should we?' Marvin protested. 'It's not our fault that someone has been stupid enough to lose a pistol.'

Resting the gun on the windowsill, he took aim at his father.

'We're going to get a bawling out if they catch us,' Erlend objected.

'That's exactly why we shouldn't tell them.'

He shifted the gun and let the barrel point at the man, who was now talking into his mobile again. He let the sight above the muzzle cover the man's head and followed him as he paced back and forth. His index finger curled around the trigger, pressing millimetre by millimetre as the resistance increased.

The shot came suddenly. The kickback from the fired weapon propelled him backwards. The loud bang filled the tight space and made his ears hurt. His heart was hammering as if it wanted to escape from his ribcage. For a moment or two he lay in total confusion before moving forward on his knees and hauling himself up at the window.

Wisting had been barking brief messages into his phone, summarizing what Johan Eskedal had told him about the white estate car and directing the various units to cover all the surrounding roads.

He realized what the loud bang was before he felt any pain. He flung himself down behind his car. Something warm and sticky was trickling down the right side of his face. He ran his hand over his cheek and saw it was red. The pain spread from his shoulder all the way down his arm.

Johan Eskedal crouched down beside him, his eyes shifting from Wisting up to the barn.

'Those boys!' he shouted, swearing under his breath as he got to his feet. He took a few steps away, but turned and stooped down again. 'Are you OK?'

Although Wisting nodded, he was not really sure. He wrenched off his jacket and saw that his shirt was ripped on his right shoulder and also stained red with blood. A sizeable gash had been torn in his skin, but it looked like a flesh wound. Moving his arm, he rotated his shoulder and nodded again.

The farmer turned to the barn again, roaring his son's name and striding forward.

32

Wisting sat on the paper-covered doctor's couch with his feet dangling above the floor. The doctor who was studying the wound on his right shoulder was short, had dark hair and a dark complexion, and spoke Danish.

'You've been lucky,' he said, getting a needle and thread ready. 'The bullet has only damaged some of the top layer of skin and torn it off.'

Nils Hammer stood at the entrance of the treatment room. He took a step forward and tossed a transparent evidence bag on to the bench beside him.

'A month's house arrest,' he said, pointing at the pistol. 'The boy told us he found it down at the roadside yesterday morning but he didn't realize it was loaded.'

The doctor stole a glance at the gun before bending over the wound again, deep in concentration.

'Those men must have dropped it when they picked up the stave on Sunday,' Hammer continued. 'And then come back to look for it today.'

Wisting had worked that out for himself. Pieces of the puzzle were falling into place.

'How's the search for the car going?'

'We put up roadblocks on most of the routes, but it could have slipped through before they were in place.' Hammer took out his snuff tin and tucked a pinch under his lip. 'We're making door-to-door inquiries across the village. I think that car belongs somewhere up there and they're holing up in a cabin or disused smallholding somewhere. Probably they've driven past Johan Eskedal's milk platform a few times before and so they stopped at the roadside and helped themselves to a stave when they needed one.'

Wisting grimaced, feeling the needle go in as the doctor made the first stitch.

'Johan Eskedal didn't think he'd ever seen either the car or the men before. Two guys like that would stand out and get noticed in that neck of the woods.'

'Not necessarily,' Hammer objected. 'All that farmland is chock-a-block with cheap labour from Poland, Lithuania and Romania.' He looked at his watch. 'Anyway, an arrest warrant will be issued at the press conference at 5 p.m. I've told them you won't be there.'

'I hope Vetti has considered keeping this from the press for a while longer,' Wisting commented.

'I think that'll be difficult. We're talking about the discovery of a possible murder weapon in a case where the newspapers are giving an impression that the police have nothing to go on. He has to give them something to restore the trust of both the media and the public in the police force.'

Wisting nodded. He could see the point but would have preferred to wait until the ballistic examinations had been completed. It would be a setback if it turned out that the gun had nothing to do with the case.

'What do we know about it?' he asked.

'Quite a lot,' Hammer replied, producing some documents from a folder.

'It's a Colt M1911, 45 calibre,' he said. 'More than three million of them were made but, according to the gun registry, this particular pistol belongs to Pål Stensby.'

The name chimed immediately in Wisting's head. Pål Stensby was a firearms collector who was active in competitive shooting. Five weeks ago, burglars had got away with the entire contents of his gun cabinet. Thirteen handguns and five rifles were missing. In addition, the cabinet had contained an envelope containing nearly 30,000 kroner. Traditional methods of investigation had led nowhere, but sources had claimed to the Police Security Service that Cato Dalen and the Patriotic Front were behind the theft.

Hammer handed Wisting the case papers. Wisting skimmed through the crime-scene report to refresh his memory:

CRIME SCENE

The crime scene is a farm at Omsland in Kjose. The farm itself is situated 300 metres east of the Kjoseveien road and 10 kilometres from the exit road from the E18. The farm comprises a farmhouse, garage and barn. The victim of the crime, Pål Stensby, lives here with his wife, Grete Stensby. The couple left the farm on Friday 3 October around 16.00 to visit their son, who lives in Kristiansand. They returned on Sunday 5 October and discovered the break-in when they arrived home around 17.30. The situation was reported to the police at 17.37.

MODUS OPERANDI

Access to the farmhouse was gained by breaking through the verandah door at the rear of the house. A crowbar was pressed between the door and frame at the height of an external cylinder lock. Damage sustained to door and frame.

The verandah door leads into the living room. From here there is free access to the rest of the house. The victim's gun cabinet was in an adjoining guestroom/study. There are obvious scrape marks on the parquet flooring from the cabinet being dragged through the living room and out to the verandah.

The marks on the doorframe from the crowbar measure 16 millimetres. Photographed and secured in plastic moulds. Traces of blue varnish were found from the crowbar.

On the verandah door and other places in the house, prints have been taken from gloves. Footprints were secured from the living-room floor that may be suitable for comparison with footwear (see separate folder of illustrations).

On the lawn around the house, tyre tracks were left by a vehicle. The axle base is measured at circa 270 cm and wheel gauge at circa 135 cm.

STOLEN GOODS

The gun cabinet, brand name Seifuva SG149, was taken. The cabinet weighs net 158 kg and is 150 cm in height, 60 cm broad and 40 cm deep. Containing the following weapons in addition to the injured party's firearms licence:

Weapon no.	Weapon type	Calibre	Manufacturer
24401	Rifle	45	Pedersoli
3460	Revolver	451c	Uberti
27891	Revolver	44	Colt
462032	Shotgun	12	Boito
J05645	Revolver	38	Uberti
229065	Shotgun	S/S 12/70	Husqvarna
J08914	Revolver	451c	Uberti
237893	Rifle	22	Marlin
Y26671	Rifle	6.5	Sauer
803422	Pistol	45	Colt
483995	Revolver	22	Smith & Wesson
484653	Revolver	38	Smith & Wesson

Weapon no.	Weapon type	Calibre	Manufacturer
SP1419	Pistol	9	Vektor
010102	Pistol	7.65	Mauser
002112	Pistol	6.35	Browning
65274	Pistol	22	Ruger
654651	Pistol	9mm	Walther
125454	Pistol	22	Margolin

The victim further reported that the gun cabinet also contained ancillary ammunition as well as a grey C5 envelope containing 29,500 kroner, mainly in 500-kroner banknotes.

Also, various items of gold jewellery belonging to Grete Stensby were stolen from a chest of drawers in the same room. The total value is estimated at 100,000 kroner. A specific list will be produced.

Wisting leafed further through, to the forms produced as a result of the door-to-door inquiries made in the local village. A neighbour had seen an old-style Ford Mondeo turn into the gravel track leading up to the farm. There were two men with close-cropped hair in the car. They were wearing camouflage clothing and he had thought they were teenagers intending to go fishing at the small lakes on the Telemark border. Another witness had spotted the same car making its way out of the village an hour later and had noticed it had a heavy load. They were unable to provide a registration number or any more detailed description of the men.

The type of car that had been seen was one of the most-sold cars in Norway over the years.

Torunn Borg appeared at the door, wearing a concerned expression and holding a Dressmann carrier bag.

'Any news?' Hammer asked.

'No sign of the car,' she told him as she unpacked a checked shirt and a brown sweater. 'Mortensen has secured the bullet. It had bored into the verandah bannisters. He's going to take the pistol to Kripos tomorrow for ballistic examination. Hopefully, Forensics will also find a bullet in the body we dragged from the river last night, so that we can establish without doubt that it's the murder weapon.'

The doctor had finished stitching and was now bandaging the wound. Wisting handed the papers describing the weapons theft back to Nils Hammer.

'Something here doesn't stack up,' he said, hopping down from the couch. 'If the Patriotic Front are behind the gun theft, I can't for a minute imagine that they would hand the guns over to foreigners of any kind.'

'The Security Service could be mistaken,' Hammer said. 'Their sources may have other motives for pointing the finger at a right-wing nationalist group.'

'Yes,' Wisting agreed, 'but a couple of skinheads were spotted at the scene and we know that Cato Dalen stored ammunition in his house. Hundreds of cartridges exploded in the house fire.'

'A couple of crime-scene technicians from Tønsberg are investigating the site of the blaze as we speak,' Torunn Borg explained, holding up the new shirt.

Thanking her, Wisting began to get dressed.

'What about Cato?' he asked. 'Has anyone spoken to him?'

Torunn Borg shook her head. 'We can't get hold of him. He's disappeared.'

'Disappeared?'

'Both him and his girlfriend. It's rumoured that he's gone to Sweden. Maybe not so strange that he wants to lie low after someone tried to torch him and his house.'

A nurse came in and handed Wisting his damaged clothes.

Wisting took the bag, moved over to the couch where he had been sitting and lifted up the transparent bag with the pistol that had been seized as evidence. He stared at the black gun barrel, wondering how many people had done that before him.

33

It was still raining when Wisting left the hospital. Grey and pouring. The last golden leaves, sad and forlorn, were plastered to the walls and windowpanes of the surrounding buildings. He dashed across the car park and clambered into the passenger seat beside Torunn Borg. Hammer drove off in his own car.

Taking his mobile phone out of his trouser pocket, Wisting switched it on. Line had tried to get hold of him. He accessed his voicemail and listened to her brief message. The clock on the display showed 16.07. The message was seventeen minutes old.

'Drive to Bøkelia,' he said after hearing the message. 'To the residential unit for children from overseas.'

Torunn took a right turn and followed the old road, laid with worn, shiny cobbles, down towards the Farris river. The uneven road surface made the car shake and rattle and he felt every bump, but at the same time a connection he should have thought of long ago began to dawn on him.

Line's car was parked at the kerb. As Torunn drew up behind it, she gave Wisting a quizzical look.

'A fourteen-year-old girl has gone missing from here,' he explained.

'Do you want me to –'

'You drive back to the station,' he broke in. As long as Line was involved, he would prefer to deal with this on his own. 'Tell the others we'll have a meeting after the press conference. I'll get Line to drop me off.'

Torunn nodded.

Wisting stepped out and walked up to the broad door. At last the case was moving in one direction. He had experienced this before, when a phone call, a tiny detail, could shift the investigation on to the right track.

A young lad let him in and showed him the way to a simply furnished office at the end of a long corridor.

Line was seated in front of the window beside a dark-haired woman. They both stood up as he entered. The tall, slim stranger gazed at him with sceptical eyes behind thin glasses.

Line introduced them and the woman offered him tea or coffee. Wisting turned this down, keen to get straight to the point.

Suzanne Bjerke repeated her story about Layla Azimi.

'When did you see her last?' Wisting asked.

'Last Friday.'

Four days, Wisting calculated. He refrained from asking questions about why she did not appear on the list of missing persons or why the unit had not made contact with the police. That was unnecessary criticism. He could see from the woman's expression that she was already full of self-reproach and despair.

'Do you have a picture of her?' he asked instead.

Suzanne Bjerke opened up a folder and took out a portrait photo. 'That's three months old,' she said, handing it to him.

It was her.

The pictures of her head still lay spread out on his office desk. He had studied every detail of the child's face and now recognized the familiar features. The placement of the ears, the moles above the right-hand corner of her mouth and on her chin, the small scar above the bridge of her nose and the striking green eyes. In the picture in front of him they shone like stars.

Wisting gulped as he took time to scrutinize every detail again before nodding his head in affirmation.

'Can I keep this?' he asked.

'Is it her?'

Wisting nodded again.

'Of course, we'll have to carry out a formal identification, but I'm afraid I can't offer you any hope.' He took a deep breath. 'It's definitely her.'

The expression on the woman's face changed from faintly hopeful to despondent and her eyes filled with tears. She struggled to say something but failed to articulate the words. He saw how sorrow had affected her while her eyes searched his for some kind of explanation. He felt like a doctor faced with a grievously ill patient who expected both an immediate diagnosis and a cure.

As for himself, he felt some kind of release now that one of the major questions had been answered and they had come one step closer to the truth. The beheaded girl had been given a name, Layla Azimi. A beautiful name. At the same time he felt a strange sense of relief that there were no surviving relatives in Norway. A murder always had several aspects. Wisting liked to think he had come across them all in the course of his career: an inconsolable mother, a despairing spouse, hysterical siblings and tearful children. He was pleased that he was spared having to cope with a heartbroken family right now.

At the same time, the total absence of relatives raised the investigation on to a completely new level of complication. The possible motive of protecting family honour had vanished. The idea that this murder, like most homicides in this country, might have been committed by someone in the victim's family or close circle was also now a remote possibility.

Clearing her throat, Suzanne Bjerke composed herself

and adopted a professional persona. 'What happens now?' she asked.

'I need a detailed statement from you,' Wisting replied. 'At the police station,' he added, glancing across at his daughter. In reality, she was the one who had brought the investigation to this crucial point, but he could not permit her to take part in the follow-up work. 'Everything to do with Layla will be of interest to us,' he went on. 'Did she have a boyfriend? Did she hang out with any specific groups? Did she have enemies? Or is there anything else you can tell us?'

The two women exchanged glances.

'There's more,' Line said.

Wisting sat hunched forward, waiting. Suzanne Bjerke took hold of the half-empty teacup in front of her, twirling it between her slim fingers. She wore no ring, he noticed. Her walnut-brown eyes had flint-like splinters scattered around the pupils that caught the light when she scanned the room.

'In August, you came to pick up one of the teenagers here, Khaled Athari,' she began, putting down the cup.

Wisting frowned.

'The Police Immigration Service,' Line interjected by way of explanation.

Suzanne Bjerke nodded.

'He was deported and sent to his grandparents in Afghanistan. I received a letter from him a month ago.' She stole a glance at the desk. Wisting could detect disquiet and bitterness in her voice but had no inkling of where she was going with this story. 'It makes me feel awful to read how things are with him there.'

'He told a story before he left,' Line took over. 'About how he had been forced to smuggle a suitcase over the border from Sweden to Norway.'

'A suitcase?' Wisting repeated, noticing a knot begin to tighten at the back of his neck.

'Suzanne is afraid that the youngsters here may have been forced into service by criminals,' Line went on. 'That they've been used as drugs couriers.' She took out the pictures of the blue suitcase containing 14.3 kilos of almost pure heroin from the police press conference. 'And Layla's been punished for a delivery gone wrong.'

Wisting ran his hand over the stubble on his chin. Like an aircraft carrier starting to change course, it dawned on him that the case was slowly, surely and inevitably making head-way in a new direction.

All of a sudden he sprang to his feet. 'Could I see her room, please?'

Suzanne Bjerke nodded and stood up and Line followed suit.

'On my own,' Wisting said, fixing his eyes on his daughter. 'I'd like to see it, and then we'll lock it up.'

The room allocated to Layla Azimi was tidy and plain. The walls and ceiling were painted white and the bed was covered in a lime-green spread and soft cushions so that it functioned as a settee when she had visitors. On the bedside table there was a book in English with a title Wisting had never heard of and just under the window stood a dark-brown desk. A mug was filled with pens and, beside that, school textbooks were neatly piled up. The wardrobe that lined one wall had large mirror doors that reflected the whole room and made it seem light and airy.

Crossing to the window, Wisting saw that the room on the upper floor faced west and had a view of the rest of the sloping town that stair-stepped down to the sea. A white cat with a black tail sauntered through the light cast by a street-lamp towards the wall enclosing a neighbouring property.

'It's not always so tidy in here,' Suzanne explained, speaking from the doorway.

'Were you the one who tidied it?' Wisting asked.

Suzanne shook her head. 'It's been like this since she left. We don't have any cleaning staff. The teenagers here are responsible for their own rooms and take turns to clean the common areas.'

Wisting surveyed the room. He had visited children's rooms like this in the past in connection with his work, searching for answers to why a daughter had chosen to end her life by slitting her wrists or why a son had raided a filling station while high on drugs, rummaging through teddy bears and drawing paraphernalia while parents watched him with red-rimmed eyes. As a rule he found nothing other than sorrow, anguish and frustration.

'I think you can understand and learn a lot about a young-ster's everyday life through seeing how they furnish their rooms,' Suzanne said, perching on the edge of the bed. 'They go to bed there and they wake up there. They play their music there and do their homework there too. They sit in the room when they're soul-searching and reflecting on their lives.'

Wisting turned to face her. In the harsh glare from the ceiling light she looked paler and the faint bags under her eyes looked more prominent.

'The choice of posters, decoration and colours expresses how a teenager wants to present themselves to the world in a search for their own identity,' she added. 'The boys usually plaster their walls with posters of football heroes or cars; the girls usually hang up film posters or pictures of famous pop groups. But some young people don't allow themselves to be influenced and, in their rooms, different things pop up.'

Wisting looked around at the bare walls.

'There's nothing here,' he summed up, thinking of how often it was what you *didn't* see or find that could betray so much about a person. In the case of Layla Azimi, there were no posters, no pictures and no cuddly toys. There were no CDs, no records, no computers. No make-up. There wasn't as much as an ornament of any kind.

'It says something about how empty her life was,' Suzanne concluded.

34

Darkness now surrounded the police station. The wind had picked up and was hurling rattling squalls of rain at the windowpanes. The streetlamps tugged at their cables like tethered animals.

Wisting stood at the window, waiting until the sound of scraping chair legs around the table had ceased. He had invited his closest colleagues to a meeting – Torunn Borg, Nils Hammer and Espen Mortensen, as well as Superintendent Audun Vetti.

Suzanne Bjerke had let him take the large portrait photo of Layla Azimi. She had placed it in a brown envelope and he now drew it out, placing it on the table and saying her name aloud.

The others stared at him as he told them what he himself had learned only an hour earlier. When he had finished, they sat in silence, absorbing this new information, which represented a major breakthrough in the investigation. Then it was as if a dam broke and suddenly they were all speaking over one another.

The superintendent's voice cut through all the others: 'We need a definite identification.'

Wisting agreed. This was the first formal step they had to take.

'I've brought her hair and toothbrushes,' he said. 'There should be enough biological material for a DNA analysis.'

'Is she not in Eurodac?' Hammer asked.

Wisting looked at Mortensen with a question in his eyes. Eurodac was a shared European data register with fingerprints from all those who had sought asylum or been caught staying illegally in one of the member countries.

'That only registers asylum-seekers over the age of fourteen,' the crime-scene technician explained. 'Anyway, the fingerprints are deleted when the asylum-seeker is granted asylum or the right to remain permanently.'

Wisting moved on: 'Suzanne Bjerke will come in to make a more exhaustive statement. However, she's gone through her records and found out that Layla Azimi was also missing from the residential unit from 13 to 17 October. The seventeenth of October is the day the suitcase full of narcotics was left on the platform down at the railway station.'

'It seems a bit unlikely that professional smugglers would hand over narcotics worth many millions to a child, though,' Torunn Borg mused aloud.

'It's actually ingenious,' Hammer said. 'What would cause either customs or the police to be suspicious? The customs checks on the train from Sweden are a joke anyway, but by using children the organization runs no risk of losing one of their own gang if they did it themselves and got caught. There are loads of solitary asylum-seeking children throughout Europe and if they use youngsters – who know no names, or anything about the smuggling apart from the suitcase they have in their hand – then they avoid the danger of the courier revealing who's behind it all. Also, it's completely risk free for the couriers, as long as they're below the legal age of criminal responsibility. I know of teenage girls who have done far worse things for money for a pay-as-you-go card or a new mobile phone.'

'But all alone on a train?'

'She probably wasn't alone. People she didn't know would have been with her on the train journey, making sure everything went smoothly.'

'But something did go wrong. The suitcase never reached its destination. It was left sitting on the platform.'

'Yes, something did go wrong,' Wisting nodded, 'and Layla Azimi had to pay a high price for that.'

As the others round the table went on discussing this, Wisting leaned back, having glimpsed something of the big picture. The newspapers had run many headlines about lone asylum-seeking children who had gone missing from various reception centres. Each year, a large number disappeared without any kind of investigation being set in train. Forms were filled out and statistics compiled but no purposeful work was undertaken to find the youngsters. It was pretty much assumed that the children had moved on to family or friends in another country and sought their fortune there.

He flicked through to a blank page in his notepad and spoke up again.

'There are six youngsters left in that unit,' he said. 'We have to interview all of them. We'll make a start tomorrow morning.'

'What do we say to the press?' Audun Vetti asked.

Wisting looked at the superintendent and bit his bottom lip before explaining Line's role to him.

'*VG* intends to write about Layla, but they'll hold back on the link to the blue suitcase and the narcotics,' he concluded.

Vetti scowled. 'We can't withhold this from the rest of the news media,' he protested.

Nils Hammer gave a snort from the other side of the table. 'We can't confirm that the victim has been identified. Were you thinking of issuing a press release about who we believe her to be?'

Audun Vetti shrugged. 'What will I say when they ask?'

The chair almost toppled as Hammer suddenly leapt up. 'Haven't you just held a press conference and told them we think we've found the murder weapon?' He headed to the coffee machine and filled a plastic cup. 'We're running an investigation, not a fucking guessing game. Do you really have to say anything else before we know for certain?'

The silence that filled the room felt awkward. Wisting broke into it: 'You can say we've made great strides in the work of identifying the victims. If you can manage to withhold the narcotics lead from the media, that would give us a valuable head start.'

'Have we actually made any progress with the identification of the body from the river, though?' Torunn Borg asked.

Espen Mortensen straightened up in his seat.

'I've examined the keys we found in his pocket. One had been filed down, with no type of system number to tell us where it belongs. The car key is from a Mazda, most likely an old 626. The last key might open some kind of locker.' The crime-scene examiner leaned back, thrusting his hands under his armpits. 'In addition to the keys, he had fourteen Danish kroner in his pocket. I've called in the passenger lists from the Danish ferry for the past week and worked back to see if there are any interesting names. If I'm lucky, I'll find some guy driving an old Mazda.'

Wisting nodded to acknowledge his colleague's initiative. Then he leafed back through his notepad to find what he was looking for.

'This is Layla Azimi's mobile number,' he said, tearing out the page. 'If there's a connection between her and the man from the river, then his number will be somewhere in the telecoms traffic.'

'Where is her phone?'

'No idea, but she had it with her when she went missing.'

He handed the paper to Mortensen. 'The historical telecoms data might also confirm that she's travelled between Norway and Sweden and who she's been in contact with.'

Mortensen held the page carefully in his hands, as if it was in itself an important piece of evidence.

'What about other electronic traces?' he asked. 'Bank card and that sort of thing?'

'Let's get Jan Osther to check that out,' Wisting suggested.

He got to his feet, mostly to mark that the meeting was at an end. The others went on sitting and talking.

Wisting moved to the window again and stood looking out with his back to the others. Sheets of rain swept over the rooftops and drummed on the windowpanes. The streets lay deserted and desolate. He thought of what Suzanne Bjerke had told him about Khaled Athari, who had been sent home to his grandparents in an Afghan mountain village. The person who would probably be the most vital witness in this case was a thirteen-year-old boy who was now 5,000 kilometres away. Where the Norwegian authorities had sent him.

35

Morten P. opened the door of room 302 in the Grand Farris Hotel when Line knocked a second time. He looked as if he had been sleeping. His long black hair was pressed flat on his scalp and he had pillow marks on his cheek.

Line glanced at her watch. It was just after 6 p.m., fifteen hours since the last time she had woken him and dragged him down to the river, where they had witnessed the police hauling a body ashore. She quickly calculated that she had slept for just over three hours in the course of the last day and a half, but she did not feel at all tired. The hours had raced past, crammed with new incidents that had pumped her full of adrenaline.

'What have you got?' the older journalist asked, waving her in.

The hotel room was spacious and inviting with light walls, parquet flooring and red velour seating beside the window. Old photographs hung on the walls, showing what the town had looked like in the past. The bed was located in a small alcove.

Line sat down in a high-backed chair with lots of cushions and placed her handbag down on the floor at her feet. Morten P. put on his cheerful smile and ran his hand over his bearded chin.

'I know who she is,' Line told him as she produced a picture of the Afghan girl from her bag. 'Her name is Layla Azimi,' she added, handing him the photograph.

Morten P. took it from her, his mouth opening and closing

as if he had no idea which question to ask first. Line related the story of the lone refugee girl. Morten P. walked back and forth across the floor as he listened. When she had finished, he came to a halt in front of the minibar. He took out a bottle of beer but then put it back again and produced a bottle of Farris mineral water instead and poured out two glasses.

'Bloody hell, Line,' he said, handing her a glass. 'This is good. We don't just have her name but her photo and practically her whole life story. And we're the only ones who have it.'

Line took a gulp of the water before setting the glass down again and taking her laptop from her bag. Morten P. stood by the window, nibbling at his bottom lip. The evening darkness, heavy with rain, had settled outside. She could see what he was thinking.

'When are they going to make this public?' he asked, turning to face her.

'In twenty-four hours at the earliest. They must have a definite identification before they can do that.'

Morten P. nodded. He knew how the police worked.

'But can we be sure it's her?' he asked. 'We can't risk printing the name and picture of a girl who just turns out to be on the run.'

'The police are certain,' Line assured him, taking back the photo, which Morten P. had set down on the coffee table.

'Your father?'

Line nodded, running her finger across the small scar on the girl's face in the photograph.

'The severed head has an identical scar,' she explained. 'And three little moles like that. One at the corner of her mouth and two on her chin.'

Morten P. drew the photo back again.

'She's beautiful,' he said. 'Radiantly beautiful. This is going to be a hell of a good story. But we must have some official confirmation.'

Line took out her reporter's notebook with the notes she had made before leaving her father.

'*The police believe the victim to be fourteen-year-old Layla Azimi, missing from local authority housing for minority-language young-sters,*' she read out. 'Or possibly *Police confirm they are working on the theory that the murdered girl is fourteen-year-old Layla Azimi and are awaiting the results of the forensic tests that will establish her identity.*'

'That's more than good enough,' Morten P. said, grinning. 'What's the deal?'

'That we don't write anything about the drugs connection. At least not yet.'

Morten P. pressed his lips together and stood, working his jaws. Then he nodded.

'It can wait. What can we write about the link to the body in the river?'

Line glanced down at her notebook: '*Police sources regard the cases as connected.*'

'Do they have any opinion on who he might be?'

'No.' Line flicked through her notebook. '*This could be some-one with no permanent residence in Norway. The police therefore anticipate a lengthy and time-consuming investigation in order to uncover the man's identity.*'

'Sit down and write,' Morten P. instructed her, pointing at the computer.

'I need your byline,' Line said. 'I can't have my name on an exclusive story confirmed by my father.'

Morten P. gazed thoughtfully at her.

'You realize you're giving up one of the year's most sensational front pages?'

She nodded. 'There will be other front pages,' she said with a smile.

Morten P. reciprocated with a broad grin and took out his phone.

'I'm ringing the news editor,' he announced. 'They'll have to clear some space for us.'

They took four hours to stitch together what was about to be the next day's main headline and story. Line had been granted two pages for the feature on Layla Azimi. In addition to the portrait photo of Layla, the article would be illustrated with a bleak image of the building where she had lived. It had been taken at dusk and in rain, enveloped in a yellowish sheen from the streetlights. They had considered including quotes from people connected to the residential unit but came to the conclusion that it would be best to wait. If they began to poke around too much, there was a danger that the story would break.

Morten P. read it through one last time before clicking to dispatch the story. It took three minutes for the news editor to phone. When Morten P. answered, the broad smile was abruptly wiped off his face.

'Fuck,' he swore, and beckoned Line away from the computer. '*Dagbladet* have beaten us to it.'

Line felt something contract within her ribcage as she waited for the browser to download the pages from *Dagbladet*.

VICTIM PROBABLY UNDERAGE ASYLUM SEEKER.

The headline was divided into two lines above archive photos from the crime-scene work at the town square. The story was signed off by Erik Thue.

Police Superintendent Audun Vetti confirms that the victim is probably an underage Afghan girl who had been granted asylum in Norway. She has been missing from a local authority home since Friday.

'Fuck.' Line echoed her colleague. They had been pipped at the post.

Morten P. was still holding the phone pressed to his ear. He listened to the caller and agreed to a couple of things before ringing off.

'The online editor is publishing a similar story,' he explained. 'We'll hold back the name and photo for the paper copies, but they're borrowing a lot of what you've written and are writing a more comprehensive account than *Dagbladet* has managed.'

Line touched her forehead, feeling dizzy. She was in a cold sweat, her face was burning and she could not catch her breath. She wanted to scream and shout, to run away, but she was rooted to the spot. She had worked so intensely for the last few hours, scarcely lifting her eyes from the screen and keyboard, and when she had finally finished, the *Dagbladet* journalist with the shark-fin hair had been served up the story through a leak from a source in the police. Her father had warned her that something like that might happen. The police superintendent was exactly the naive sort that she and her journalist colleagues loved. He quite simply could not keep his mouth shut but adored standing up and announcing every single step forward made by the police so that he could claim the credit for it.

Morten P. took a beer from the minibar, flipped off the lid and put it to his mouth. She watched as he guzzled half the bottle. He was right, of course. They still had a good story. She doubted whether any of the other newspapers would manage to find a name, photo and background story for Layla Azimi in time to get it in print. They had a solid lead on the others that would last, for a while at least.

'Would you like a beer?' Morten P. asked, wiping around his mouth. 'We still have good reason to celebrate.'

Line thought about it. A cold beer was exactly what she needed.

'You could spend the night here,' Morten P. continued. 'Well, I don't mean right here in this room, but the paper can pay for a room for you. If there are any vacancies.'

Line looked at the time and saw it was nearly 11 p.m. Then she shook her head. She wanted to head off.

36

It had rained non-stop all afternoon and evening. The town was shrouded in a veil of grey, the streets black and glistening like a beetle's back.

Line dashed out of the hotel, making for her car. She sat in the driver's seat, peered into the rear-view mirror and ruffled her wet hair. Her eyes were red and sore with a hint of dark circles underneath. With a sigh, she put her hands on the wheel and stared out through the grey windscreen in an effort to look straight ahead.

She had set herself the goal of finding out who the murdered girl was. The solution had come, as it often does, suddenly and from an unexpected source. Her next task was to tell her readers why the girl had died. The loss of fourteen kilos of pure heroin could be a good enough motive, but there must be more to this story than that. This had been a brutal, reckless execution in which the victim's head had been displayed almost triumphantly to the outside world. It seemed like some kind of internal showdown.

However, the blue suitcase was the starting point for the subsequent story. It had to do with organized crime and a narcotics network that extended well beyond national borders.

She cast another glance in the mirror and tidied her hair again. She knew someone who would be able to give her an introduction to those circles.

Tommy Kvanter released the security chain and let her in.

'I hope it's not too late,' Line apologized.

Tommy smiled and shook his head. 'I'm a night bird. I think the bedcovers taste better in the morning.'

'That makes two of us,' Line said, returning his smile.

She walked in front of him into the living room and sat down. The room was less tidy than it had been the day before, with four empty beer bottles and a dinner plate with leftover food on the lid of the chest that served as a coffee table. The ashtray was overflowing and a writing pad with elaborate notes lay open beside it.

Tommy closed the pad and cleared away the plate and bottles to the kitchen.

'Would you like anything?' he called out to her. 'Beer or wine or something?'

'I'm driving,' Line told him. 'Maybe a cup of tea?'

'Not much tea to be had in this house, I'm afraid,' he said, back at the kitchen door now. 'Cola?'

She accepted with thanks. Tommy disappeared into the kitchen again and re-emerged with beer for himself and cola for her. He sat down on the settee and used the remote to turn down the stereo system.

'Blackmore's Night,' he told her, nodding to the atmospheric guitar notes reminiscent of music from the Middle Ages. 'Have you heard them before?'

Line shook her head.

'Have you heard of Deep Purple?' he asked. '"Smoke on the Water"?'

'Of course.'

'Then you've heard Richie Blackmore's guitar playing. This is the band he formed with his wife.' Tommy took a drink and put the bottle down on the table. 'How's the story going?' he asked.

Leaning forward, Line told him what was going to be the next day's latest news. Tommy sat still, listening. She could see the curiosity and amazement grow in his eyes as she spoke.

'But why?' he asked when she had finished. 'When she doesn't even have family here in this country? Why would anyone kill her and display her head on a stake? That was the sort of thing they did in the olden days.'

'I think it has to do with drugs,' Line said, leaning back.

Tommy Kvanter frowned.

Line produced the photographs of the blue suitcase with the Mickey Mouse stickers. She had held that part of the story back. Now she told him the events Khaled Athari had confided in Suzanne Bjerke about before he was deported from Norway.

'I think Layla Azimi was forced to take part in the same operation,' she explained. 'She was punished when something went wrong and the suitcase did not arrive at the intended place and her head was put on display to warn other couriers against making the same mistake.'

Tommy Kvanter shook his head.

'You're living in a fantasy world,' he said. 'A fanatical delusion of how awful and dangerous drugs are, and the people involved with them. A distortion created by the police and the authorities with good help from you lot in the media.'

'Do you believe that narcotics aren't dangerous?'

'Everything that's forbidden is dangerous,' Tommy said.

'You mean we should legalize drugs, then?'

'Well, then at least Layla Azimi would still be alive,' he challenged her. 'If we're going to follow your theory, at any rate.'

She gave him a questioning look.

'In the first half of the twentieth century all stimulants with the exception of nicotine were criminalized in the US,' Tommy went on to explain, reaching out for his tobacco pouch. 'Alcohol was banned in 1920. It was said that the ban would solve the great social problems of the time and prevent crime. That's exactly the same argument that is used for the current policy of banning narcotics. But the Americans wanted alcohol even though it was forbidden, and the local mafia became the new distributors and the income from the sale of alcohol skyrocketed. The ban became a catalyst for smuggling and organized crime. After only a year of prohibition, the total number of murders and break-ins in America increased by almost twenty-five per cent. Also, the Americans drank far more after prohibition than before. After thirteen years of an increasing crime rate, more people in prison and gigantic health costs, alcohol was legalized again. In reality, the ban had made everything far worse. We could say the same about the effects of the present-day ban on drugs.'

Tommy Kvanter said nothing for a moment but sat with his rolled cigarette in his mouth, lighting it with a match.

'However, the US has become a global driving force in the battle against all stimulants other than alcohol and nicotine,' he went on, taking a drag. 'They enforce the ban on narcotics consistently and militantly. The rest of the world has followed their lead. Hundreds of billions of dollars are spent on the so-called war against drugs, but the results have failed to materialize. Never before have more people used illegal stimulants and never before has access to them been greater. Drugs like crack and crystal meth have destroyed American communities. There's nothing to suggest that use and access are diminishing.'

'So the solution is to make them legal?'

Blowing out a cloud of grey smoke, Tommy Kvanter stood up and walked over to a bookcase.

'It's time to learn from history,' he said, taking out a faded magazine. 'It's certainly time to change course. Switzerland is the country in Europe with the most liberal narcotics policy. They have twenty-three clinics that dish out free heroin, morphine and methadone to addicts. Health professionals work at the clinics and addicts can inject heroin in clean, clinical surroundings. It has given drug addicts a better life. After the clinics opened, both the number of new addicts and the total number of overdoses were halved. The homeless statistics fell from eighteen to one per cent in the course of a year and a half. Crime dropped drastically and addicts have been given the opportunity to live an almost normal life.'

'We surely can't allow and accept the use of damaging poisons?' Line protested.

'Heroin is not harmful to health in itself,' Tommy retorted with a smile. 'It's a pain-relieving natural substance. Hospitals in England administer it to children. It's the criminalized lifestyle and dependency, with all the consequences, that destroy the user. There are other reasons why people who abuse heroin today look so completely ravaged. If an addict had unrestricted means of buying heroin, then you wouldn't be able to tell that he was on heroin by looking at him. The way of life, the continual debasement of the very worst kind, stealing from friends and family, stealing from your own children's piggybanks, bad dope, dreadful health care, no money for dental treatment, hostels, being chased around . . . Most heroin addicts would be able to walk tall and function in working life with arrangements like the ones they have in Switzerland. It's actually incredible that neither Norwegian nor Danish politicians have taken that to heart.'

'We do have supervised injection sites in Oslo,' Line reminded him.

Tommy Kvanter burst out laughing and sat down again.

'That says something about how ignorant Norwegian

politicians are. Smoking heroin is, despite everything, less dangerous than injecting it, but in Norway it's forbidden to smoke heroin in the injection sites because it is characterized as a breach of the smoking laws.' He shook his head. 'Lots of politicians also believe that methadone is lifesaving medicine and heroin is lethal dope, without understanding that they're both opiates and you can become addicted to either of them, and many people suffer worse side effects from methadone. You do have to wonder what basis we have for the practice of our narcotics policy.'

Taking a final drag on the cigarette, he crushed it out in the ashtray and put the beer bottle to his mouth.

'But you're absolutely right, of course,' he said, as if afraid he had scared her with his views. 'Fourteen kilos of pure heroin would, for many people, be worth killing for. After the oil and weapons industries, narcotics is the most lucrative activity in the world. The ban is a gift to organized crime, and the whole market is in the hands of ruthless criminals, with all the tragedies that brings. Well over ninety per cent of all heroin sold on the streets of Europe, including Norway, originates from the Taliban regime in Afghanistan. Norwegian drugs policy finances the war against Norwegian soldiers.'

Tommy Kvanter put the beer bottle to his mouth again and drained it. He got to his feet, took the bottle into the kitchen and returned with a new one.

'Sorry,' he said with a smile. 'I like to be provocative.'

Line reciprocated the smile. She liked people who managed to give her a different perspective and view of things she took for granted. Tommy Kvanter had succeeded in swaying her personal opinions. She also liked his enthusiasm, zeal and engagement.

'Who would be in a position to take and distribute a delivery of fourteen kilos of heroin?' she asked.

He looked at her over the neck of the bottle. 'Why are you asking me that?'

'It seems as if you have some knowledge of this.'

Tommy Kvanter's face took on a serious expression and his eyes grew darker. Something in them suggested he knew something.

'This is *dangerous*, Line,' he warned her. 'I don't think you ought to follow up this lead.'

'It's my job.'

'Isn't it the job of the police?'

Line leaned further forward. 'Do you trust them?'

The smile was back on Tommy Kvanter's lips. He took another swig of the beer and fixed his eyes on her.

'If you don't involve the police, then I may be able to help you.'

'Complete protection of sources,' Line assured him, aware of her pulse racing.

'I can only think of one person who could handle that quantity,' Tommy told her.

Line considered taking out her reporter's notebook but decided against it.

'Who would that be?' she asked.

'They call him the Night Man.'

37

The meteorologist on the radio promised the rain would ease off overnight. Wisting stopped the car in the empty courtyard and clambered out, stooping his back against the weather. He jogged over to the mailbox in the street and took out the contents before letting himself in. Line had still not returned.

He hung up his jacket in the hallway and found his way to the kitchen, where he spread out the post on the table, sorting out a couple of bills and dropping the junk mail into the recycling container behind the door.

The bread in the bin on the worktop felt dry and stale. He could not recall how many days it had been since he bought it. He cut three slices and lathered on a thick layer of butter. Adding some cheese and ham from the fridge, he placed the plate in the microwave. While he waited for the cheese to melt, he took a bottle of pilsner from the fridge, flipped off the lid and took a deep gulp. The lager ran down his throat and tasted good. He felt his shoulders relax as he drank.

He stood with his back to the worktop while he ate his simple supper. Outside the window, everything was just dark. Not even the birch trees were visible against the night sky.

The wall clock showed almost half past midnight. He followed the second hand round with his eyes. He realized how tired he was but was reluctant to go to bed until Line was back. He thought about phoning her but dropped the idea. He would make good use of the silence by going through everything that had happened. He needed to go over old ground and required peace and quiet to look at it from every angle and be able to stop to absorb various details in the hope of discovering or hitting upon something he had not already thought of.

He found nothing.

The connections and motives were still unclear. The strategic retreat simply led him back to the starting point. A young girl had been killed in a terrible, brutal way and at the same time a man had been shot in the neck. Both bodies were then dumped in the water. There seemed to be no direct link between them, other than that the victims were probably both of Asian origin. All he had was a shadowy feeling that the cases were somehow connected. And that they most likely had to do with narcotics smuggling on a grand scale.

He was just gathering his thoughts and wondering what might take them forward when he heard a noise at the front door. Although startled by the sound, he smiled when he heard Line shout from the hallway.

Soft cat's paws pattered across the floor. The black male cat with thin tail and white chest was first to reach him. He rubbed against his legs and looked expectantly up at him with bright yellow eyes. Wisting crouched down and gave him a scratch behind the ear. The fur was wet and smelled damp.

'Long day?' he asked, glancing up at Line.

She nodded. 'You too?'

'I only got home half an hour ago.'

He rose to his feet and took out a tin of cat food from the cupboard. The cat began to purr as he opened it and thrust his head impatiently into the food dish while Wisting was still pouring out the contents.

'Are you hungry?' he asked, turning to face his daughter.

She peered sceptically at his plate on the table, with half a slice of bread left on it, and shook her head.

'*Dagbladet* beat us to it,' she said, taking a seat at the table.

Wisting gave a heavy sigh, suddenly feeling weary and exhausted.

'I don't want to talk about the investigation,' he said.

She nodded and gazed at him with tired eyes.

'She knew Mum,' she said.

'Who?'

'Suzanne Bjerke. They worked together on some school projects for pupils with behavioural difficulties.'

Wisting sat down. 'Did she tell you any more?'

'Just what a good person Mum was. That she hoped I had inherited the same belief in the goodness of every person that she had.'

'And indeed you have,' Wisting replied with a smile. His eyes struggled to penetrate the darkness outside.

Line followed his gaze. 'Have you heard of someone called the Night Man?' she asked all of a sudden.

Wisting frowned as he looked at her.

'The executioner's assistant,' he said, nodding, and tried to bring to mind what he had just read about beheading and old methods of execution.

'Eh?'

'The sanitation worker of the 1800s,' Wisting said. 'The night man's job was to empty privies, castrate horses, remove dead animals and human suicides. In addition, he helped the executioner to remove the body after execution and bury it outside the city perimeter. Dirty work that had to be done at night.'

Line's eyes were full of questions.

'The night man and his family would live almost like outcasts,' Wisting went on. 'When his wife was about to give birth, it would be virtually impossible to get hold of a mid-wife. No one wanted to touch the children of the night and it was difficult to obtain godparents for baptism.' Leaning back in the kitchen chair, he studied his daughter. 'Why do you ask?'

She shook her head. She had no desire to tell her father where she had been or why she was back so late.

'It was just a name I heard.'

Wisting leaned tentatively forward again.

'It was also the night man's job to place the severed head on a stake,' he said in an undertone.

38

It was Wednesday 12 November, the third day of the investigation, and the day on which they could expect to start getting results from all the tests that had been sent in.

Wisting cast a glance out of the office window. The meteorologist had been right: it had stopped raining. Instead, it was windier and had turned colder. The large beech tree behind the car park was shaking off the very last of the autumn leaves.

The girl in the chair opposite him was from Somalia and she looked at him, very ill at ease.

In reality, Somalia was a country that had disintegrated, Wisting thought. After decades of rival clans and groups in changing alliances fighting for power in bloody skirmishes, the country had been torn to shreds. The population was so affected by the ravages of war that the ultimate dream was to flee abroad in the hope of a safer and more peaceful existence.

Hanan Aden was one of the teenagers in the residential unit who had known Layla Azimi best. If Layla had confided and shared her thoughts and experiences with anyone, it would have been with her.

But the young Somali girl seemed sullen and uncommunicative. It looked as if she had decided not to say anything.

Before fixing his eyes again on Layla's friend, Wisting leaned forward and looked at the child psychologist who sat in the chair beside her, but found nothing of help.

'I've thought of her all night long,' he said. 'Every minute that has passed since we found her, I've thought of her. Wondering who she is and asking myself thousands of questions. About anything and everything: what kind of music did she like to listen to, what did she like to watch on TV, what books did she read, what was her favourite colour, did she have a lucky number, what did she dream of, how did she get that little scar beside her nose?' Wisting leaned back, sighing, and lowered his eyes. 'But most of all I wonder why she was not allowed to live.'

The psychologist shifted uncomfortably in her seat. Wisting avoided looking at her. He had come to the conclusion that social skills were more important than advanced psychology. To persuade a person to open up he had to create some kind of equilibrium between himself and the person brought in to make a statement. He had to find ways of reaching the witness and facilitate a situation in which that person would also reach out to him.

'She fell when she was little,' Hanan said all of a sudden, rubbing her nose.

Wisting looked straight at her.

'She was with her cousin, watching over the goats. The flock was attacked by a snow leopard. She ran to save one of the kids but fell and hit her face on a rock.' The young girl met his gaze. 'But she got up again, picked up the rock and threw it at the leopard. That was what she was really like.'

'What do you mean?'

'She got to her feet and won. She never gave up. But not this time.'

Wisting remained silent, allowing her the peace and quiet to continue in her own words.

'She had deeper scars inside,' Hanan said in a tone that

told of how she herself had gained more life experience than should be expected of a girl in her early teens. 'She had wounds on her soul that meant she was always looking for something, though she didn't even know what that was. It made her get mixed up in things that weren't good for her.'

'Such as what?' Wisting asked when her voice trailed off.

The eyes of the young girl in front of him became restless. They did not flicker but grew searching. In the end she met his eye and it seemed as if she found the reassurance she was after.

'Like the men with the suitcase,' she answered, casting her eyes down again. 'They were from Sweden. It happened a month ago. They dragged her into a car and drove off with her. She was sure they were going to rape her.'

Wisting pushed the glass of water slightly closer to the girl, but she did not touch it.

'They drove for hours and hours, though nobody said a single word,' she went on. 'They drove over the border to Sweden and arrived at a city. They locked her in a room high up in an apartment block, but nothing happened. She got food and drink and they asked only one thing.'

The girl trailed off again. Her hand was shaking when it reached out for the glass.

'What was that?' Wisting asked once she had taken a drink of water.

'They wanted to know who she was fond of. That was the only thing they asked. Who she missed and worried about. Who she had shared secrets with and confided in. Who she longed for.'

Wisting leaned forward again. He felt that the girl facing him was about to lead them in the right direction, into the dark heart of the case.

'What was her response?'

Hanan Aden sobbed, her eyes suddenly filling with tears. The psychologist sitting by her side put her hand on the girl's, but she snatched it away.

'She said it was me,' she whispered. The words almost disappeared in a burst of painful, pent-up weeping.

Wisting opened the desk drawer and produced a box of paper tissues. Hanan took one and dried her eyes, wiped her nose and then sat staring down at her lap.

'She had to write down my name and address on a sheet of paper,' she eventually continued, clutching the box of tissues so hard that the knuckles on her right hand turned white. 'After two days, they let her go. They gave her a suitcase and a train ticket. She was told, if she really loved me, she had to take this suitcase back to Larvik.'

Wisting nodded as a sign that he wanted to hear more.

'They didn't say anything else. Just that she had to take good care of it and that a man would come to meet her at the station. If she didn't deliver the suitcase to him, then she would take me with her into death.'

Wisting looked at the child psychologist. He could see from the expression on her face that what Hanan was saying was news to her and the staff of the residential unit.

Hanan took another drink of water.

'She obviously knew it was something illegal,' she said. 'If she spoke to the police, they would kill her.'

'What happened?'

'You found the suitcase, didn't you?' The young girl's voice was barely audible. 'We saw the picture of it in the newspaper, along with you.'

Wisting nodded.

'It was left on the platform,' he told her. 'Why did she leave it there?'

'She got scared. When she got off the train, the station was full of police.'

'Police? Why was that?'

'I don't know, but she got scared. She just put down the suitcase and ran home.'

Wisting leaned back in the chair and clasped his hands on his knee. The story he had just heard was roughly the same as the one Suzanne Bjerke had been told by the young lad who had been sent back to his grandparents in Afghanistan. This investigation was linked with a modern form of the slave trade. Children who were threatened into being used for the trafficking of narcotics.

'We believe Layla was murdered on Sunday night.' Wisting cleared his throat. 'But she disappeared from home on Friday. Do you know where she went?'

Hanan Aden shook her head.

'She was gone when I got home from school, but I knew she was going to leave. She was afraid and said she would go to people where she could feel safe.'

'You don't know who they were?'

'She didn't feel safe at home and wanted to go somewhere else. I don't know where. I guessed she had gone to Oslo. That's where she usually goes when she runs away.'

The child psychologist leaned forward.

'Is Hanan in danger?' she asked.

Wisting hesitated to answer. The men behind this had used the fear of reprisals against Layla's best friend to force her to undertake the journey. However, Layla had probably been killed because she could identify the men behind it all when the smuggling trip had gone awry. At the same time, the brutal murder would also be used against future trafficking victims as a terrifying example of what would happen if they put a foot wrong. There were no reasonable grounds for them to take revenge on Hanan, but it was difficult to know how rationally these criminals thought.

He inhaled deeply and held his breath for a moment.

'Maybe you could send her away somewhere for a few days?' he suggested.

39

Wisting leafed through the printouts from the case log while the participants gathered around the conference table for the meeting.

Hanan's story made sense. He had read the printouts earlier. At 13.43 on Friday 17 October the police had received a message from the staff at the railway station about an extremely drunk man who was making a nuisance of himself to passengers and behaving in a threatening manner to the railway employees. The first patrol on the scene had been unable to control him and a second patrol was called. The man had drawn a knife and the officers had been forced to use pepper spray before the man gave himself up. When the train arrived at the station at 13.50, the police presence on the station platform was massive.

One hour later, traffic controller Kyrre Anker Fredriksen from the National Railway Administration had picked up a suitcase with Mickey Mouse stickers on it that had been left behind.

The man who was arrested was Sindre Hovden, aged thirty-eight and a drug addict for the past twenty-three years. In addition to countless narcotics offences, his criminal record contained a long list of thefts and several instances of violent and threatening behaviour. One of the possibilities they had looked into was that the suitcase had belonged to him and had been left sitting there after his arrest. Even though it was highly unlikely that an addict would walk about with a suitcase that held more than fourteen kilos of heroin, he had been interviewed. His statement ran to one line: he had no knowledge of the suitcase or the drugs.

Wisting put the papers away and glanced up at the clock: one minute past twelve. The chairs had stopped scraping and silence had fallen. He let his eyes circle around the familiar faces. Espen Mortensen was missing, but otherwise everyone was present.

He began by outlining the statement given by the Somali girl he had interviewed.

'Things are starting to come together,' he finished off. 'Layla Azimi was threatened and forced to import a large quantity of narcotics. In the tumult at the station when she got off the train, she panicked and put down the valuable luggage and disappeared.'

He let the investigators who had interviewed the other children in the residential unit give accounts of their interviews, but they comprised only general comments and confirmed that Hanan was the one who had known Layla best.

The next point was the pathological reports from Forensics. Wisting handed over to Torunn Borg, who thumbed back and forth through her papers.

'Layla Azimi died of an air embolism,' she explained, glancing up. 'A kind of thrombosis. Her head was cut off with a blunt implement of iron or steel. Probably a saw. It has left flecks of rust on the edges of the wounds. Fragments of skin and muscle tissue were slowly wrenched off. Cutting through the blood vessels in the neck has led to air being sucked in and carried to the heart and the brain. As soon as the saw reaches so far into the throat, death occurs quickly. There would have been massive blood loss.'

Torunn Borg looked down and leafed further through her papers.

'There is no sign of sexual assault. She was not a virgin but had no injuries or indications of violence in the pubic area. She did have several bruises on her arms and legs. Two diagonal wounds across her torso are described, suggesting these injuries are consistent with her being tied and bound.'

The participants around the table remained silent. Wisting pictured in his mind's eye how the defenceless girl had lain trussed up on a table or something similar while her head was chopped off.

'As far as the unidentified body in the Lågen river is concerned, the cause of death, unsurprisingly, is given as a gunshot wound. He has one large entry wound at the back of his neck but two projectile paths. We're talking about two close shots in rapid succession. He has one exit wound immediately below the larynx, but the other bullet path has a more perpendicular angle. A bullet was found in his vertebral canal.'

'What kind?' Nils Hammer asked.

'Full metal jacket, 45 calibre.'

'The weapon from the pig farm at Hagtvedt is on its way to Kripos as we speak. It's the same calibre. They may even be doing the ballistics tests on it right now.'

'The same applies to the bullet they've found at Forensics. I reckon we may have answers to the comparisons of these bullets by the end of the afternoon.'

'Any news from the village?' Wisting asked, looking now at Hammer.

'No.' Hammer shook his head. 'A couple of possible sightings of the car, but nothing specific.'

Wisting made a few notes and then turned to Jan Osther, seated at the far end of the table. The young policeman had come up with his own theories and strong opinions when the investigation had started. He had been a prime advocate of what was described as the racism hypothesis but had been forced to acknowledge that the motive was likely to be found elsewhere.

'How far have we come with the collection of electronic traces?'

Jan Osther picked up the top sheet of paper from a thick bundle.

'The video footage is of course affected by night darkness and fog,' he told them. 'The most interesting aspect is probably the printouts that show the telecoms traffic on Layla Azimi's mobile. The person she talks to most is, naturally enough, her Somali friend, but apart from that the data traffic confirms she has been to Gothenburg. On 13 October, her phone was in use at 14.23, and after that it was probably turned off. There is no movement until she receives a few text messages early on the morning of 17 October. At that time she seems to be within a coverage area that Swedish Telia identify as Drottningtorget. That includes Gothenburg's central railway station. After that, the phone moves parallel to the railway track all the way to Larvik. However, she does not phone anyone during the journey. All that confirms what we already know.'

'Who was the last person she was in contact with?'

'The last time the phone was used was on the morning of Friday 7 November. There are a few text messages to and fro between her and Hanan. We haven't gone into the rest of the telecoms traffic as yet, but it doesn't look as if she used the phone after she went missing. The data tells us nothing about where she was in the days before she was found.'

Wisting thanked him, keen now to hear from the investigators who had worked on assignments that had ended up being fruitless. Even though these were steps in the inquiry that had not led them any further, it was important for everyone to feel they had contributed and done a good job. Before that could happen, Espen Mortensen, carrying a large brown envelope, opened the conference-room door.

'This is bizarre,' he said, taking position at one of the empty chairs around the table.

Giving no further explanation, he opened the envelope and took out the contents of a sealed plastic bag: a high-calibre revolver, spattered with soot, the rubber stock melted and distorted. A layer of ash was left at the bottom of the bag.

'This was found in the ruins of the fire at Cato Dalen's house in Scheensveien,' the crime-scene technician explained. 'It's an Uberti 45 with the serial number Jo8914. Stolen from a farm at Omsland in Kjose just over a month ago.'

'That reinforces the suspicion that Cato Dalen and the Patriotic Front were behind the theft at Pål Stensby's place,' Hammer said.

'The weird thing is those young boys finding a weapon from the same theft at Eskedal.' Espen Mortensen stole a glance at Wisting.

'Then something here doesn't add up,' Jan Osther piped up. 'The Patriotic Front incite war against all foreign cultures. The men who were seen in the white Toyota at Eskedal were described as looking as if they were from somewhere in the Middle East, I seem to recall. Cato Dalen and his people would never have handed over firearms to them.'

Wisting touched his forehead in bafflement. Something about all this simply made no sense.

40

Torunn Borg and Nils Hammer remained with Wisting when the meeting was over.

'I'll arrange for surveillance on Cato Dalen,' Torunn Borg said, making a note on her pad. 'We'll charge him with theft of weapons. We can get help from the Security Services to track him down.'

Wisting nodded. He had the feeling they were groping around the periphery of a number of incidents that were somehow connected. There was still something shadowy about the case, but he was beginning to discern the outlines of something significant. The past twenty-four hours had provided them with a direction.

'The statement given by the Somali girl leads one way,' he said. 'To Sweden.'

'To Gothenburg,' Nils Hammer corrected him. 'Aren't there nearly a million inhabitants there?'

'Just over nine hundred thousand in the whole metropolitan area, to be exact,' Torunn Borg commented.

'The route to Sweden goes via a mountain village called Qaramqul in the north of Afghanistan,' Wisting went on.

'You mean we should bring back the Afghan boy who was deported so that he can point out the apartment in Gothenburg for us?'

'That's the only thing we have.' Wisting reached his hand out for a glass of water. 'He told Suzanne Bjerke that he was held captive in an apartment block in Gothenburg for two days before he was given a suitcase and a train ticket back to Larvik. It's the same story that Layla told to Hanan.'

Nils Hammer was shaking his head. 'Even if we break out our entire travel budget and find the boy, what are the chances of him managing to make his way back to the apartment in question?'

'It was a traumatic experience for him,' Wisting said. 'The chances that he'll be able to help us are actually pretty good. Anyway, as I said, he's all we've got.'

Crackling from the intercom interrupted the discussion and Espen Mortensen's voice suddenly filled the room. 'Are you still there?'

'Yes.'

'I think you should pay me a visit at the lab. There's something here you ought to look at.'

Espen Mortensen was standing at the far end of the forensics room on the first floor, stooped over a stainless-steel work bench. A frame with two infrared lamps was mounted above the area.

The crime-scene examiner beckoned them and pointed down at a small piece of paper. Wisting recognized the crumpled note that had been in Layla Azimi's pocket when her body had been hauled out of the harbour basin in Stavern.

The penetrating heat from the infrared light had permeated the paper and given the washed-out text sharper edges and distinct contours.

'A name and phone number,' Nils Hammer said at once.

Wisting squinted at the paper and nodded. He saw one word and a series of numbers, but they were still unclear. The letters could be the name Akhmet. The first three digits were 959, like a mobile phone number, followed by two indistinct figures before the number ended in 459.

'Ahmed – 959 42 459,' Mortensen read out.

Wisting bit his lip as he studied the two middle numbers again. The second of them was either a two or a seven, but the first one was impossible to make out.

'Ahmed Saad, Unnersbogate 4 in Torstrand,' Mortensen continued, handing Wisting a printout.

He looked down at it. It was the telecoms data from Layla Azimi's mobile phone usage. Three lines were highlighted. The day before she disappeared, she had rung Ahmed Saad on phone number 95942459.

'Who is that?'

Espen Mortensen walked across to the computer screen at the other end of the room.

'He is from Iraq,' he said. 'Thirty-seven years old. Came to Norway as a quota refugee in 2001. No family. He was given asylum and granted leave to stay.'

The crime-scene technician tapped on the keyboard and logged in to the computer system for immigration and asylum cases. After a few seconds, the picture of a thin man with a round face and a wispy beard appeared on the screen. The image made the breath vibrate in Wisting's nostrils. The photo was a few years old, but Wisting recognized him all the same. It was the man they had dredged up from the Lågen river the night before last with two bullet holes in his neck.

41

After the morning meeting with Morten P., Line drove home and transformed the kitchen table into a small office. The chief news editor had two stories he wanted them to do more work on. They were to discover the identity of the body in the river and find out what connection there was between him and Layla Azimi. And they had to follow the narcotics lead.

Morten P. would take care of the unidentified body. Admittedly, the police had suggested it was far from certain that he had any fixed residence in the town or even in Norway. However, someone had phoned the paper and tipped him off that the police had obtained the passenger lists from the ferries to Denmark. Morten P.'s extensive network included journalist colleagues in the Danish newspapers *Ekstrabladet* and *Jyllandsposten* who had good contacts in the local police in Copenhagen as well as the national police force. He believed that if the man came from Denmark, they would learn of this before the message had gone via official Nordic police channels.

Line had taken on the narcotics lead. Her mobile phone lay in the middle of the kitchen table. She had given Tommy a hug and received in return a promise that he would call her. She wanted to wait a while longer, but if she had not heard from him by 3 p.m., she would phone him.

She had searched through the text archives and on the Internet for information about the Night Man, but had not found any references other than what her father had told her about the executioner's assistant.

Thereafter she had spent an hour reading various online newspapers. None of the media outlets had come out with anything that could be regarded as news in this particular case.

Then she switched to the overseas news agencies. This was a habit she had picked up that had provided her with a number of interesting stories. The editor's office, of course, had electronic news agencies that alerted the paper each time Reuters, Associated Press or any of the other international press agencies mentioned Norway, Norwegian towns or had any kind of Norwegian angle in their stories. However, often a manual search with key words from what was on the day's agenda in Norway could result in interesting items she could revamp into a national version. Last week several Norwegian media sources had run stories about the increase in household break-ins. The police blamed Eastern European gangs. In Deutsche Press Agentur she had found an in-depth interview with a young Lithuanian man who had served a lengthy sentence for various crimes, including burglaries. Along with two others, he had travelled through a number of European countries, including Norway, before he was arrested just outside Hamburg. He had unblushingly described how they had operated. The article enabled her to delve deeper into the story and give the media picture a fresh slant.

She searched on the term *beheading* and came up with several hundred hits with reference to the war in Afghanistan and Al-Qaeda. Adding the search word *drugs* caused the results to dwindle significantly, but she found nothing of interest. She ploughed on with a search using the words *beheaded* + *head* + *stake*. The first page of results was international coverage of the story she was working on in which *VG* was mentioned several times.

When she clicked straight into the last page of search

results, one headline made her frown. *Head on stake still mystery for German police.*

The report was almost three years old and referred to an article in the East German regional newspaper *Sächsische Zeitung* about a case in which the head of a young man was found displayed on a stake in the middle of a park in the city of Dresden. The rest of the body was not recovered, and the police had no inkling of who the boy could be, apart from that he was one of the many hundreds of thousands of illegal immigrants living in the country. The theory the investigators had come up with was that it had to do with a *blood feud* and *honour killing*.

Line leaned back in her chair and stared at the computer screen, unsure what this might mean. It felt like more than a coincidence.

She hunched over the computer again and conducted further searches on German websites, where she found a collection of pages about the story. Her proficiency in German was a few years old but sufficient for her to understand that the police had shelved the case after seven months of investigation with no resolution. A few of the articles contained references to *der Liberecfall*. Line negotiated her way through these and discovered that the Liberec case was the name given to another story in which a young boy was found beheaded on the Czech side of the border, near the city of Liberec, two years earlier. His head was placed *auf einer Stange* in a popular recreation ground near the Neisse river. In this case too, the police investigation got nowhere. The police in the Czech Republic had been unable to identify the young victim and described the case as a *ritual murder*.

Line doubted whether the police in Norway knew of these two cases, but under cover of the narcotics angle, it would obviously be of interest to the investigators. East European countries such as Poland and the Czech Republic were transit routes for much of the heroin from Central Asia that was transported through Europe to Denmark, Norway and Sweden. The criminal networks probably extended over the same land borders. If the smuggling method was identical, then the cases from Germany and the Czech Republic could also be narcotics-related executions.

Saving the pages, she sent an email to Morten P. with a link to what she had found and reached for her mobile phone to follow this up with a chat. Her older journalist colleague had lived in Hamburg at one time and spoke fluent German. He would be able to make the necessary phone calls.

42

The old workhouse and prison separated Torstrand from the rest of the town, as if the citizens had at one time in the nineteenth century wanted to build a barrier between themselves and the working-class area. Now, however, the old suburb was one of the most vibrant parts of the town, though some areas were still affected by decline and social class divisions.

Wisting manoeuvred his car through the grid of streets and found his way to the greyish-blue four-in-a-block building in Unnersbogate. He parked at the kerb and stepped out with Nils Hammer and Espen Mortensen.

The name *Ahmed Saad* was scrawled in felt-tip pen in thick black letters on one of the mailboxes that hung in the entryway leading to the backyard.

The thirty-seven-year-old man had lived an anonymous life, at least according to the records the police had at their disposal. After being granted asylum in 2004, he had worked for a cleaning company for six months before being signed off sick for a period and then being placed on a rehabilitation programme. By November 2007, he was in receipt of disability benefit, paid at the minimum level. He had no previous convictions but there were three interesting incidents recorded in the police log. Twice in May, a Syrian girl who had run away from home had been removed from his apartment and returned to her parents after her family had received a tip-off about her whereabouts. Four months earlier, the police had assisted the Child Welfare Service when two female friends who had run away from an institution in

Telemark were traced to the old working-class housing that now loomed in front of them.

Wisting opened the gate. The weather had cleared up and white fluffy clouds scudded across the skies. Inside the gravel courtyard they saw an old, dilapidated garage with its door pulled halfway down. One corner of it had collapsed entirely – the walls and roof were of corrugated iron and in some places rust had eaten holes in the metal sheets.

An old yellow Mazda 626 was parked in front of the garage. Wisting broke the seal of the evidence bag that held the set of keys belonging to the man they had hauled from the river less than thirty-four hours ago. He took a quick look at the car key before choosing the house key, inserting it into the front door lock and turning it. Then he took a step back and looked at his two colleagues. They had come to the right place. This was the home of the second murder victim.

For the moment, they were alone, but soon curious onlookers would gather out in the street. The press pack would invade the area around them and embark on their interrogation of people in the neighbourhood, long before the police detectives would be ready with their door-to-door inquiries and forms.

Lifting his phone, he rang Torunn Borg and gave her a rapid summary before asking her to send out a patrol car so that the area could be cordoned off to give them peace to work. He did not yet know what they would find behind the door but took it for granted that the crime-scene examiners would be here for a while.

Mortensen handed out the obligatory white sterile overalls along with shoe covers, gloves and hats. When they were kitted out, Wisting depressed the handle and opened the door.

In the hallway he stopped for a second to take in the scene. There was a terrible stink of cat piss in the cramped space.

The door to the living room was open a crack and a narrow strip of light spilled out on to the worn linoleum flooring. He put his hand immediately under the door handle, pushing the door open and taking a step inside.

It was a simple apartment of the type Wisting had seen many times before, and resembled all the others: painted walls, a settee, an armchair and a bookcase. A TV and a cheap stereo system. A pile of comics on the settee, newspapers and advertising brochures on the floor, empty spaghetti tins, a discarded pizza carton. Soft-drink cans and bottles of squash on the bookshelves.

It had happened in this room.

The blood had pooled in the middle of the floor in a quantity Wisting had never witnessed before now. It had dried and developed a thin black crust – most of all, it looked as if someone had poured out a bucket of deep-red paint.

Dotted around the bloody mess little imprints of cat's paws were visible. The blood had been drawn out into a path that moved to and from an adjacent room that lay in darkness.

Wisting crossed to the doorway, aware of faint noises from inside as he fumbled to locate the light switch. A dim bulb on the ceiling sprang to life and two terrified cat's eyes gleamed towards him from the bed in the centre of the room. Its nose was smeared with blood. The cat's skinny back shot in the air before it jumped down, darted between Wisting's legs and fled out through the open door behind them.

Wisting scanned the room. Thick curtains hung at the windows. He drew them aside a little and let a few feeble sunbeams shine into the room. Outside, a gust of wind snatched up an old newspaper and whipped it away down the deserted street.

As he dropped the curtain again, his eyes swept around the room. The bed was unmade with one quilt at the footboard.

A kitchen roll sat on the bedside table beside a comic book. He saw a sleeping bag on the floor and a few scattered crisp packets, one with a used condom hanging out of it.

This is where she had been living, Wisting decided. This was where she had come when she needed a place to hide. He nudged the crisp packet with his foot and shivered at the thought of the price she had paid for staying here.

Mortensen's camera flashed in the living room, jolting Wisting out of his train of thought. He went to join the others. An atmosphere of desperation, anxiety and death lay sticky and heavy in the room. The proximity of the horrors that must have played out here made him feel queasy and he had to force himself to study the individual details in the room.

On the low coffee table he could see a blood-spattered breadknife and a slightly smaller and sharper carving knife. The settee and chairs around were covered in sprayed blood.

A thick rope had been tossed on one of the chairs. It had been tied with a tight knot but, rather than being untied, the rope had been cut in two places. Blood from the knife used had stained the white nylon fibres.

Espen Mortensen was concentrating on something on the floor in front of the kitchen doorway. Wisting hunkered down beside him. A pool of coagulated blood fanned out across the floor and, in the middle, a bullet had bored into the wooden floorboards.

'Denmark,' Nils Hammer said out of the blue. He was the first to speak since they set foot in the apartment.

Wisting turned to face him.

'Denmark,' Hammer repeated, pointing to a couple of carrier bags, clearly from the tax-free shop on the Color Line ferry, that had tipped over just inside the hallway door. One of them had been scratched open with the cat's claws and the thawed contents, a bag of frozen chicken fillets, hauled out.

'His name is on the passenger lists,' Mortensen said. 'He was just on a day trip and came home on Sunday night. We would have found our way here sooner or later regardless.'

Wisting walked to the door. He had no more business here. The crime scene was not difficult to read. Layla Azimi had been tied to the coffee table with her head jutting beyond the edge. Then the killer had taken a knife from the kitchen and cut off her head. When he was finished, the householder had come home and dropped what he was carrying when he saw what had happened. As far as the murderer was concerned, the intruder was simply a troublesome witness who had to be executed with two shots to the back of his neck in front of his own kitchen door.

Wisting envisaged Layla Azimi crawling on her hands and knees to escape her killer's clutches in the final minutes and seconds of her life. Scratching her way across the living-room floor. Scrambling and floundering, yanking at an overturned lamp and tugging at over-toppled chairs in a desperate attempt to find something to defend herself with. Even though it was not difficult to imagine what had happened, the technicians would spend hours in here in their search for evidence that would link the perpetrators to this brutal crime scene. He was in no doubt that traces would be found. There was something almost disquieting about the way the killer and his accomplices had left the crime scene. They had made no attempt to conceal their crimes. On the contrary, they had taken Layla Azimi's head with them and displayed it in the middle of the town square, while the rest of her body was dumped like a piece of rubbish.

Wisting's eyes narrowed. An uneasiness he had never felt before washed through him and made him feel restless and agitated.

43

There was a special atmosphere in the Criminal Investigation Department, as always when something out of the ordinary was happening. The rumours of the discovery of an important crime scene had reached the police station even before Wisting and his colleagues returned from Torstrand, initially in the form of widespread whispers and disconnected mutterings circulating through the corridors. Gradually it had all become more specific and tangible, extending into the offices and finally taking shape in log reports and completed forms. It was as if the excitement and anticipation had charged the air with electricity and filled it with breathless silence, just like the moments leading up to a huge, unavoidable blow.

Wisting heard the noise of the fax machine as he passed the department office and, looking in, he saw Torunn Borg hunched over it, removing the sheets one by one as they emerged. The sunlight from outside sliced through the venetian blinds at the window, reflecting on her black hair and shading her face. She glanced up and smiled when she realized she was not alone.

'From Forensics,' she told him, waving the papers. 'The DNA analysis is ready. Shall we take a look at it in your office?'

Wisting agreed before fetching a cup of coffee and heading towards his office.

Torunn sat down in the chair opposite him and put the reports down on the desk.

'Taking first things first,' she began, 'the head and body are a match. The same DNA in both body parts.'

Wisting nodded encouragingly as he sipped his coffee. It had not even occurred to him that the two parts could indicate two victims. The very idea was terrifying.

'The forensic odontologist has identified her,' Torunn continued. 'The dental records confirm that it's Layla Azimi. The DNA analysis shows no relationship between her and the male body from the river. Quite the opposite, in fact; it suggests they have different ethnic origins.'

'Ahmed Saad,' Wisting said. 'He was Iraqi. Layla Azimi was from Afghanistan.'

Torunn Borg pushed half the bundle of papers across to him and now concentrated on the remaining ones.

'The analysis of the blood-spattered T-shirt found in the backyard near the town square is also here,' she told him.

Wisting's brows knitted as he leaned back: he could see from her face that something did not add up or the information she was about to give would be sensational. He cast a fleeting glance at the pile of case papers that included the interview with Tommy Kvanter.

'Two profiles were found on it,' she went on. 'The sweat at the armpits and skin cells on the neckline come from an unidentified male. The same DNA profile was also retrieved from the wooden stake the head was placed on.'

Wisting bit his bottom lip as he grabbed the crime-scene report from the bundle. In one of the supplementary points, Mortensen had described finding cutaneous tissue and blood 113 centimetres up on the hay stave the perpetrator had used. It was suggested that the killer had got a splinter on his hand and would have a small scratch or cut as a result.

He had been unsure whether the discovery of the T-shirt headlined in the media had in fact anything to do with the case. This link established that the garment probably belonged to one of the killers.

'What about the blood?'

'That's been analysed and we have a match on the ID register.'

Wisting swallowed audibly.

'Who?' he asked.

Torunn pushed the final report towards him.

'Sindre Hovden,' she replied.

Wisting's brain began to work overtime. Sindre Hovden was the man who had caused such a commotion in the railway station when Layla Azimi had arrived from Gothenburg.

'Get hold of him,' he said.

Torunn Borg nodded and stood up, leaving him with the new case documents, just as Wisting's phone rang.

The number that appeared on the display struck Wisting like a claw on his chest. He had not seen it for two years – his own home number. Ingrid had been in the habit of phoning him when he was working late, just to find out how he was. He glanced quickly at her photograph beside the computer screen on his desk, one of the last ones taken before she died. He had snapped it himself, at home on the verandah. He had said something that had made her laugh and a small gust of wind had given extra life to her hair. The sea and sky merged, blue on blue, in the background.

The phone rang seven times before he answered.

Line was pacing to and fro across the kitchen floor, the phone pressed to her ear.

'Hi, it's me,' she said when her father finally answered.

He said something she failed to catch.

'I've come across something I think might be of interest to the investigation,' she continued, snatching a glimpse at the computer screen and the picture she had found in a German online newspaper. It showed a metre-high pole behind police barriers in a park. 'I don't know if you're aware of it, but similar murders have been committed in at least two other countries.'

She heard her father clear his throat at the other end.

'What do you mean?'

Line told him what she had discovered through the international press agencies. She heard him catch his breath and then breathe more rapidly while she explained. When she heard the rustling of paper, she understood that he was taking notes.

'I'll send you a link,' she suggested.

The cursor danced across the screen and, with a few taps on the keyboard, she sent off an email. She heard a signal in the background at the other end of the line to indicate that it had arrived.

'What do you think?' she asked.

Wisting took a deep breath. 'Interesting,' he replied, obviously reading from his computer screen.

Line's mobile phone vibrated on the kitchen table as a call came in. She saw that it was Morten P. and dismissed it.

'Can we write that you're familiar with these cases?'

'Well, we are now, at least,' Wisting answered with a touch of merriment in his voice.

'What do you intend to do with the information?'

She heard her father take a couple of seconds to prepare a professional response: 'We'll seek further details from our colleagues in Germany and the Czech Republic.'

'Do you think there's any connection?'

'The similarities are so striking that it would be natural to take a closer look.'

Line was searching for a follow-up question when her

mobile gave a peep. Assuming it was a message from Morten P., she drew the phone towards her.

Danish Tommy, she read on the display.

Her heart was in her mouth at the thought of what kind of information he might have uncovered. She clicked on to the message: *Let's have a chat.*

'Any news of the narcotics lead?' she asked, starting to key in a reply. 'Do you have any idea of where the drugs were headed?'

As Wisting gave a negative response, her mobile emitted another signal before she had finished answering Tommy, this time a message from Morten P.: *The police are cordoning off Unnersbogate 4. White overalls going in and out of the house. Possible crime scene. Go!*

Line cleared her throat. 'What's happening in Torstrand?' she asked her father.

Wisting did not answer.

'You've closed off an address down there.'

'That's right.'

'Why is that?'

'We have identified the man who was found in the Lågen river,' her father explained. 'He was a thirty-seven-year-old Iraqi. We're examining his apartment now.'

The response sounded rehearsed, as if he had begun to string together what he would say to the press as soon as they rolled out the crime-scene tape. At the same time, she gained the impression that there was more to what was going on than her father was prepared to tell her.

'Is there a connection?' she pressed him.

'Our investigations have strengthened our theory that the two victims knew each other,' Wisting answered guardedly.

Line deleted parts of the text message she had begun to write to Danish Tommy, suggesting a time that evening instead.

'There's more to it, isn't there?' she asked, switching off her computer.

'Yes, there's more,' Wisting replied, closing his eyes. The splattered blood from the crime scene seemed to be imprinted on his retina.

44

Wisting stood by the window, watching the white foam of the breakers out on the fjord. Grey clouds scudded across the sky and a couple of seagulls spread their wings, wrestling with the wind.

His plan had begun to take shape. He could see parts of the big picture now.

He had often regarded an investigation as a long journey, with a window seat and lots of stops along the way. A journey into unfamiliar, unknown territory.

However, if this journey were to come to an end, he would have to do more than visualize it in his imagination. He turned around as Nils Hammer entered the office.

'Cato Dalen's been arrested in Oslo,' he said, slumping down into a chair. 'The Security Service caught up with him at Oslo Central station.'

Wisting skirted around him and sat down. Hammer lifted his long legs and perched his feet on the edge of the desk.

'He's on his way here now,' he continued, fishing out his snuff tin from his pocket. 'In an hour or so, you can have him in this chair here.'

'Good,' Wisting replied. 'Because we're leaving tomorrow.'

'Leaving? Do you really mean to travel to Afghanistan to find that young boy?'

'I'm just arranging the last details right now,' Wisting said through tight lips. 'The army has an airlift departing from Gardermoen airport tomorrow afternoon.'

Hammer sat with his mouth open. 'An airlift?'

'They fly down replacement personnel, mail, food, machine parts and other equipment.'

'But it's not just a matter of *going* to Afghanistan, surely?' Hammer protested. 'There are laws and rules for international cooperation. Procedures and processes that have to be followed.'

Wisting shrugged. 'Afghanistan is a lawless country. We don't have time to attempt to enter into formal arrangements.'

'Afghanistan is huge, though,' Hammer objected. 'How on earth can you believe we'll even be able to find our way or set up anything at all if we travel under our own steam?'

'We'll get help,' Wisting assured him. 'Norway is leading a stabilization force in northern Afghanistan. Representatives from the whole legal apparatus are in place down there, both police lawyers and prison advisers, even a defence counsel. We have six colleagues working there to build up a competent and fair police force. The head of the drugs squad in the province has a Norwegian mentor who will assist us.'

'Isn't that where Thomas is?'

Wisting nodded. He had not seen his son for eighteen months. Thomas had trained as a helicopter pilot in the military and was serving the fourth of his twelve years of duty. He belonged to 720 Squadron and his home base was at Rygge in Østfold, but since October he had been stationed with the Norwegian forces in Maymana that had been tasked with rebuilding the surrounding province.

Hammer got to his feet and crossed to the window, where he turned on his heel and walked to the shelf unit on the other side of the room before resuming his seat.

'Are just the two of us going?'

'No.' Wisting picked up his jacket, which was draped over the chair back as he stood up. 'I want to bring someone who knows the country. Someone who can speak the language and has some insight into the culture.'

'Were you thinking of anyone in particular?'

Wisting nodded again. Suzanne Bjerke had been in his thoughts a great deal in the twenty-four hours or so that had elapsed since he had met her.

A solitary candle was burning in Suzanne Bjerke's office, with liquid wax running down the candlestick and across the table. The delicate flame flickered in the draught from the door and the glow of candlelight enhanced the radiance of her eyes. Holding his gaze, she gave him a friendly smile and invited him to take a seat.

'I've been thinking about Khaled Athari,' Wisting said. 'We're considering bringing him back.'

'What do you mean?'

'Do you think he could manage to locate the apartment block where he was held prisoner?'

Suzanne Bjerke rose from her chair and walked over to the window. The dim light distorted her features. Her eyelids slid shut, as if she was struggling to gather her thoughts.

'Yes, I think so, almost certainly,' she said with a sigh. 'Children exposed to trauma have too much memory. They remember all the dreadful details far too well. Just think of yourself and the day your wife died. I'm sure you recall every-thing from that day. Maybe not in the right order or context, but you remember little trivial and inconsequential things that have become seared into your mind.'

Wisting dipped his head. She was right. He kept trying to chase away the memories from the day Ingrid died, but it was impossible to get rid of them. He could recollect almost every step he had taken that day. Meetings he had sat in, assessments he had made and important decisions that had been taken – as well as how insignificant everything had suddenly seemed when he had looked into the pastor's eyes. He could call to mind the rain and how the dark clouds had blown away to reveal a blood-red moon in the heavens as day had turned to night.

'But bringing him back will damage him even more.' Suzanne turned to face him with her arms crossed on her chest. 'He's still only a child. The Norwegian authorities have decided that the place he belongs is a poor village in North Afghanistan. To you, he's just a piece in a jigsaw puzzle.'

'An important piece,' Wisting said softly. 'If we're to catch the people who took Layla's life and put an end to this madness, then we need to find him.'

She smiled again, as if she had known all along that he was right but had felt compelled to protest all the same.

'It won't work, though, if he feels afraid and unsafe,' Wisting added. 'If he's to help us, then he has to trust us.'

Suzanne walked back to her desk and sat down again. 'How are you going to manage that?'

'I was hoping you would come with us.'

Suzanne's black eyebrows shot up so that they arched and almost met in the middle. She maintained eye contact with him and he could see something light up in her eyes, which took on a different glow. Of warmth and yearning.

She stared at him doubtfully and he moved closer and placed his hand warily on her forearm.

'I would really appreciate it if you said yes,' he concluded.

She answered by putting her hand on his, giving him a smile and nodding her head.

45

'There are two visitors for you down in the basement,' the duty sergeant at the front desk told Wisting when he returned to the station.

Wisting glanced at the board where the names of prisoners were chalked up. Cato Dalen was in cell 8 and Sindre Hovden in cell 4.

'Dalen arrived with the transport from Oslo a quarter of an hour ago. Hovden was hauled in from a boozing session in Bøkeskogen. He needs an hour or so to sober up before he'll be ready for you.'

'Then I'll take Dalen up with me,' Wisting said, marking *at interview* beside cell 8 on the board.

'He's asked for a lawyer and specified Heitmann,' the sergeant said.

Wisting mulled this over. Reidar Heitmann was one of the town's most high-profile defence lawyers and had also made a name for himself well beyond his own legal circles by being thorough and efficient in his job. He seized upon mistakes, taking hold of ragged edges and loose threads in cases until they had large holes in them. Often these holes were big enough for his clients to wriggle through when the cases ended up in court. However, this was not a matter of bringing Cato Dalen to court but of obtaining information from him that could progress the investigation.

'Then I'd better hurry,' Wisting commented as he rushed to the staircase leading to the floor below.

His footsteps echoed off the grey concrete in the basement.

On the floor outside the cell door there was a pair of black boots, with a blue pack of Petterøe rolling tobacco sticking out of one of them.

Wisting slid the iron bolt and let the heavy door swing slowly open. The walls were smooth and bare and the air inside was stuffy and oppressive.

Cato Dalen sat on a thin blue mattress at the far end of the cramped room with his knees drawn up to his chin. His eyes squinted at the light that fell diagonally from the corridor outside.

Wisting stepped in and reached out an arm to help him up. 'Shall we go up to my office?' he suggested.

Cato Dalen sat without moving a muscle. 'I think we'll wait for my lawyer,' he said through compressed lips.

His body language told Wisting that this was going to be difficult. The man facing him was suspected of stealing firearms. A pistol found in the burnt-out ruins of his house tied him to the case and would give him a potential sentence of six years' imprisonment. He had nothing to gain by talking to the police. Lies and silence would be the easiest route for him, whereas telling the truth would result in immediate, guaranteed disadvantage.

'Can't we wait up in my office?' Wisting ventured, in the hope of sparking some conversation.

'I've nothing to tell you.'

'I have a lot of questions for you.'

Cato Dalen shrugged and looked away.

Wisting gazed at him. He had been in similar situations before. But time was short. The defence lawyer was probably already on his way.

Shrugging off his jacket, he threw it down on the mattress beside Cato Dalen.

'Have you heard of the Butterfly Effect?' he asked, starting to unbutton his shirtsleeves.

Cato Dalen glanced up at him, looking scared and perplexed.

'Chaos theory? Are you familiar with it?'

Wisting calmly walked from one side of the cell to the other while he talked.

'The world we live in is really a dynamic chaos in which everything affects and is in turn affected by everything. The Butterfly Effect is a term for how tiny variations in the initial conditions in a dynamic system can cause major variations in the longer term. Such as when a little flutter of a butterfly's wings somewhere on earth can theoretically cause stormy weather on the opposite side of the globe.'

Wisting stopped and looked down at the prisoner. He could see that he had whetted the man's curiosity, at least.

'What are experienced as small random events can have a great deal to say in the life of a human being,' Wisting went on. 'I would not be standing here if it hadn't been for someone stealing my father's car when I was eight years old. That was when I made up my mind to become a policeman. You might not have been sitting within these narrow walls if it hadn't been for Maria Schicklgruber.'

Cato Dalen shifted uncomfortably over to the corner of the cell.

'Maria Schicklgruber was Hitler's grandmother, his father's mother,' Wisting continued. 'We don't know who his father's father was. She became pregnant when she was working for a Jewish family in the nineteenth century and gave birth to an illegitimate son. It's fairly likely that Hitler was one quarter Jewish. When he came to power, he forbade all discussion of his family and had his father's birthplace razed to the ground by turning it into a military training area. He also banned non-Jewish women from working in Jewish households. Soviet propagandists during the war insisted that Hitler was Jewish. Anyway, chaos. If Maria Schicklgruber had not become pregnant in 1836, the world would look very different today. We would not have had Nazism as we know it. The thoughts and ideals you hold would probably not have brought you to that corner where you're sitting now.'

Wisting began to unbutton his shirt from the top of his chest.

'You find yourself in the midst of chaos now,' he said, looking straight into the uncertain eyes facing him. 'The actions you've taken and can't escape from have made you into an important piece of a bigger picture. We found a pistol in the ruins of your house. You've been charged with stealing it and seventeen other firearms from a house in Kjose. One of those weapons was used when Ahmed Saad died with two shots to the back of his neck.'

'I don't have any –' Cato Dalen tried to speak.

'A few hours later the killer accidentally drops the gun in a ditch,' Wisting broke in. 'The next day an eleven-year-old boy gets off the school bus. Someone has tossed a can of cola out of a car and it lies at his feet when he gets off the bus. He kicks it away, following it with his eyes along the road verge until it rolls down into the ditch, where he finds something far more exciting. He takes the pistol with him, hides it in the barn and shows it to the boy next door just as I park my car in the farmyard.'

Wisting wrenched off his shirt. Yellowish liquid had seeped through the bandage on his right shoulder.

'The young lad pulled the trigger almost as soon as I stepped out of the car.' He peeled off the bandage to reveal the rough stitches that held the wound together. 'The shot tore through skin, tendons and tissue. I've never been closer to death. A sum total of coincidences that spread out like rings in water from the day you broke in and stole those guns.'

Cato Dalen cleared his throat but still said nothing more.

'Right now you're like a stone on the top of a mountain,' Wisting ploughed on. 'Depending on small variations in position, it ends up rolling down into one of many possible valleys, some of them deeper than others. The simplest way out is for you to tell me who you delivered those firearms to.'

A vein in Cato Dalen's forehead had become more prominent while Wisting had been talking. Now it was throbbing distinctly on his smooth scalp.

'A lot of things could have been different,' the young man said finally, running his hand over his red goatee beard. 'It's not possible to control everything in life, but I'm willing to answer for the choices I've made.'

Wisting clenched his fist on his shirt to hide his excitement. He had led Cato Dalen exactly where he wanted him to be.

'That's exactly what it's all about,' he commented, going on to find the words he had used many times before: 'It's about standing up for what you've done. Taking responsibility for your own actions.'

Something came over the young extremist's face as he realized he was about to talk his way to an admission. Then he stretched his arm up towards Wisting and accepted help to get to his feet.

'It's not true, what it said in the newspaper,' he began. 'That 30,000 kroner was stolen as well.' He began 'There was an envelope in the cabinet, but there were only 2,000 kroner in it. And we didn't take any jewellery. The rest must be an insurance scam. We were just interested in the guns.'

Wisting put his shirt on again. The chill air had made his skin contract.

'You know what happened to my house,' Cato Dalen added. 'We had to be able to defend ourselves.'

'There were enough guns in that safe to start a small war,' Wisting remarked.

'We just kept one pistol each and sold the rest.'

'Who did you sell them to?' Wisting asked, swallowing audibly. Cato Dalen was on the point of informing on another person. Wisting had seen this before and knew how difficult it was, what conflicting emotions were battling for supremacy in Cato Dalen's soul. All his experience suggested that it was the instinct for self-preservation that would gain the upper hand, but often the price for that was self-hatred. It was the same for him, the observer: he had persuaded many a weak and emotional suspect to squeal, but when he succeeded the taste of victory often contained a tinge of disgust. But not this time, Wisting thought. The desire to move the case on another notch towards resolution was so strong that he could not be less concerned about what mental agonies and fear of reprisals it might lead to for Cato Dalen.

The prisoner opened his mouth to answer but closed it again when the heavy door leading into the cell area slammed noisily. Footsteps could be heard out in the corridor.

Wisting poked his head out to see Cato's lawyer, Heitmann, dressed in a suit and check shirt and carrying a briefcase. A guard walked behind him with a large bunch of keys. They both stared wide-eyed at Wisting, whose shirt was still flapping open.

'What's going on here?' the lawyer demanded, looking from Wisting to Cato Dalen.

Wisting had no answer for him and concentrated instead on buttoning his shirt.

'Who?' Wisting tried again, in one last hope of getting something out of the young man.

'I must be allowed to speak to my client,' Heitmann said. 'Do you have a room we can use?'

The guard nodded as he fiddled with the keys.

Wisting picked up his jacket, keeping his eyes fixed on Cato Dalen. He could see that his eyes were filled with despair, but his mouth was firmly closed.

46

Only photographers now stood outside the crime scene in Unnersbogate as the yellow streetlights cast their shadows along the ground. They hung around with their lenses, waiting for one of the white-clad technicians to appear outside.

Line sat in her car some distance down the street. She could see the red-and-white police crime-scene tape fluttering in the wind. She had spoken to several distressed neighbours and written a couple of paragraphs to be interwoven into Morten P.'s story.

She clicked her way into the folders to see what the other members of the team were working on. One of her colleagues, located in Akersgata, had been in contact with a senior investigating officer in Dresden and obtained comments on the three-year-old case in which a severed head had been found in a city park. The unsolved inquiry had been shelved. They had not heard from their Norwegian police colleagues as yet but the German police were prepared to reopen their case if a request was received.

A new folder with the title *Fire Victim Arrested* aroused her curiosity. She clicked into it. The status of the story was still 'unfinished', and Line skimmed through the text. The leader of the Patriotic Front had been apprehended in Oslo and charged with firearms theft following the discovery of a pistol in the ruins of his house, which had burned to the ground two days earlier. A spokesperson for the Police Security Service was unwilling to comment. However, Superintendent Audun Vetti at Larvik police station had confirmed that he had been taken into custody. He had been transported to Larvik and would be interviewed in the course of that evening.

In the stored background material, she saw that the journalist had made a note of the same thoughts that had struck her. About the racism theory that had been prominent at an earlier stage with both the police and the media. The Iraqi who had lived in Unnersbogate had been shot dead. The Patriotic Front had obviously acquired an arsenal for themselves. Could the police have a hidden agenda with the arrest? Did they suspect the right-wing nationalists of having more to do with the case than they were willing to make public?

However, that did not stack up with the theory that the murders were connected with the narcotics trade. From what she had read of the organization, she did not have the impression that they were in favour of that sort of thing. Neither had she read or heard of any of these nationalist groupings financing their activities through the sale of narcotics.

The clock down in the right-hand corner of the computer screen showed 20.34. She opened the program from which she could send text messages and found Tommy Kvanter stored in the contacts list.

Could I come over in ten minutes? she asked before switching off the machine.

OK pinged in on her mobile phone.

Line glanced in the rear-view mirror and moved a couple of stray hairs from her blonde fringe. Her eyes looked tired and needed a fresh application of mascara. She rummaged around in her bag to find what she needed to make her eyes look brighter and applied a fresh coat of lipstick before she moved off.

She considered stopping at a petrol station to buy something. A box of chocolates, maybe, but she ended up empty-handed outside the apartment block beside the town square.

The security chain rattled when Tommy Kvanter came to open the door. He unhooked it and gave Line a welcoming smile.

He had put on a long-sleeved shirt that covered the tattoos on his arms – he had also shaved recently and smelled of fresh aftershave.

The lights in the living room were dimmed and the curtains drawn. A pillar candle was flickering on the coffee table and soft music filled the room.

'I've bought some tea,' he announced from the kitchen doorway. 'African flowers, green peach, Mabula lime or Evening Star?'

Laughing, she realized that what she really wanted was to sample one of the wine bottles on the rack beside the stereo system. She was on the verge of suggesting that, but there could be further developments in the story and she would prefer to be fit to drive.

'Evening Star,' she accepted with thanks, and sat down in the same chair as last time.

Tommy disappeared into the kitchen and she heard cups clinking.

'Any progress on the story?' he shouted through to her. 'Any imminent arrests?'

'It doesn't seem so,' Line told him. She stood up and crossed the room to join him. 'Other than the arrest of the leader of the Patriotic Front.'

'I saw that on the Internet,' Tommy commented as he filled a tea strainer with green leaves.

'Are they mixed up with drugs?'

'Well, they do have to get their crazy ideas from some-where.' He filled the cups and watched sceptically as the water changed colour. 'They most likely sit in some small room somewhere, smoking until they're completely stoned, but in no way are they major players in the market. They don't have the brains or the balls for that.'

He handed her a cup.

'Sugar? Milk?'

'Sugar,' she said.

Tommy Kvanter took out a sugar bowl and carried it through to the living room, where they both sat down. The hot drink smelled of apple and lemon. Line stirred the tea-bag around in her cup and then looked for somewhere to lay it aside.

Reading the expression on her face, Tommy disappeared back to the kitchen and returned with a saucer.

'It's nine o'clock,' he said, grabbing the remote control. 'Let's watch the news.'

She nodded as she sipped her tea. They just managed to catch the theme tune for the TV2 evening news. The head-line item was the discovery of the crime scene where the beheading had taken place. Images of the old workers' block in Unnersbogate filled the screen while a reporter announced that the police had confirmed they were confident they had now located where fourteen-year-old Layla Azimi had been murdered. The location in question was the apartment belonging to a thirty-seven-year-old Iraqi whom the police had identified as the man who had been found shot dead in the Lågen river thirty-six hours ago.

Line heaved a sigh of resignation. When she had left Tor-strand twenty minutes ago, the police had still been unwilling to comment on the case. They had not even been disposed to answer direct questions about whether there was a definite connection between the two murder victims but had referred her to the press conference at 9 p.m. TV2 must have applied some pressure to capture the news in advance in order to make the evening news bulletin.

'*We'll return to that story, direct from a press conference being held at the police station in Larvik now, at nine o'clock,*' the newsreader said, moving on.

Line picked up her mobile to send a message to Morten P., but decided not to bother.

The arrest of Cato Dalen was the next main item on the news. Archive footage from the dramatic fire flickered across the screen. The camera zoomed in on the frontman's shaved head as he stood behind one of the fire engines talking to Line's father, the flames casting an orange glow over them.

Police Superintendent Audun Vetti appeared with a microphone in front of him. He repeated parts of what the reporter had said, as confirmation. The same reporter had also covered the murder cases. Line recognized him as a persistent, ingratiating character who never took no for an answer. She guessed that it was to his credit that TV 2 had obtained the spectacular newsflash.

The figure of Reidar Heitmann, the lawyer, now filled the TV screen. The camera lighting made his prominent ears look bright red. He was wearing a stylish tie and matching shirt. It crossed Line's mind that she should buy something similar for her father on payday, something different from those boring old Dressmann shirts of his.

The lawyer made a few brief comments before the segment was over and the programme moved straight to the police station. Her father was seated at a table at one end of the spacious conference room. He had put on his uniform and appeared calm and composed. All the same, Line could see that he felt uncomfortable.

The superintendent read out a prepared statement containing little new in relation to what had already been publicized in the broadcast and ended by encouraging any-one who had noticed anything out of the ordinary near Unnersbogate 4 last Sunday afternoon, evening or during the night to come forward.

'They're saying nothing about it having anything to do with narcotics,' Tommy said, turning down the volume. 'There was nothing about that in the newspapers either.'

'I've finished writing a story on that,' Line told him. 'But I need more information and some confirmation from the police.'

'The import and sale of heroin to Scandinavia are con-trolled by Albanians,' Tommy explained, leaning back. 'That's the way it's been ever since the war in Kosovo in the nineties. The USC guerrillas financed the war against Serbia and Slo-bodan Milošević using lucrative narcotics traffic through what was called the Balkan route. Opium from Afghanistan was processed into heroin in Turkey and from there distributed on through the Balkans to Europe and the Nordic countries. Then there was the war in Afghanistan. The Taliban fell and local warlords needed finance. Narcotics have found new routes. Raw opium and heroin are transported to Tajikistan and then on to Russia and Western Europe.'

'The Silk Road,' Line commented, thinking of the old trade route that centuries ago had brought spices and silk to the West.

Tommy agreed. 'The new networks have stretched out those threads to reach as far as here. They've become entan-gled and gained access to established organizations by importing purer and cheaper drugs.'

'Who are they working with?'

Tommy Kvanter lifted his cup to his mouth and drank. He made a face to show he did not care for the taste.

'A Norwegian is pulling the strings,' he said, putting down his cup. 'He lives here in Larvik.'

'The Night Man?'

'That's what they call him.'

'Why is that?'

Tommy shrugged. 'They always have. I imagine it must be because he only shows himself at night.'

'But who is he?'

'There are a few stories about him.' Tommy leaned forward conspiratorially. 'He worked in the local bank in the seventies. Used safety-deposit boxes as depots for hash brought in on fishing boats from Denmark. Then he was caught and received a lengthy sentence. The money he had earned was invested in securities and property. When he was released, he had built up a fair amount of start-up capital and established a unique network of contacts in all sorts of criminal circles. He is that rare beast, an intelligent criminal, with a cynical business sense.'

Line had taken out her notebook. 'He must have a name, though?'

'Werner Roos.'

The name sounded familiar, but she was unable to place it. She was tempted to take out her laptop and do some searches but decided against it.

'Where does he live?'

'Outside the town, at Lamøya. I don't think there's as much as a street name or anything like that out there.'

Line put her pen in her mouth and nibbled at it. She sat in silence, staring into the candle flame in front of them. Melted wax ran over the edge and solidified in a puddle on the table-top. Then she fixed her eyes on Tommy.

'Can you show me?'

Smiling at her, he nodded his head, leaning forward to blow out the candle.

47

As the last journalists were ushered out of the police station, Wisting headed into the toilets to splash his face with cold, refreshing water. The rough paper towel from the dispenser on the wall chafed on his bristles as he dried himself, studying his reflection in the mirror. His eyes were bloodshot and he had to squint to see in the harsh light. His head was filled with thoughts that were difficult to disentangle, but he knew he would sleep when he got home, as soon as his head hit the pillow. There was just one thing he had to do first.

He walked slowly down the corridor towards the interview room. Despite the thousands of interviews he had behind him, he always felt a strange tingle in his gut when he knew that a forthcoming conversation might be crucial to the progress of an investigation.

Sindre Hovden was sitting on a simple wooden spindle-back chair, a plastic cup of water on the table in front of him. He glanced up when Wisting entered the room. His face showed clear signs of the life he had led – broken nose, bad teeth, swollen gums and a yellowish tinge to his eyes. His hands and arms were covered in abscesses and little cuts from countless needle pricks.

Wisting introduced himself and they shook hands. He could see how hostile the man was. At the same time, he seemed detached, as if his thoughts were elsewhere, far from this small room and what was about to happen. He scarcely listened when Wisting rattled through the introductory, formal parts of the interview. From a technical point of view, he was charged with the acquisition and use of narcotics. That gave him the right to refuse to provide the police with a statement and to be assisted by defence counsel. Most people in Sindre Hovden's situation ignored both of these and were only concerned with talking their way out of the room as fast as possible. Many of the confessions given in here had come about as a result of withdrawal symptoms.

'What time is it?' Sindre Hovden demanded in a hoarse, rasping voice.

'Five to ten,' Wisting replied without checking his watch.

'In the morning?'

'In the evening. You've been here for five hours.'

Sindre Hovden raised his eyebrows, reached out his hand for the cup and drank the last gulp of water.

'Have you got time to bother with me, then?' The voice had become smoother after the drink of water.

'What do you mean?'

'I do follow things, you know.' Hovden shifted in his seat. 'People are chopping heads off one another in the town. Thought you'd have more important things to do than sit here talking to me.'

Wisting did not answer. Instead he drew a grey envelope out of a bundle of case documents and took out a photo of the blood-spattered T-shirt. Sindre Hovden did not seem to react in any way. Then he opened out the copy of *VG* with Line's article about the find. Sindre Hovden leaned forward, his eyes skittering over the newspaper pages.

'It's *your* blood,' Wisting told him.

Sindre Hovden sat bolt upright. 'No fucking way,' he said.

Wisting thumbed through to the report from the DNA register where the conclusion was typed in bold print.

'No fucking way,' Hovden said again.

'Let me see your hands,' Wisting asked him.

Sindre Hovden showed his grubby palms, turning his hands over, studying them with a befuddled expression.

'Where did you get that?' Wisting asked, pointing at a cut on his right palm. It was almost five centimetres long and ran diagonally down from his little finger. It had healed slightly but was still red and puffy. Yellow pus had collected at the edge of the wound and it looked infected.

The reply was hesitant: 'I cut myself.'

'How did that happen?'

The confused look on Sindre Hovden's face changed to something resembling a triumphant smile.

'You must already know that, surely?'

'What do you mean?'

'You hauled me in when it happened. There was such a fucking circus down at the railway station.'

Wisting scowled and began to flick through the papers.

'A few days afterwards you came and picked me up again and tried to tell me I had left a suitcase full of heroin.'

Sindre Hovden burst out laughing and the guffaws echoed through the little room.

Wisting had gone through the papers several times before but had never read anywhere that this man had sustained an injury. He took out the report and skimmed through the simple rubric. It stated that pepper spray had been used and that he had been treated with running water but nothing about a cut.

'Tell me,' he asked in a serious tone of voice.

'All of it? Again?'

'About the cut.'

'I don't know exactly how it happened.' He shrugged. 'I was pretty much out of it but I remember that foreign guy getting really angry. That was just before the cops turned up.'

'A foreigner?' Wisting skimmed through the previous

interview form. 'You've never mentioned any foreigners before now.'

'No, why the hell would I talk about foreigners?'

Wisting felt the lack of sleep making him impatient. Sindre Hovden's account was disjointed and he had to try to take him through it step by step.

'How did you get that cut on your hand?' he asked.

Sindre Hovden leaned across the table. 'When I broke the mirror on his car.'

Wisting said nothing and waited for Hovden to continue.

'Well, I was messing about down there. Had problems staying on my feet and stepped off the kerb at the car park and used a car to steady me. I nearly tore off the mirror and cut my hand.'

As he held up his palm again, the light on the ceiling flickered.

'What kind of car?' Wisting asked.

'White estate.'

Wisting felt the pieces falling into place. The connection had dawned on him before Sindre Hovden had given him the details. It was the Butterfly Effect again. A tiny mis-step by the man in front of him had cost two people their lives. Random events had taken charge. Just as Layla Azimi arrived on the train, Sindre Hovden had quarrelled with the man who was supposed to collect the narcotics. He had damaged the man's car and cut himself on the mirror. There could be several explanations for how the blood had got from the car to the T-shirt. The simplest one was that the man in the car had wiped the blood off with a discarded T-shirt lying in the vehicle. Then the rag could have fallen out when the man and his sidekick had parked in a backyard the night they placed Layla's head on a stake.

The man had panicked when he heard the police approach

and left Layla Azimi standing with her luggage before she also ran off. Later, she was the one who was punished.

'Was he alone?' Wisting asked in the hope of coming closer to the heart of the matter.

Hovden nodded.

'What did he look like?'

Sindre Hovden spread his hands in bewilderment: 'Like a foreigner.'

Wisting tapped his pen on the notepad in front of him. He asked a few more questions but received no answer that might help him make progress. What had appeared to be an opening had closed up again.

48

Lamøya was situated a quarter of an hour's drive east from the town. Line followed the Kaupang road all the way out, her car headlights slicing through the night darkness, lighting up the surrounding countryside that was blanketed in black-ploughed fields.

Despite the name, Lamøya was not an island. The area may well have been surrounded by water during the first settlements of the early Iron Age. Now the old pastures had long been attached to the mainland after the shallow straits near the shore had been filled.

Line had been out here once before, when she worked at the local newspaper and was writing a story about the sale of what at that time had been Norway's most expensive holiday home. An entrepreneur in the fashion trade had put his cabin up for sale with a price tag of 28 million kroner. The property lay at the far edge of the coastal rocks with a shoreline of more than a hundred metres. The owner had purchased it fifteen years earlier for a quarter of that sum, but when the local authority removed the obligation to reside there full-time the value had soared to a record high. The financial newspapers and other business publications had picked up her article and rehashed it with bought-in photographs.

'Right here,' Tommy said when they came to a fork in the road. The tracks here were narrow and Line dropped her speed.

'What are you actually planning to do out here?' Tommy asked.

Line shrugged. She did not really know. The greater part

of her job was usually done with her phone in front of a computer, unearthing information from archives and contacts, finding links and connections. But she always worked better when she knew who she was working with and what they looked like. Her father had talked about the same kind of thing. When a major case was on the go, he always wanted to visit the crime scene. Touching and feeling, seeing what things looked like, made it easier for him to envisage the chain of events when he read reports and witness statements.

'I'll just drive past,' she replied. 'Have a look at where he lives.'

'That's not possible.' Tommy took out his tobacco pouch. 'He lives at the end of a cul-de-sac.'

'Can we park and go for a walk?'

Tommy scattered the tobacco on the cigarette paper.

'Yes, we can do that,' he said. His tongue slid across the paper. 'Drive to the right at the hill over there.'

'Do you know the area?' Line asked, following his directions.

'I've been here before,' Tommy answered with a sly smile as he returned his tobacco pouch to his inside pocket.

The road ran past a few summer cabins and several side roads with gates and notices forbidding unauthorized access. After two hundred metres or so, the road continued over an uneven, twisting cart track of crushed shells that led up a slight slope and ended on a plateau with the sea directly below.

Tommy Kvanter was first out of the car. The flame from his lighter glowed on his face as he lit his cigarette.

Line rummaged through her bag to take her mobile phone with her but could not find it. She went through her pockets and searched around the car seat before it dawned on her that she had left it at Tommy's apartment. She could see it in her mind's eye, on the coffee table with a message she had started writing to Morten P.

Hiding her bag under the seat, she locked the car. The night air, filled with the tang of the sea, was silent around them, broken only by the swell of the water and the breakers pounding on the shore. In the skies above them, there were more stars than she had seen for a long time. The moon afforded enough light for her to make out the outline of a ridge in the murk, humpbacked and rugged against the night sky. While she watched, a star fell through the darkness, leaving behind a thin, milky-white trail.

She could see her breath when she exhaled.

'Shall we go for a walk, then?' she asked, fastening up her jacket.

'Down there,' Tommy said, using his cigarette to point in the direction of lights from a house on the shore, just over a hundred metres further north.

A sudden gust of wind rushed through the crooked pine trees. Somewhere in the darkness, a bird screeched, and then silence returned.

'I'm not sure that's such a good idea,' he said from behind her.

'What do you mean?'

'Werner Roos is not a man who would like to find anyone lurking around his house. Now you know who he is and where he lives. There's a reason he lives in such an out-of-the-way spot.'

'It's that reason I've come here to find out,' Line protested. 'Since we've come so far now, we might as well try to go all the way up to the house, don't you think?'

'It's up to you.'

Line turned towards him with a smile on her face. 'Put out that cigarette.'

He did as she asked and they moved on.

The track was easier to follow in the darkness than she

had anticipated. The most difficult part was down from the heights where they had parked the car. After that, it was simply a matter of skulking along the water's edge.

Werner Roos's house had to be one of the oldest ones out there. It sat on a tall basement and was two full storeys with several glass verandahs, balconies and gabled dormers. The roof rose steeply, jutting out into the starry sky.

The garden surrounding the large house was fenced in with black wrought-iron railings that looked really dilapidated. Autumn leaves had collected in heaps at the house wall and other places sheltered from the wind.

Line took up position behind a huge oak tree outside the property. The distance from here to the house was approximately twenty-five metres. Almost all the windows were brightly lit, but there was nobody to be seen inside.

At the rear of the house there was a small annexe, less brightly lit, but they saw a flickering blue glow from a TV set at two of the windows. Down beside the water a boathouse and a storage shed were hidden in the darkness.

'He's at home,' Line whispered, pointing at a four-wheel-drive vehicle parked in the courtyard in front of the house with a smaller sports car beside it. She squinted but was still unable to read the registration plates.

'And he has a visitor,' Tommy told her, gesturing towards one of the windows. A woman in a white turtleneck sweater was standing inside. With tanned skin and blonde hair, she was speaking to someone, gesticulating and tossing her head back and laughing, showing her dazzling white teeth.

A man appeared behind the windows. He must have stood up and now walked towards the woman. Tall and broad-shouldered, he had blond hair with an unruly fringe and his complexion looked pale, as if he had not been out in daylight for a long time.

'The Night Man,' Tommy confirmed.

He was older than Line had imagined, but when she thought about what Tommy had said about him having worked in a bank in the seventies, she figured he must be about the same age as her father. The woman in the room was much younger and could scarcely have been born when Werner Roos had used the bank vaults as a depot for narcotics.

Werner Roos caressed the woman's cheek before heading into an adjoining room. When the woman sat down, she disappeared out of sight.

'Can we go now?' Tommy asked, looking around and rubbing his hands.

Line was feeling the cold too. She had no idea what more she could achieve with her visit out there, but if this man was the intended recipient of the narcotics haul, then he was also responsible for the deaths of two people. He was the drugs baron who pulled the strings and was never caught. But those same strings could lead her to the killers, so well camouflaged that they would never succeed in reaching him.

Assuming that Tommy Kvanter was right in claiming that Werner Roos and his organization were where the heroin was destined to end up, she was now facing the pinnacle of the criminal hierarchy. It would be easier to work down through the network, in a direction where there was unlikely to be so much effort made to hide their tracks. She also knew how she could do that. *Follow the money.*

As she turned towards Tommy and nodded a sign that they should leave now, they heard the noise of a vehicle further down the track. The headlamps swept powerful beams across the undergrowth.

Line crouched down and crept further forward so that she could keep the entrance in her sight. Tommy held her close to him, behind a straggly bush.

A black Mercedes swung up into the yard and parked behind the other two vehicles. The cabin light lit up when the door opened. Line let out a gasp when she saw who had arrived. Reidar Heitmann, the lawyer helping Cato, fumbled with a document folder as he stepped out of the car. He had on the same clothes he had been wearing at the TV interview an hour ago.

Werner Roos welcomed him on the front steps and ushered him into the house. Line shifted position again in an effort to gain a better view.

The woman inside greeted the lawyer before disappearing out of the room. Heitmann's lips were moving: he obviously had a lot to communicate. Werner Roos's expression changed from anxiety to anger and he began to pace back and forth across the room. The raised voices reached all the way out to them. The lawyer held his hands up in placatory fashion, as if trying to subdue his client.

Line put her hand on the cold iron railings. If the two men continued to talk so loudly, she desperately wanted the opportunity to hear at least part of what they were discussing and thought she could manage that unseen if she stood beside the wall of the house.

Tommy protested, but she ignored him, raising her leg to straddle the fence. At that very moment, the two men indoors froze and, looking straight at the window, they moved towards it. Line, paralysed with fear, stood completely still. She knew that from inside the brightly lit room they would be unable to see anything other than darkness if she stood entirely motionless.

As she took a deep breath, a door crashed open at the other side of the house and the barking of hot-tempered dogs filled the cold night air.

49

Studying the contents of his wardrobe, Wisting took out a couple of T-shirts, some underwear and a few pairs of socks and packed them into his travel bag.

He had not yet had a chance to tell Line that he was taking a trip. And if she was going to be late, he was not sure that he had the energy to sit up and wait for her. He was already suffering from lack of sleep and could never manage to sleep well when he was travelling. The long journey that lay ahead of him, lasting as much as twenty-four hours, was going to be exhausting.

Although he had no idea how long he would be away, he packed four shirts anyway. Then his thoughts turned to what Suzanne Bjerke had told him about the climate and the weather and swapped two of them for a thick sweater and a cardigan. The winter was hard and tough in Afghanistan, especially in the northern provinces where they were headed.

It crossed his mind that he had taken a liking to Suzanne Bjerke. There was something about her that invited some kind of trust, though he could not quite put his finger on what it was. Even though they had met in tragic circumstances, he felt comfortable and at ease in her company. He also had to admit to himself that she was beautiful, but there was something else that caused his thoughts to return continually to her. She seemed warm and caring and she possessed a calmness and gravity that he found attractive.

He found some heavy woollen socks at the bottom of the drawer and tossed them into his bag. This was the first time he had thought about another woman since Ingrid's death. It pricked his conscience, but he could not chase away the feeling that he was looking forward to becoming better acquainted with Suzanne.

He jumped when the phone rang in the silent house.

'I think we've got something,' Torunn Borg said at the other end of the line. She was still at the police station and would be in charge of the investigation while Wisting and Hammer were away. 'The patrol's been called out to a fire at a cabin in Solbergvannet.'

'I see,' Wisting replied. He reached out for a scarf and waited for her to continue. In his mind he pictured the map of the police district and located Solbergvannet in the northern part on the border towards Lardal, where Route 306 snaked along the shore towards Andebu.

'The cabin is situated fifty metres from the road,' Torunn Borg went on. 'There's a car on fire down there in a layby. An old white estate.'

'Christ,' Wisting swore as he tossed the scarf on top of the travel bag.

Torunn Borg had no need to explain anything further. This was the car and the hiding place of the men they were pursuing. He put on his jacket and boots and rushed out to his own car. He had no idea what lay behind this sudden development, but most likely it was a scorched-earth tactic. The killers were setting fire to everything that could link them to the inquiry while they drew back. It could cause complications, but at the same time it had exposed them.

He kept his speed just under the limit as he drove through the centre of town and stamped his foot on the accelerator as he left it behind.

The shortest way went exactly as he had anticipated, past the farm at Hagtvedt and the pile of staves lying at the road verge.

The drive took more than half an hour. He could have saved himself the bother and replaced it with a few hours' sleep. The fire brigade had taken almost as long as he had to get there and there was nothing left to see. Very little traffic moved on these country roads in the evenings and the flames had raged for a long time before being discovered by a chance passer-by. The cabin had nearly burned to the ground by the time the first fire engine arrived on the scene. The car was nothing but a twisted wreck in a layby.

The media had still not made an appearance, but they would soon be here. Fires always provided good pictures, even after they had been extinguished.

Wisting followed the thick hoses rolled out along a path through the woods.

Hot steam rose from the ruins that were hidden from the road. The stink of wet ash, charred timber, burnt plastic and rubber hung in the air, irritating Wisting's throat when he inhaled.

Espen Mortensen had arrived minutes before him. He stood expectantly while the fire crew packed away their equipment.

The site of a fire was completely different from other crime scenes and presented problems not encountered elsewhere. Not only was a blaze in itself incredibly destructive but also the work of putting it out often damaged what traces had been left. By the time Mortensen was able to examine the debris, the fire officers had already been there, trampling over vital evidence. But mostly it was the degree of eradication in a fire that created the problems. Fire could be completely catastrophic and make the simplest of objects unrecognizable.

Espen Mortensen produced a particle mask and handed it to Wisting. 'There's a lot of shit in the ash,' he said, putting on similar protective gear.

Wisting tied on the mask and followed him to the site of the blaze. Mortensen was carrying a powerful flashlight that swept over the black, charred remains. The roof and most of the walls had been burned away, revealing a jumble of carbonized, warped rubbish. Settees, shelves, beds, chests, roof timbers, all blackened by the flames and soaking wet following the onslaught of the firemen's hoses.

Through the mask, he could not smell how bad it stank, but the typical acrid odour was fixed in his memory. Wisting stopped just beyond the stone steps. He had seen enough and there was no need for him to venture any further. With a heavy sigh, he ran his hand through his hair. Fires were often used to cover other crimes or to destroy evidence. Here, the flames had consumed everything.

'Perfect spot,' Mortensen commented, glancing behind at the spot where the firefighters were huddled. 'The cabin isn't visible from the road.'

Wisting agreed. Only the car betrayed that people had been staying here, but it was parked on the opposite side, in the small lay-by with a path leading into an area popular with hikers.

'Was it a mistake, do you think?' he asked. 'Publicizing the search for the vehicle. The media coverage must have led to the fire.'

'Did we have any choice?' Mortensen retorted. He hunkered down, picking at something.

Wisting did not respond. 'Have we traced whoever owns the cabin?' he asked instead.

'Headquarters has been in touch with him,' Mortensen replied. 'An old man from Høyjord who lives in a care home now. The cabin's been empty for years. He thought someone must have decided to squat in it.'

'What about the car?'

'That can probably be traced. The number plates are gone, but it should be possible to find a chassis or engine number. I wouldn't be too optimistic, though, if I were you. It's almost certainly stolen.'

Wisting pivoted round and gazed out over the nearby lake. The fire ruins still gave off some heat but the moon was reflected in a thin layer of ice on the water. Behind that, tall spruce trees loomed against the black sky. Everything was shrouded in darkness.

50

Line understood what was about to happen, but it took time for her body to react to the danger. Something had clearly triggered a silent alarm and warned the residents of the house that someone was lurking outside.

Two huge floodlights on the house wall directed their beams across the garden and the surrounding area. A large brownish-black dog, its ears flapping and mouth frothing, came bounding towards the railings.

Tommy yanked her away from the fence and dragged her with him into the woods. Pine needles and twigs scratched at her as she moved and she tripped on a root and fell headlong to the ground but managed to totter to her feet and run on. Her pulse was hammering in her ears and sweat was pouring off her. The taste of blood filled her mouth. The last thing she saw behind her was a stocky man trying to lift the eager dog over the railings.

Tommy ran ahead of her, holding one arm in front of him to clear a path through the vegetation that was becoming thicker and thicker. Picking her way across a stream, she lost her balance on the wobbly, slippery stones and stumbled again. She floundered in the water then got up and was able to pick up her speed. Her jacket was flapping around her and her wet jeans were plastered to her legs. In front of her, Tommy had found a path leading up to the track. At her back, she could hear the dog forcing its way through the trees.

All of a sudden, Tommy was above her, stretching his arm out towards her from an overhang beside the path. Grabbing hold of his hand, she found a foothold and hauled herself up the steep incline until her chest and torso were resting on a rocky ledge. The hulking brute of a dog was left standing on the ground below, barking at them.

Line stretched straight out and slowly but surely her breathing became less laboured.

'Come on!' Tommy said. 'We need to get away from here!'

She staggered to her feet and struggled to find her bearings in the unfamiliar terrain. Tommy pointed out the right direction and darted ahead. She could still hear the dog, but the yelping grew increasingly distant. Her thoughts were whirling. It was not really surprising for Reidar Heitmann to turn up at the Night Man's house. The guy obviously made his living from crime and very probably needed to consult a lawyer from time to time. However, the timing was significant. Heitmann had just taken on the high-profile task of defending Cato Dalen. On the TV interview, he had seemed to be on his way into the cells to talk to his client. He must have come straight here from the police station with information he wanted to share with Werner Roos.

'Do you have the keys?' Tommy panted. They had now reached the track and the car was parked in the open just under sixty metres away.

Line searched through her pockets, feeling a touch of panic at the thought that she could have dropped the keys in the stream or when she crawled up the ridge. At last she found them and pressed the button to unlock the car remotely.

Clambering in behind the wheel, she turned the ignition and just had time for a glance in the mirror before the wheels began to spin on the uneven ground. Her face was spattered with splashed mud and she was wet, cold and filthy.

The car radio came to life automatically, playing some kind of ill-timed ballad. Line flexed her fingers on the wheel and forced herself to breathe more calmly with every metre they put behind them. Once they had turned out on to the main road and were mingling with the other traffic, she began to laugh. At first somewhat nervously, then breaking into hearty laughter when Tommy joined in.

She changed to a different station with more upbeat music.

'That was a close shave,' Tommy said.

She agreed.

'Did you see who was visiting him?'

'Reidar Heitmann.'

'What do you think he wanted?'

Tommy shrugged. 'Well, it did at least look as if he was the bearer of bad news.'

'He must have come straight from Cato Dalen down in the police cells. Are you sure there can't be any connection between the Night Man and the neo-Nazis?'

'Not when it comes to narcotics,' Tommy said, 'but there is of course another possibility.'

'Guns?'

Tommy Kvanter nodded. 'Money talks. Second to narcotics, the illegal trade in weapons is one of the most lucrative things you can get involved in.'

'Eighteen guns disappeared in the theft Cato Dalen is charged with,' Line mused. 'Only one of them was found at the site of the fire.'

'The others could have been handed over to someone in Werner Roos's organization.'

Line glanced across at him. 'You mean that Reidar Heitmann is operating as an informant for Roos?'

'He's one strand of the network. A link that can provide intelligence and convey instructions through prison walls.'

'That must surely be a breach of good legal practice? Possibly even criminal?'

'Money talks,' Tommy repeated. 'Some lawyers are willing to stretch the boundaries to preserve their client's interests, at least as long as it meets their own financial interests. There are also dishonourable police officers. Money and drugs disappear from evidence stores. Of course, there are black sheep among the legal profession as well.'

Line swung into the backyard behind Tommy Kvanter's apartment block. It was the nature of the beast for members of the police force to be vulnerable to corrupt offers from individual criminals or organized-crime groups. It was almost a matter of course that lawyers would be offered payment for providing information and it was naive to think that it did not take place. No matter how it had come about, she felt compelled to make this into a story and came to a decision as she stopped the car. The Norwegian Bar Association must have an overview of warnings given and licences revoked. She could call the media-savvy left-wing politician who had jumped out of a legal career in hopes of a parliamentary seat at the next general election.

'Are you coming up?' Tommy asked as he opened the car door.

'I have to collect my phone,' she replied. 'I left it on your coffee table.'

'You need to change into some dry clothes too,' Tommy told her, taking the measure of her with his eyes. 'I've got jogging bottoms you can borrow.'

'I don't know . . . it's not so far for me to get home.'

Tommy was out of the car now. 'You'll catch a chill, Line. And you didn't even drink your tea.'

With a smile, Line followed him. Tommy let them in and disappeared into the bedroom, returning with grey joggers, a T-shirt, a hoodie and a pair of thick socks.

'Have a hot shower,' he said, using the bundle of clothes to motion along the hallway to the bathroom.

Line studied him, trying to work out whether his suggestion had ulterior motives.

'You can just relax,' he assured her, as if he had read her thoughts. 'No pressure. I'll put on some more water for tea in the meantime.'

Accepting the clothes, she cocked her head and looked at him, coming to the conclusion that she really had no objection if his intentions were less than pure anyway.

'OK then,' she said with a smile. 'But I'd prefer a glass of wine afterwards.'

He appeared taken aback by her answer. His brows shot up and his eyes took on a roguish expression. Then he stepped forward and gave her a hug.

'You deserve it,' he said, smiling.

The tiled bathroom had a heated floor. It was tidy and clean and a fresh fragrance of vanilla wafted through it, though she was unable to find the source of the scent.

Stripping off, she folded her wet clothes and put them in a pile on the floor. Naked, she stood for a moment in front of the mirror and gazed at her body. The chase through the woods had left her with a little scratch on her left cheek. Apart from that, she could not complain, really. Her skin was still tanned from her autumn holiday in Spain. She had always been slim and three visits to the gym every week had given her distinct muscles in her arms, legs and stomach. Her breasts were small but firm.

She pulled a face at her reflection and ran her fingers through her blonde hair. Then she turned on the shower and waited for the water to heat up.

In addition to the hand-held shower, she could regulate

the water so that it sprayed out of three nozzles on a wall panel. She adjusted them so that powerful jets of water hit the small of her back, twirling round a few times, revelling in the hot water before picking up the shampoo bottle. It smelled fresh and masculine and produced plenty of lather.

When she had finished, she heard that music had been turned on in the living room. She did not recognize the tune, but it was a subdued, sentimental ballad.

The T-shirt he had given her had a picture of Jimi Hendrix on the front with the simple text: *Heaven Rocks*.

She pulled it on without putting on her bra underneath. It was slightly tight across her chest, and she covered her nipples, visible through the thin fabric, with the two sides of the hoodie.

A couple of minutes in front of the mirror and she was all set.

He had lit the candles when she came out. Two glasses were filled with red wine. Tommy got to his feet and offered her a place on the settee before he sat down again and raised his glass.

'Cheers.'

She returned the toast and tasted the wine, full bodied and deep red with a lingering aroma of cherries. The bottle was on the table and she tried to make a note of the label to remember it for another time. She was fond of wine, but the bottles often had names in languages she could not understand. That meant she seldom remembered which wines she had tasted and enjoyed, which ones were just palatable, and which were nothing more than diluted dishwater.

'Brolio Chianti Classico,' Tommy said, though he did not have the accent quite right.

'Do you know much about wine?'

'No,' he laughed. 'So I always buy something that costs

about 150 kroner a bottle, to be sure I get something worth serving.'

She took another gulp and began to feel the effects as a blush came to her cheeks.

'Your phone was buzzing,' he said, motioning towards it.

She picked it up. There were three calls and one message from Morten P. He thanked her for the story she had submitted and suggested that she get a good night's sleep. There was also a message from a number she had saved as *Dagbladet Dude*. The young online journalist with the shark's fin haircut had been wondering if they could have lunch together the following day.

She answered neither of these but sent a message to her father to say she would be back late and not to wait up for her. What she did not add, though if she were being completely honest she should have, was that she reckoned she would not be home that night at all.

51

The outgoing flight took them over Kabul before they turned and landed from the east. Everything below them looked brown and bare. No buildings. No roads, just deep valleys and massive peaks with snow-capped summits before the metropolis appeared like an immovable grey mass in a narrow glen high in the mountains.

The flight had taken eleven hours, including a stop in Istanbul. The time difference of three and a half hours meant that it was 7.30 a.m. local time on Friday morning.

Suzanne leaned over him and peered out while Nils Hammer blinked wearily from his aisle seat.

'Kabul was once beautiful,' she said.

Her eyes surveyed the scene below, the details becoming clearer as they neared the landing strip. Dusty piles of ruins and battlefield debris with occasional signs of reconstruction work, new buildings and cranes.

That was all they got to see of the war-weary city. A logistics officer from the National Support Element at the air terminal greeted them and escorted them into a container building, where they were served breakfast.

The Focker plane hired from a Dutch airline took them up into the air three quarters of an hour later. A vast mountain landscape opened up below them on the flight north, where scattered roads zigzagged between snow-covered mountain ridges.

On the gravel runway at Maymana they were met by a burly man in Norwegian police uniform.

'Welcome,' he said in a broad Bergen accent, taking each of them by the hand. 'Idar Spenning.'

'We spoke on the phone,' Wisting replied.

'Yes, I understand the situation and appreciate that you're keen to get started.' The Norwegian policeman picked up Suzanne Bjerke's luggage and showed them to a waiting four-wheel-drive vehicle with a local driver. 'I've arranged transport to take you further after lunch. Qaramqul is a hundred kilometres from here, but the road is bad. The drive takes almost two hours. We'll meet up with a local police officer, Hanif by name. He's one of my instructors and might be able to help you. Speaks fluent English as well.'

Wisting slung his travel bag into the cargo space of the jeep. The driver, a short, bearded man with a face covered in acne scars, glanced apathetically at him.

'Instructor?'

'We've trained twenty-four Afghans who travel around the provinces to instruct the local police forces. Military forces can't win the peace on their own. Our strategy involves integrated attempts to solve the challenges faced by Afghanistan. We work alongside the inhabitants and local authorities to contribute towards stability and development. The people best placed to train the Afghan police are the Afghans themselves. This week they've been running courses in arrest techniques.'

The Norwegian officer waved them into the back seat before jumping in beside the driver.

'Arresting people in a decent and humane manner is perhaps the simplest thing we pass on,' he continued, signalling to the man behind the wheel to drive off. 'Only one in five Afghan policemen can read and write. When I came here, the police didn't even have pens and paper.'

He gave a brief order, most likely a place name, to the driver, who nodded in response.

'I'll show you something so you can see how far we've come.'

The driver negotiated his way out through the built-up area towards an elevation in the barren landscape. Sand from the dry road whirled up into the air.

'We've established a headquarters in the town here,' Idar Spenning went on, pointing towards a radio mast in the rundown huddle of buildings below them. 'We have radio and phone links with all the police districts in the province. That is something of a revolution, in fact. The police in Faryab are the only provincial police force in Afghanistan with permanent telecoms links to all of their subsidiary units. That's vital for the security of the Afghan police officers as well as the effectiveness of their operations.'

The policeman from Bergen interrupted his flow of conversation when the vehicle stopped on the crest of a hill.

'There!' he said, gesturing down to an open plain. Three large vehicles were parked in a semicircle and black smoke rose from a bonfire in the centre. A group of men in uniform stood a short distance from the blaze, watching the flames.

'They're burning opium,' Spenning explained. 'The raids and checkpoints are becoming more frequent and efficient. Last week the police found 350 kilos under a false floor in a goods van. Now they're burning the confiscated raw material. One of the smuggler routes to Europe goes through this province. The opium was probably intended to be turned into heroin.'

'How much heroin do they obtain from 350 kilos of opium?' Hammer asked.

'As a general rule of thumb, it takes ten kilos of opium to make one kilo of heroin. In Nygårds Park in Bergen, one gram of heroin is sold for around 1,200 kroner.'

Wisting did the mental arithmetic and realized just how enormous the sums of money involved were.

'Here in Afghanistan, a gram of heroin costs the equivalent

of only ten kroner,' Spenning said, smiling. 'The profit for the people who smuggle the drugs as far as Norway is enormous.'

'Who does profit from it?'

'The UN has calculated that the Taliban has earned more than three billion kroner from the sale of opium. It's ironic. When they controlled the country, they declared narcotics un-Islamic and received millions of dollars to join the Americans in the war against drugs. Then came the war against terror, and the Afghans realized they could no longer depend on the support of the USA. The farmers ploughed up their wheatfields and planted opium again. The Taliban rake in the profits and use the money to finance their guerrilla war against the Northern Alliance and the NATO-led forces.'

'It's a double problem,' Suzanne Bjerke commented. 'Both for the countries the narcotics are smuggled to, and for Afghanistan, where the farmers, instead of cultivating grain for their starving population, depend on crops that yield a larger income.'

'Exactly,' Idar Spenning said, nodding. 'Thousands of hectares of good earth are sown with poppy seeds. The narcotics are the root problem. As long as the narcotics industry is given free rein, there will never be peace in Afghanistan.'

Wisting's mind strayed to the suitcase full of heroin that had been left on the railway platform in Larvik. If it had reached its destination, it would not be only the dealers and drugs barons who would have made a fortune. The flow of money followed the narcotics network all the way down to small villages and caves in the mountains of Afghanistan, or wherever the Islamic fundamentalists hid themselves. The money was spent on landmines and weapons, for fighting against an enemy army in which his own son was a soldier.

Idar Spenning pointed down at the bonfire, where orange flames were spiralling up to the sky.

'This is a good start,' he said. 'But there are other problems too. Poverty has led more than a million people to find refuge in a drug-induced haze. Addiction is seen as a personal problem, something for which you can only blame yourself and that you have to sort out for yourself.'

He signalled to the driver that they had seen enough, and they headed towards the camp where the Norwegian reconstruction troops were based, at the end of a runway.

The low buildings were surrounded by a high stone wall topped with barbed wire. Uniformed soldiers with automatic weapons, helmets and bulletproof vests bore testimony to the seriousness of their purpose.

'I've organized a room for you all in the barracks,' Spenning told them as the jeep drove up in front of an ochre building. 'It's a room with four bunk beds,' he added, glancing at Suzanne Bjerke. 'I'm afraid we don't have anything else to offer.'

'That's fine,' she reassured him.

'As you no doubt realize, there's no mobile network here. You can call home from a landline in my office. I've also got Internet access there. I suggest you unpack and then we'll have a bite to eat and head off. It gets dark at five o'clock, and by then we should really be back here.'

'Are we to travel on our own?'

Idar Spenning nodded. 'We live alongside the task force, but day to day we try not to be too closely associated with the military. It's difficult to build trust in the local population if we're continually accompanied by heavily armed soldiers. But we have a practical arrangement to ensure that in any given situation we can receive support and if necessary be evacuated by them.'

Wisting grabbed his bag and gazed out over the wall at the waves of sand in the brown and yellow landscape. On one of the ridges beyond the camp, he glimpsed a guard patrol as a dot on the horizon.

52

They drove first through the centre of Maymana. The driver was smoking a lopsided cigarette and trying to blow the smoke out through a gap at the window.

The streets were crowded with cyclists, scurrying pedestrians, horse-drawn carts and rickshaws that chugged along, belching smoke, as they weaved in and out of the traffic. Street sellers with thin blankets draped over their shoulders sold lampshades made of animal skins, rugs, embroidered shawls and copper utensils from rows of small, overflowing sales booths.

Beggars at every street corner on sacks held out grubby hands for money. Mostly children, they were gaunt with serious faces; some of them looked no more than five or six years old.

'Seventy thousand people live here,' Idar Spenning told them.

Wisting nodded. The place buzzed with noise and activity and pungent smells drifted through the jeep's windows. The exciting aroma of spices mixed with the sharp reek of diesel, the stink of putrefaction, rotting vegetables and excrement.

Never before had he experienced the dark side of the world for himself. He had only seen such destitution on television and read about it in newspapers. The squalor surrounding them made him feel uncomfortable and aroused a hopeless desire to help. Now he understood what had drawn Ingrid back time and again to aid work in Africa. She had experienced want there, but also the benefits brought by the organized relief work.

The road to Qaramqul snaked along steep cliffs and over desolate sand plains that looked like blankets of lead under the grey sky. Poverty confronted them everywhere they looked. On either side of the road, small villages clung to the mountainsides. Tumbledown houses made of clay and shacks that consisted of nothing but four wooden poles and a threadbare rug for a roof. Old men sat beside these ramshackle buildings. The blankets wrapped around them fluttered in the wind. A group of children in tattered clothes ran barefoot after their vehicle. It could not have been more than six or seven degrees Celsius outside.

'There are so many of them.' Suzanne Bjerke sighed. She was leaning over him, looking out at the children. 'Not just here but throughout the world. Millions of kids, starving and suffering, but Norway doesn't want to take care of the ones who manage to flee from this misery.'

He realized she was thinking of Khaled Athari, the boy they were hoping to find at the end of this twisting road.

She turned to face him. 'It seems so hopeless. I spend every single day helping the teenagers that live with us. Trying to give them back their lives. There are seven of them. Here, in this country, nearly a thousand youngsters die every single day.'

Wisting leaned his head against the jeep window. He did not know what to say and instead let his eyes follow the potholed road as it rose and fell and curved around the hillsides.

Before this visit was over, he wanted to see Thomas. It felt strange to be near him so suddenly, without his son knowing anything about it. It gave him almost the same feeling as when he had sneaked into the boy's bedroom, back when he had lived at home, and looked through his belongings on the sly in an effort to gain some insight into how his quiet lad spent his time and what he thought about.

He had seen the helicopters and kept an eye out for him

among the uniformed soldiers, but without catching sight of him.

Along the verge, a goatherd was leading five or six scrawny goats. An old man dressed in rags trudged over a field with a large sack of grass tied to his back. The poverty Wisting saw made him feel melancholy and long for home.

He had only just managed to catch Line on the phone before he left and had been evasive when she asked him where he was going. For some reason she had not asked any more questions. She seemed preoccupied and in a hurry to end their conversation, which had suited him. He had no wish for the press to know about this trip. Going away and handing the investigation over to Torunn Borg also gave him the opportunity to avoid the problematic dual role of investigator and father to a journalist at the newspaper that was following the case so closely.

After an hour and forty minutes they drove into a town that was slightly larger than the other places they had put behind them. It was situated on an arid plain, surrounded by precipitous mountains.

The driver turned on to a narrow dirt track and parked the Land Cruiser beside a dried-up gutter. Low-rise stone houses flanked the street.

Wisting stepped out, stretched his legs and took a deep breath. A stiff wind blew along the narrow street, carrying unfamiliar smells with it.

The building in front of them was two-storeyed. Traces of the original matt sienna paint were visible through the peeling flakes on the walls. A sign with Arabic letters was displayed beside the entrance. In slightly smaller letters underneath, it read: *Afghan National Police*.

The door leading out to the street was open. Inside, there was a cramped waiting room with hard wooden benches.

Behind a grate sat a man in a blue cotton uniform. When Idar Spenning went up to him and gave a name, the policeman stood up and disappeared out of the room. One minute later, bolts on a side door were slid open and a tall man with a large thick beard and tousled mop of curly brown hair came out to meet them. He welcomed them with a smile and double handshakes all round, letting his dark eyes linger on Suzanne Bjerke before ushering them all along a narrow corridor into an office. *Sergeant Muntadahr Hanif* was engraved on a copper plaque on the door.

The room smelled of tobacco and cinnamon and the windows overlooked the backyard, where two grimy police vehicles were parked. One had its bonnet flipped up and two tyres missing. Behind them lay an orchard with rows of cherry trees.

'Welcome to Qaramqul,' said the Afghan officer in a deep voice, showing them to a circular conference table.

He moved across to a copper samovar in the corner and poured out cups of steaming hot tea.

'You've travelled far and look very tired,' he said in English. 'The information you seek must be of great importance to you.'

Wisting explained that they were investigating two murders related to narcotics and human trafficking of children who were being used along the smuggling route.

The sergeant diffidently sipped his tea.

'And for that, three investigators come all the way here to Qaramqul,' he summarized with astonishment in his voice. 'To talk to a boy who knows who these dreadful killers might be.'

He stole a fleeting glance out at the dusty backyard, where four policemen had laid down their rifles and were playing cards around a barrel.

'Our two countries are very different,' he said. 'These dirty drug-dealing dogs also kill one another here, but their pathetic souls are not avenged by the police.'

Wisting looked across at Idar Spenning, understanding how patient and persevering he must be.

'Have you checked things out for us?' the policeman from Bergen asked.

'I've found out what you wanted to know,' the strapping sergeant replied. Getting to his feet, he walked to the wide office desk and picked up a sheet of paper.

'The boy's grandfather, old Rashid Athari, is a respected citizen of Qaramqul. Many good Muslims unroll his rugs for their *salah.*'

'Prayers,' Suzanne translated.

Idar Spenning nodded. 'They pray five times a day,' he explained. 'That makes it more difficult for a believer to sin, since they know they must bow down and prostrate themselves before God five times daily. The prayer rugs are probably top sellers.'

'The old rug merchant lives with his wife. All his sons died in the North Alliance battles. His brother's son took the orphaned children with him to Pakistan and sent them on out into the world. Three months ago, old Athari received a message to come and fetch one of his grandchildren from Kabul. He lives with them now and helps his grandfather in his trade.'

'Can you take us there?' Wisting asked.

'Of course,' replied the Afghan police sergeant. 'After our tea.'

Hanif drank slowly while he proudly told them of the progress the police unit was making. The Norwegians listened and made approving comments. Finally the Afghan rose from his chair, hoisted his Kalashnikov on to his shoulder and motioned towards the door.

The driver was waiting in the jeep outside. He straightened up as a rickety pickup drew up in front of the entrance with four armed policemen seated on the cargo bed.

'This won't work,' Suzanne Bjerke said in an undertone. 'We're going to scare them out of their wits.'

Agreeing, Wisting addressed himself to Idar Spenning: 'Do you think we could visit them on our own? Without a bunch of police officers?'

Spenning agreed. He approached the sergeant and spoke to him in hushed tones. The policeman seemed to protest, making energetic use of his arms and hands to bolster his argument, but in the end he nodded his head.

'Hanif will show us the way,' Spenning said. 'Then I'll accompany him back to the station.'

The small group headed off. At a willow tree where two winding roads met on the outskirts of the little town, they drew to a halt. Sergeant Hanif got out of the vehicle and pointed up at a cluster of houses on the parched hillside. Sunlight was reflected on the windows in the buildings that clung tightly to the foot of a cliff.

'The rug seller's house,' he told them.

53

Barefoot children were playing in the street outside the cluster of low houses. They were hitting a threadbare tennis ball with a stick but stopped and stared when the car drew to a halt and the driver switched off the engine.

Suzanne Bjerke asked them about the man who sold rugs, and the kids pointed to a house with an enclosed garden. A spotted dog, sleeping inside the low wall, looked lazily up at them as they approached.

They had no need to ask for directions. Hanks of red and white woollen yarn were hanging up to dry between old maple trees in the extensive garden and large balls of wool lay waiting to be collected and spun into yarn.

An elderly man with a turban impressively balanced on his head was stirring a pot full of dye. He wore baggy, pyjama-like trousers and a long shirt with a loose-fitting knitted waistcoat on top. His grey-white beard lent him an air of authority.

Suzanne greeted him from the gate: '*Salaam. Khush Aamdeed?*'

Straightening his back, the man looked at them, bowing politely, and gave an answer.

Suzanne took the first step inside the wall and spoke to him with the kind of dignity and respect demanded from a woman addressing an esteemed man.

The rug seller, Rashid Athari, asked a few questions, which Suzanne answered with a long sentence containing the word *Norvek* and the name of the police sergeant. As the exchange batted to and fro, the rug seller's eyes grew probing and his voice antagonistic. He turned aside and spat on the ground before fishing coloured wool out of the simmering pot, pensively studying the result and dropping it on the ground. Then he put down the stick and came to a conclusion.

'He's willing to talk to us inside the house,' Suzanne explained. 'But he doesn't like the rich country that refused to take his grandchild.'

They followed the old man through a weaving workshop, where dried plants that would probably give colour to the woollen yarns were hanging in bunches, and on into a living room. The low ceiling was made of clay and straw, with a lamp full of dead flies suspended from it, and there was a picture of the holy mosque in Mecca on the wall.

Removing their shoes, they walked in, over the mats that covered the floor, and were shown to large cushions that lined the wall. The rug seller disappeared into another room and they heard an angry exchange of words before he returned and sat down opposite them, his back ramrod straight. The glow from the gas lamp on the ceiling made his wrinkled face look serene.

He rattled off a couple of short sentences that Suzanne Bjerke translated for them: 'His grandson will be here soon. We shall drink tea while we wait.'

They sat in silence for almost ten minutes before a woman entered with a tray of white porcelain cups full of steaming-hot tea. Her hair was covered in a shawl and they assumed her to be the rug seller's wife. Deep lines were etched on her tanned face and her eyes and mouth were also outlined with wrinkles.

Suzanne thanked her in Dari. Wisting noticed that the woman had lost the tips of three fingers on her right hand. The other nails were painted with red varnish.

Suzanne saw him looking at this and waited until the woman had gone before explaining: 'When the Taliban were in power, nail varnish was forbidden. Some unfortunate women had their fingertips cut off.'

All at once, the boy was standing in the centre of the room.

He was wearing harem pants, a baggy shirt and a woollen hat. He looked skinny and his dark eyes flitted from one face to the other. Wisting could not resist smiling at him. It was two days since he had mooted the idea to the others of travelling to Afghanistan and talking to this young lad. He had to admit that he had not really expected to be able to meet him in person.

The boy's confused eyes finally fell on Suzanne, who met his gaze, her own eyes brimming with unshed tears.

The rug seller barked a gruff instruction and the boy bowed briefly and delivered a polite phrase before sitting down at his grandfather's side. A ray of sun that spilled in through the window divided the room in two between them. The dust quivered in the bright light, making the scene look even more dismal.

'Are you doing OK?' Suzanne asked.

The boy shrugged without giving any verbal response.

'I've come with bad news for you,' she added, swallowing audibly. 'Layla is dead.'

'Layla?'

Nodding, Suzanne explained how one of the girls he had lived with and who had been like a sister to him had been found beheaded. The boy frowned, the deep wrinkles outlined against the dark eyebrows on his forehead.

'I've brought two of the investigators with me,' Suzanne went on, telling him that they suspected the people who had threatened Khaled and forced him to smuggle a suitcase into Norway had probably been the same ones who had murdered Layla. Khaled listened in silence.

The rug seller let his prayer beads slide through his fingers.

He seemed uncomfortable about being kept outside the conversation, which was in Norwegian. His grandchild, who must have understood his disapproval, translated some snippets for him.

Wisting leaned forward. 'Can you tell us about the men who took you to Sweden?' he asked.

'I've already told Suzz everything,' he replied, his speech showing signs of not having spoken the Norwegian language for a long time. His words sounded staccato and stilted.

Wisting smiled at the nickname the child obviously used for Suzanne Bjerke. Suzz. Although he had not heard it before, he thought it suited her.

'We've travelled a long way,' Wisting said, clearing his throat. 'I'd like to hear it from you for myself.'

The boy's grandfather shifted uncomfortably. Khaled's eyes wandered. Nils Hammer cautiously took out a pen and notebook from his inside pocket.

'Can you remember what the weather was like, the evening they took you?' Wisting continued, in an effort to take the boy back mentally in time. 'Where you had been? What you had been doing?' He used open questions in his search for details that might jog the boy's memories of six months ago.

'I usually hung out at Kebab Corner in the evenings. Me and some of the boys in my class. Frank, Alexander and Richard. It was a few days after the Norwegian National Day. The trees in the square at Lilletorget were covered in green leaves. The birds had started singing. It was light until late in the evening.'

Wisting saw that the boy was casting his mind back. Memories he had locked out were now rushing through his brain. Wisting waited patiently for him to continue.

'I was on my way home. I was walking alone. Then a car came along. It was just outside the butcher's shop.'

266

Wisting listened intently, picturing how it had happened. From the Abrahamsen butcher's shop in Kongegata, he would have had only a few hundred metres to reach home. He ventured a simple question: 'Do you remember what the car looked like?'

'It was white,' he said. 'An estate car. Old and dirty. It smelled fusty inside. The seats were blue. It had a black dashboard with two large and a few small gauges. One was a clock.' He gulped, as if the detailed memories were becoming almost too much for him. 'It was quarter to ten.' He glanced at Suzanne. 'I was meant to be home by ten.'

Wisting saw that Hammer was taking notes.

'It wasn't a Volvo or a German car,' the boy went on. 'Maybe a Toyota or something like that. They were playing loud music. Pakistani and Indian.'

'What about the men?'

'There were three of them. The man who was driving called out to me in Norwegian. When he realized I was Tajik, he changed language. He said they had driven far and were hungry. They wondered where they could buy some proper meat. I told them about Kebab Corner, but they didn't understand how to get there. Even though it wasn't far or difficult. They were my brothers, they said, so I had to go with them and show them the way. I said I was short of time, but they said they would drive me home afterwards.'

He looked down at the floor.

His grandfather asked him something and Khaled answered softly, having to explain what he was talking about to the strangers. The old man used his hands to gesticulate and sounded indignant when he spoke.

'What happened?' Wisting asked.

'They didn't stop at Kebab Corner. They drove past and stopped far down the street. The man in the front passenger seat moved to the back so that I was wedged between two of them. His mouth smelled horrible and he had a cut on his face. The man on the other side took out a knife.'

'Where did they take you?'

'They drove fast, sometimes so fast the car was shaking. All the same, it took many hours. None of them said anything more. I asked where we were going but they just told me to keep my mouth shut.'

The rug dealer drank his tea slowly and thoughtfully, as if reluctant to be part of a conversation in his living room that he neither understood nor participated in.

'We stopped at a petrol station and the man who was driving bought cola and chocolate. I got a bottle and then they drove on. I watched the signposts as we went by. We drove over the border to Sweden. In the middle of the night we stopped outside a block in a Swedish city.' He glanced across at Hammer, who was writing notes. 'It was Gothenburg. That was on the train ticket I got when I had to go home again.'

Wisting moved restlessly. He was beginning to feel uncomfortable sitting on the low cushions.

'The two men sitting beside me took me up to an apartment on the fourth floor. There was a lift. The driver came a couple of minutes later.'

Wisting, listening avidly now, could not refrain from asking the question: 'How many storeys were there in the building?'

'There were two more above us. The walls were pale yellow and there was a balcony on each floor. They locked me in a room. There was a finely knotted Kazan rug on the floor.' He snatched a sidelong glance at his grandfather who had obviously recognized a word. Khaled gave him a few sentences of explanation before he moved on: 'I could see other blocks all around. Further behind them there was a large fairground.' He used his left arm to point obliquely as if to clarify its position. 'The next day I saw people on the roller coaster.'

'Liseberg,' Hammer muttered.

Wisting had brought a map of the city of Gothenburg. Taking it out, he unfolded it and studied it closely. The rug seller peered at it inquisitively but remained silent.

'Did you see any street signs or door plates?' Wisting asked optimistically.

Khaled shook his head. 'But one of the men was called Mamhood. He was the one who drove the car. I didn't hear the names of the others.'

'Did you see anything else from the window?'

'There were a lot of people outside. In front of the fair-ground I could see a road where a blue tram passed. Behind that was a river and behind that again there was a huge motorway.'

Wisting studied the map. This was almost more than he had hoped for. Khaled Athari must have been transported to an area of the city called Johanneberg.

'I was given roast chicken, rice and naan in the living room,' Khaled went on, still translating for his grandfather in an effort to play down the drama. 'And more cola. After I'd eaten my fill, they asked if I would cooperate.'

'Cooperate? With what?'

'They didn't say. Not then. They had been kind and given me food. I just said yes. I don't know what they would have done if I'd answered no.'

'Did the men live in this apartment?'

His response was merely a shrug.

'There was a kitchen, a living room and a bedroom. Two of the men slept in two beds in the bedroom. I slept on the floor. The third man lay on the settee in the living room. They locked the bedroom door at night. Next day, another two men came to visit. They had pistols with them. I saw them sticking up from their trousers at the back.'

'Do you remember anything else about the apartment?'

'There wasn't much in it. A long, curved settee, a table and a TV. In the kitchen there was a table with four chairs. A cooker, a fridge, a coffee machine and a microwave. They used only the microwave. After we had slept, they ordered pizza.'

'Was there a phone there?'

'No, but they spoke on mobile phones. Then they shut themselves in the bathroom so I couldn't hear.'

'Was there any more talk about cooperation?'

'No, they asked me what my situation was. Where I lived and what school I went to. I told them about Suzz and the others. About Layla and Hanan.'

'Did anything further take place?'

Khaled nodded and, if possible, his expression grew even more serious.

'Early in the morning of the second day the man with the cut on his face and the other man who had sat in the back of the car were not there with me in the apartment. The man with the cut turned up an hour after I got up and he had brought a black suitcase and said I would be allowed to travel home again. He had a ticket for the train with him.'

'Tell us about the suitcase.'

'I was to take it with me. It was heavy and I had to take good care of it. They had stuck some childish stickers on it, but I had to keep it with me all the time.'

'Did they say what was in it?'

'No, but I realized what it was. At least that it was something illegal. They said it was worth a lot of money and if

54

The helicopters had gone from the base when they returned to the camp. The soldier on duty explained that the crews were on assignment in Mazar-e-Sharif, headquarters of the ISAF forces, situated forty-five minutes' flying time further to the north-east. They were not expected back until the following morning.

Wisting had hoped to spend what was left of the day with Thomas. His son had always been more attached to his mother. He did not know why, but it could of course be connected to the fact that Wisting worked long hours. For the first few years he was seldom home before the children were in bed. In conversation, his son had always been fairly reserved, and it was to his mother he turned when he needed advice or someone to confide in. He had taken it very badly when she had died.

It was different with Line. She had always been his. Whereas his son had withdrawn slightly when he spared time to play with them when they were little, she had crawled on to his lap, chattering and laughing, always delighted. This had meant she was the one Wisting had shown more interest in, and there weren't many handball games or end-of-term school activities he had not found time for. When he looked back, he had to admit he had divided the attention he paid his children unevenly, but it had been difficult to do things differently with a daughter who sought him out and a son who backed away from him.

Wisting spent the hour before their late dinner at the camp

in the police office. He perused a couple of online newspapers and saw that the case was still holding the media's attention but that no developments were reported in the coverage. Then he rang Torunn Borg. It was almost half past four at home in Norway, but he did not think she would have left the office yet.

She answered at once. Wisting gave her a brief summary of the meeting with Khaled Athari. He realized this would be uplifting news.

'Any progress at your end?' he asked.

'Not really. Cato Dalen has been remanded in custody for four weeks. He admits the firearms theft but has not been willing to tell us who he was with or what has become of the weapons.'

Wisting swore under his breath. He had been so close to getting that information out of him down in the cells.

'His lawyer must have given him some bad advice,' Torunn Borg continued, as if she had read Wisting's thoughts.

Wisting agreed: 'The confession he's given won't count as unqualified and he'll get a minimal reduction in sentence. He's risking one year extra for keeping his mouth shut about what he knows.'

'Unless he's more involved in the murders than we think,' Torunn replied. 'At the moment it hasn't leaked out that the murder weapon has been traced to the theft. It wasn't mentioned at the remand hearing.'

'Have you got hold of his girlfriend?'

'Yes. She knows nothing.'

'What about the fire up at Solberg lake?'

'Arson.' He heard her riffling through documents. 'Espen has found a lot of flammable liquid. The car's been traced. According to the chassis number, it's a 1993 model Toyota Carina, but something about it doesn't add up. The vehicle the chassis was on originally was deregistered in Germany four years ago. We're doing further work on it, but it looks pretty hopeless.'

Having wrapped up the conversation, Wisting wondered whether to phone Line, but dropped the idea. She would only bombard him with questions as soon as she knew where he was calling from.

He moved back to the computer. No matter how things went with Khaled Athari, their next stop had to be Gothenburg. He began to draft a report for the Swedish police, requesting assistance with fresh moves in the investigation. He presented the apartment in Gothenburg as the central focus for a narcotics network that distributed huge quantities of heroin in Scandinavia and that their activities had resulted in two executions in Norway. He knew that putting forward the hard facts would lead to them receiving all the assistance they required. In the first instance he was only looking for corresponding intelligence from them, but he did not exclude the possibility of the Swedish police having to take action at some point.

He sent the request by email to Torunn Borg, accompanied by a short explanation, and asked her to send it via the appropriate channels to their neighbouring country. She would have to see to it that Audun Vetti attached his signature and gave it the stamp of authority.

After dinner in the noisy canteen, Wisting sat down with Suzanne Bjerke in a seating area outside Idar Spenning's office. Nils Hammer had found a poker team in one of the adjacent barracks.

According to local custom, the Bergen policeman laid out dried fruits, nuts, caramels and tea for them.

'I have a meeting with the police chief here in Maymana tomorrow,' he said. 'I can't come back with you to Qaramqul, but you can borrow my car and driver. An MOT squad will accompany you and Hanif will meet you.'

'MOT?'

'Military Observation Team,' Spenning explained. 'It means in practice that you'll be accompanied by two vehicles with seven men from the Home Guard. I've arranged for you to leave at 10 a.m. Does that suit?'

Wisting accepted with thanks. Excusing himself, Spenning took his cup of tea into his office. He had fallen behind with a lot of work in the course of the day.

'I don't know if it's good for Khaled,' Suzanne Bjerke mused aloud when they were left on their own. 'For us to take him back with us, I mean, just to use him and then send him back here again.'

'You're probably right,' Wisting agreed, 'but I can't see any other solution.'

'I know,' she said with a sigh. 'He is in a good situation. He has family and a roof over his head. Food on the table. But it gets difficult for many people now when the ice-cold winter months come. All the years of war have caused the country to suffer from a precarious shortage of food. When winter sets in, it becomes far more difficult to provide those who are poverty-stricken in the population with food. In addition, relief work gets stopped by bandits on the country roads. The aid consignments have become the Taliban's supply lines.'

'They steal food from the people who need it most, the most vulnerable of all,' Wisting commented.

'It's actually not the attacks on the food supplies that are the problem,' Suzanne told him. 'Afghanistan is a fertile country and could easily be self-sufficient, but agriculture is shaky.'

It was easy to discuss difficult topics with Suzanne Bjerke. She was insightful and engaged, and she listened and weighed things up. She was unafraid to come out with her own opinions or say what she believed in, or to show her feelings. They talked about politics, religion, power and possibilities. Even ethics and morality.

The long journey had tired Wisting out. Suzanne could see that and suggested they turn in for the night. The following day would also be long and difficult.

Wisting went first to the toilet block. Suzanne borrowed the computer in the office to send a few messages home to Norway.

He was about to fall asleep when she entered the small room in the barracks. The dull light from the floodlights outside on the tarmac filtered in at the sides of the window blinds. She crept over to her bag of clothes, believing him to be asleep. Taking out her toiletries, she sneaked out again.

Wisting turned on to his back and stared up at the wooden slats on the bunk above his head. Suzanne returned after ten minutes, her bare feet making no noise as she padded across the floor. She packed her toilet bag away and began to undress, wrenching her thick sweater over her head and placing it on the back of a chair and then stepping out of her jeans. She stood in a T-shirt and white underpants, applying cream to her hands. Then she pulled off the T-shirt and unfastened her bra.

He rolled on to his side and stared at the wall as he heard her wrap herself in her quilt.

'Are you sleeping?' she whispered.

'Mmhmm,' he replied, reluctant to betray just how wide awake he was. The blood rushed through his veins and he felt aroused in a way he had not done for a very long time.

'I just wanted to say thank you.'

'Hm?'

'Thanks for letting me come with you.'

55

They had slept together each night since they had shared a bottle of wine two evenings before. She crawled in under the quilt again, snuggling her naked body into his. Hesitantly, she kissed his chest as his hands wandered, his cool fingers stroking her back. He raised his head, using his lips to kiss and nibble the side of her throat, moving on down to her shoulder.

Line, feeling her skin respond to his light touch, was unable to lie still. She was breathing faster as he put his arms around her and held her tight. She felt safe in his embrace, aware of how strong he was. His hands stroked her thighs and, taking a firm hold, raised her up on to his body. She slowly sank down on him, arching her back as he entered her.

The desire she felt was almost alien to her. She let him do things she had never allowed her previous lovers to do and it was very late at night when she finally fell asleep, content and exhausted, in his arms.

When she woke with a start, she had no idea how much time had passed. Tommy's sinewy arm lay comfortably across her body, under her breasts. He pulled it back and fumbled for the mobile phone on the bedside table.

The blue glow from the display lit up his face. His black hair fell forward and he used his hand to sweep it back – his dark eyes widened as he read the text message that had woken them.

'A bite,' he said, smiling.

Line sat up, glancing across at the clock, which read 02.32, and covered her breasts with the quilt. She gave him a questioning look.

'You know we agreed that the connection between the Night Man and the neo-Nazis is guns?' Tommy asked.

Line nodded.

'I've ordered one,' Tommy continued.

'A gun?' She felt something tighten at the back of her throat.

'Sure,' he said. 'To verify the theory.'

'You can't just go ahead and order a firearm,' Line protested, aware of a knot of anxiety in her gut. 'Do you know people you can just send a text message to and then go and pick up an illegal weapon?'

He looked at her with eyes that suggested he had thought she would be enthusiastic about the possibilities this offered instead of being angry and afraid.

'I have a past,' he said warily. 'I know a lot of people who don't ask questions.'

Shaking her head, she thought of all the reasons for being careful, but at the same time began to appreciate the opportunities this might bring.

'What you do in life echoes through eternity,' Tommy went on. 'There's a lot you still don't know about me. Things that mean I'm still regarded with respect and credibility in certain circles.'

'What are you planning to do now?'

Tommy got out of bed and stood naked at her side. She wanted to stretch her arm out and haul him back.

'My contact says I can have a look at it now, tonight,' Tommy explained, holding up his mobile phone in evidence. 'It won't hurt to have a meeting.'

'But there must be loads of illegal guns in circulation. How can you be certain this one has anything to do with Cato Dalen or Werner Roos?'

'They're talking about a Vektor pistol. They're pretty rare in Norway, a South African version of a Beretta. According to your newspaper, one of those disappeared in connection with the firearms theft.'

Line mulled this over. She had her camera bag down in her car, including a tripod and a wide aperture lens.

'Where are you meeting him?' she asked.

'That's not been decided yet.'

She got out of bed and began to search for her underwear.

'It has to be somewhere that's not in complete darkness and with only one way in.'

Picking up her clothes, she began to dress, her mind racing. She would have to find a lookout spot from which she could watch the meeting and monitor their movements. A registration number could take them a long way forward.

'Say you can meet him at the barrier leading into the waste disposal plant at Grinda,' she suggested. The place was perfectly situated just outside town. There was a short stretch of road through some trees that led to the entrance of the land-fill site that was closed at night. She had previously arranged a meeting there with a conservationist informant one time when she was writing a report about illegal fly-tipping for the local paper. The spot was dimly lit and there were lots of places in the surrounding woods where she could hide.

'It's best I do this on my own,' Tommy objected.

She shook her head. 'You can drive me out there half an hour beforehand. Have you got any warm clothing I can borrow?'

She had set up the tripod behind an uprooted tree trunk. Only the long lens protruded from it, directed straight at Tommy Kvanter, who stood smoking outside her car, parked beside an electricity substation at the roadside. The entire area was lit up by a lamppost that gave off a harsh golden light. She did not need as wide an aperture as she had first thought. The images would be sharp.

She did not like that he smoked but had to admit it suited him somehow. 'Rugged' was the word that crossed her mind to best describe him as he stood there in his leather jacket, blue jeans and boots. He reminded her of Mickey Rourke in an old motorbike film she had seen. She pressed the remote shutter release on the camera and took a couple of pictures.

They had no idea who would turn up.

Through the middleman, Tommy had arranged a meeting for 4 a.m. Now it was seven minutes past. The longer she waited, the less sure she felt about the whole enterprise. She was dangerously close to the limit of what was legal and would not be able to use these photos for anything other than her own documentation. Also, it was her car that was parked down there. Although it was a leased vehicle, if the firearms seller were completely paranoid, it would take him only a few phone calls to find out who used it and uncover the connection to a journalist on Norway's biggest-selling newspaper. Anyway, both Tommy and the car would appear in the pictures.

The sound of an engine broke her train of thought. A pair of bright headlights threw long shadows between the dark spruce trees. She crouched down. The front lights dazzled her, making it difficult to see what make of car it was as it passed by and drove up to the spot where Tommy stood.

It was a black Audi with one male occupant. Line concentrated on the registration number to start with. The car was filthy and the number plate was difficult to read. *LS 70 . . .* She snapped a couple of photos. Maybe it would be easier to read when it was blown up on a computer screen.

The car stopped beside Tommy, who hunkered down and talked to the driver through the car window. Then the door opened and a man with a high forehead and a broad jaw stepped out. He looked Norwegian.

Line took another couple of photos as the two men shook hands and exchanged a few words. Then they moved behind the car and the stranger opened the boot.

Click. Click.

Tommy tossed his cigarette away. The man moved something aside and took out a small object. The distance from Line to them was almost sixty metres, but she could see that it was a pistol.

The man handed the gun to Tommy, who stood weighing it in his hand. He took out the magazine and put it back again. His movements seemed practised. Then he held the pistol out in front of him and aimed straight for Line's hiding place. The man who had brought the gun turned in the same direction.

Click. Click.

They became involved in a discussion, with the man using his arms to gesticulate and Tommy shaking his head. After a short time it looked as if they had come to an agreement and they shook hands again. Tommy thrust the gun down into his back waistband and produced a bundle of banknotes from his jacket pocket.

Line swore under her breath. This was not what they had agreed. He was not supposed to buy the gun, just look at it. She had been absolutely clear that she could not take part in any illegal transactions. It was a serious breach of the law that could cause her to lose her job.

The deal was done in less than half a minute. The man got back in behind the wheel of the Audi and drove off at full throttle.

Line packed her gear and walked down to the side of the road, where Tommy picked her up.

'That wasn't the plan,' she snarled. 'This was completely wrong. You shouldn't have bought it.'

'I've bought time and information,' Tommy struggled to explain, taking the pistol from his trousers. 'He wanted eight thousand, I haggled him down to seven and paid half. I've to pay the rest in two days' time. He'll phone me.'

'Did you give him your number?'

'Not the number you have,' Tommy said with a smile. 'When he calls, we'll get another chance to find out who he is. He's leaving a few tracks for us.'

'But you've bought an illegal pistol,' Line groaned. 'You can go to prison for that.'

'I've done worse things,' he told her.

Line was not sure if she wanted to hear any more.

56

Darkness still enveloped the streets in the town centre when she dropped Tommy off at his apartment, giving him a smile and a kiss.

'Angry?' he asked.

Line shook her head. She had felt scared, terrified even, when the gun changed hands, and had reacted with anger, but she was no longer annoyed. There was something enigmatic and a bit mysterious about Tommy that she found attractive. Anyway, there was no ill will behind what he had done. Quite the reverse, he had placed himself in an exposed position in order to help her out.

'I'll ring you,' she said, giving him another kiss. 'Need to do some work.'

He understood and hovered at the kerb, watching her leave. The town was still fast asleep. Only weary paperboys and grey cats to be seen.

She let herself into her father's house, which was remarkably quiet and empty. Her father must still be away. She wondered how she would tell him about her relationship with Tommy Kvanter and how he would react to the news.

He had not told her where he was going, but she understood his trip was work-related and was reluctant to ask him directly. Major cases tended to have links to Oslo, but she had a feeling he was further away than that. Perhaps he had travelled to Germany to follow up on the clues that suggested the case had international ramifications.

When she stepped inside, she realized how tired she was.

It was just after half past five, and she decided to snatch a couple of hours' shut-eye before she began work. Most of what she intended to do comprised phoning round various offices that would not open for another three hours at the earliest anyway.

She slept for two and a half hours before taking a long, hot shower, bringing the cat in and firing up the coffee machine in the kitchen.

When she took out her camera and inserted the memory card in her computer, a program immediately imported the image files. She sipped at her coffee while she waited, noticing she had made it a bit too strong.

She accessed the series of pictures she had taken of the black Audi after it had passed her lookout post. The images of the vehicle on the move were fuzzy but the quality of the ones taken after it had stopped beside her car was acceptable.

She clicked into one photo and managed again to make out the first four characters of the registration number with no problem: *LS 70*. But the rest was still no clearer, obliterated with mud and dirt. She adjusted the contrast to make the image brighter. It did not take much modification before the whole number plate was legible: *LS 70719*.

She could phone the Driver and Vehicle Licensing Agency but reckoned that the telephone queue would be as long as it always was. Instead she went into the online pages of the Brønnøysund Register Centre and checked the sales details. A hire-purchase agreement for 450,000 kroner with the Handels Bank had been entered into in October. The borrower was the firm Nøysom AS with a post address in Larvik.

She went on to key in the company name and was able to obtain significant information. A relatively recently established business, it invested in and rented out real estate. The general manager was given as Edith R. Suarez and a phone number was also listed. She copied and pasted the name into the telephone directory, but it was not given there. Then she did the same with the name of the general manager. Nothing. She tried the media archives instead. Suarez was such an unusual name that it ought to come up with individual results.

The most recent article was about teeth-whitening. A woman with brilliant-white teeth smiled at the camera and said how pleased she was. Edith R. Suarez.

Line had come across her before. This was the woman she had seen in Werner Roos's home.

Yet another clue pointing to the Night Man.

57

The drive took a quarter of an hour longer with the escort from the military observation team. They drove armour-clad vehicles and were equipped with helmets, vests, automatic weapons and radio transmitters. It did not feel reassuring and was more a reminder of the clear and imminent danger that accompanied their tours of duty.

The sun's harsh rays fell on the steep, stony mountain slopes that surrounded the small town of Qaramqul. The surrounding landscape was covered in dust in shades of brown that faded to grey. High above them on the cliffs they could see dilapidated old forts with walls of sun-baked clay.

They had a short meeting with the police sergeant. The MOT team would travel further into the barren mountainous areas on observation and reconnaissance exercises. Wisting arranged with the team leader to be met at the police station one hour before sunset for the return journey. That gave them four hours to persuade Rashid Athari to let them take his grandson back with them to Norway. Wisting had just over $800 in travel money and he was willing to use most of it to convince Rashid Athari. He had already organized travel documents that, together with a diplomatic passport, would allow them to take the Afghan boy through Europe with no difficulty.

The driver tossed his cigarette out of the side window and fired up the engine. As they drove along, a shepherd chased a flock of long-haired sheep up the hillside, crossing the winding road in front of their car. The driver braked and sounded the horn, accompanied by a few oaths in his own language as he waved his arms in annoyance. The shepherd walked with his back turned, seemingly unconcerned. His footsteps grew shorter until the car was right at his back.

Wisting realized something was wrong before anything kicked off. But even so he had no time to react or prepare himself. He saw the attack come as if in slow motion.

Three men stormed out from behind a shack at one side of the road and at the same time two emerged from the ditch on the other side, some brandishing raised axes and a couple armed with Kalashnikovs.

Splinters of glass sprayed out as they forced their way into the vehicle. The sound of broken glass mixed with nervous shouted commands. The driver protested but was dragged out by the neck.

The assailants wore determined expressions on their faces and their wild eyes shone with anger. Steel glittered on their axes and rifles.

Wisting tried to object when one of them pulled Suzanne roughly out of the car but was himself yanked out by a man who was frothing at the mouth.

The blows rained down on his body. He was forced to his knees and dragged for some distance along the hard-packed road until one of the men put a knee between his shoulder blades and sent him crashing to the ground. He lay there with his head pressed against pebbles and gravel. Panic made it difficult to breathe. His eyes were skittering madly around the scene, but he could see no way out.

Nils Hammer was on his knees a metre or so away from him. One of their attackers tried to push him down, but Hammer resisted vigorously. The man in front of him roared with fury and lunged at him with a knife. The blade hit Hammer on the left side of his face, cutting his cheek open from his eye to his lips. His cry of pain drowned out everything else as warm blood splattered Wisting's face and formed abstract swirling patterns in the dry sand.

Then someone placed a hood over his head. The thick fabric made it even more difficult to breathe. His arms were forced behind his back and rough rope dug into his wrists. He heard another cry of pain followed by a sudden eerie silence.

He twisted round, calling Hammer's name, but the only answer was a sheep bleating.

'Hammer!' he shouted again.

A blow from a rifle butt landed on his neck and stunned him. Myriad colours flickered in front of his eyes before everything turned black.

He heard Suzanne Bjerke's voice in the distance. It broke through in snatches, but he could not understand what she was saying.

He found himself floating in and out of consciousness. He was lying on a hard, uneven surface and everything around him was in darkness. He tried to blink but could not recover his sight. The air he breathed in was hot and clammy.

Suzanne's voice was interrupted by a man's. They were speaking a foreign language.

Slowly his thoughts began to grow clearer. He lay motionless as tiny fragments of the chain of events fell into place.

Then he jerked wide awake as an image of Nils Hammer's bloody face appeared in his mind.

'Hammer?' he asked, speaking into the darkness as he struggled to sit up.

A pair of arms grabbed hold of him, toppling him on to his side and hauling him halfway up so that he was kneeling on the floor. The hood was torn off his head and he had to screw up his eyes even though the light in the room was dim. It reminded him of an underground cave, lit only by a couple of oil lamps. The air was damp and stuffy and there was a sickly smell of mould and decay.

'Over here,' Hammer said.

Wisting trained his eyes on the voice. Hammer was sitting, his hands tied to the wall behind his back, diagonally opposite him, beside the driver. His face was pale and splashed with blood. A flap of skin hung down on his cheek, but the wound was no longer bleeding. His mouth was clenched shut and his eyes betrayed the pain he was bottling up.

A powerfully built Afghan with a rifle suspended from a strap across his chest barked an incomprehensible order. He had a full, short beard, and a colourful length of fabric was twisted around his head and neck to hang loosely over one shoulder. Wisting scanned the cramped space. Five men in total. Some had their faces covered with thick scarves. Their eyes bored through him, but he had no inkling as to what they wanted. The only exit appeared to be a crack in the cave wall behind the man with the rifle.

He knew there were hostile Taliban factions in the mountains, rebels who had thrown in their lot with the tribal leaders and local warlords. Men who enjoyed brandishing guns and who operated as bandits on the rural roads. Opposition to the Allied forces and all kinds of Western influence was widespread among some of them. A year ago, hundreds of the inhabitants of the province, armed with Kalashnikovs and rocks, had attacked the camp where the international forces were based. Norwegian soldiers had been compelled to fire on them. Four of the village's citizens had been shot and killed by Norwegian gunfire. No doubt hatred still smouldered.

'What do they want?' he asked, looking at Suzanne. She

had been given a cushion and was sitting in front of the man with the rifle, who appeared to be in charge.

'They want to know why we've come,' Suzanne explained. 'What we want with Khaled. Why we were thinking of taking him away from his grandfather again.'

The man with the rifle took a few steps to one side, mumbling something, but let them go on talking. A cold draught blew in from the opening in the wall behind him.

'Can't you explain?' Wisting asked.

'I've tried. I think they want money. They're talking about a fee.'

Wisting shut his eyes. Images of home appeared behind his eyelids. Sun-kissed beaches and smooth coastal rocks. He swallowed down his anxiety and concentrated on the situation at hand.

Rumours about yesterday's visit must have spread throughout the village. Half-truths about why they had come so far had caused the inhabitants to resort to weapons. He let his eyes roam over each and every one of the five assailants. They seemed disorganized. A group of random Afghans who had formed their own militia. He doubted that the $800 he had concealed inside his shirt would be enough to buy their freedom.

'Where are we?' he asked.

'Up in the mountains. East of the village. Ten minutes by car.'

'How long have we been here?'

'It must be a couple of hours now. We've been sitting here in darkness. The men came a short time ago.'

'Can you ask about Rashid Athari?'

Suzanne Bjerke addressed the man with the rifle. The answer was brief and dismissive.

'He speaks on his behalf.'

291

Wisting glanced at Hammer. The wound on his face would leave a permanent scar, if they managed to extricate themselves from this crazy situation.

'Say that it's OK,' Hammer said, straightening up. 'Tell him we've changed our minds. We're leaving today. Without the boy.'

Wisting looked at Suzanne and nodded his head. Maybe it could be resolved so simply.

She put forward the suggestion. The man in front of her rested his arms on the rifle he had slung over his chest and spat out a response.

'He's still demanding payment,' she translated. 'How much we can pay will determine what kind of punishment the elders will decide for us.'

Nils Hammer rolled his eyes. His expression made the man with the rifle spit on the ground and hurl out a stream of abuse that Suzanne Bjerke did not bother to translate.

The hopelessness of the situation gripped Wisting. A muggy sense of responsibility and blame made it difficult for him to breathe. He had read about local methods of punishment where death was the inevitable outcome.

58

Line pushed the sheaf of notes away and stretched. They were pages with strokes, circles, numbers and lines of connection scrawled on them. Yellow notes with brief key words and annotations.

She had drawn a diagram of Werner Roos's activities. He obviously found the woman with the white teeth useful, but she appeared primarily to be a housekeeper. Nøysom AS owned apartment blocks and housing complexes in most towns and cities in the Østland region. The common denominator appeared to be that they invested in dilapidated buildings listed for demolition then renovated them using black-market money and an international workforce. Some of the property was sold on at a good profit, while others brought in a good income.

Edith R. Suarez figured as the owner of four more companies. As well as the real estate company, there was a letting firm, a pizza restaurant, a consultancy bureau and a firm that supplied different kinds of tradesmen. All activities suitable for laundering the profits of crime and supplying lucrative goods and services to one another. The various companies were in turn involved in other companies. It was a network of shell companies. The name of Reidar Heitmann, the lawyer, turned up repeatedly as chairman of the board.

They represented solid activity that would yield millions, with an annual turnover of huge sums. All of them presumably built on dirty money from narcotics. The evidence would, undoubtedly, be well hidden. Her work was founded on speculation, but with the help of someone on the economics side of the newspaper she was certain that this business empire could be unpicked seam by seam. Regardless of whether or not it could be used in this particular story, it would make a good spread in the paper. What she was after, however, was a solid connection to the narcotics trade and these two murders. This meant she had to get close to Werner Roos again. She had to find out what he did in the hours of darkness.

She sat staring out of the kitchen window. There was still a veil of fog above Stavern that made the colours in the landscape look pale and faded. In the distance, a container ship was making its way into the fjord.

Her thoughts turned to her father, who would sit with a cup of coffee, looking out at this view, every morning. She missed it. Her home in Oslo overlooked a neighbouring apartment block where a fat man liked to walk around in his underpants.

Feeling hungry, she got up and walked to the fridge. The contents were meagre. A few brown bananas, a six-pack of beer and a few opened packs of cold meat and cheese.

In the cupboard she found some crispbread and a packet of macaroni. She was not keen to go out shopping so she nibbled at a crispbread as she boiled water for the pasta.

She sat down again at the kitchen table and ate the simple meal with some ketchup on top. It tasted of nothing, really, but at least it subdued the rumbling in her stomach.

She made up her mind to do some shopping in the afternoon so that there would be food in the house when her father came home. She dialled his number on her mobile but only reached his voicemail service.

Her gaze turned to the window again. The wind had picked up now and, far out at the mouth of the fjord, she could see a dark bank of cloud.

59

The Afghans had gathered in the furthest reaches of the dark cave and were having a heated discussion in hushed voices, throwing an occasional glance across at their hostages.

The conversation ended abruptly when a shout from the passageway leading out of the cave made them all grab their guns. Wisting saw moving shadows at the cave opening as something was tossed in. The sound of metal on stone echoed through the cave.

The explosion that followed knocked him backwards. It was not a pressure wave but a powerful detonation that reverberated around the walls and tipped him off balance. His ears were ringing and his forehead throbbing. The glimmer of light that followed was intense and blinding and he was unable to do anything other than witness apathetically what was happening.

Six soldiers in desert camouflage uniforms entered the cave with their automatic weapons raised. Although incapacitated, Wisting understood what was going on. Specially trained police officers entered buildings using stun grenades to put their opponents out of action for up to a minute.

The rope that tied his arms behind his back was cut and he scrambled to his feet. Suzanne Bjerke still sat, in total shock.

The Afghan spokesman grasped the situation quickly and moved forward, raising his rifle and using his free hand to grab Suzanne.

Wisting launched himself at the man, shoving him aside with his shoulder and knocking him to the ground. The man struggled to his feet and took hold of his rifle again. One of the soldiers responded by firing two shots in rapid succession. The man stopped, as if he had collided with a wall, blood spurting from his left shoulder. He whirled around, keeping his balance for a few seconds before falling down.

Wisting led Suzanne out towards the exit. The soldiers backed out after them, holding the rest of the Afghans in check with their guns.

They ran through the dark passageway out of the cave. Nils Hammer was standing beside one of the armoured military vehicles and a paramedic was already attending to his wound.

Two helicopters appeared over the eastern brow of the hill like enormous birds in the wide sky. They approached and hovered in the air above them before descending, whipping up the dust of the plain.

Putting his arm around Suzanne, Wisting ran in a crouched position to the nearest helicopter. Nils Hammer and their driver were escorted to the other one.

The door was pushed up and they were hauled aboard. The pilot took off a pair of reflective sunglasses to give them a quizzical look.

Wisting did not recognize him. He had hoped that his son, Thomas, just might be the pilot to lift them out of the mountains, but this young face was unfamiliar to him.

'Ready?' the pilot asked.

Wisting nodded. The rotor blades sped up as they were lifted from the hillside. Soon they had left the barren mountain landscape far behind.

Grasping his arm, Suzanne Bjerke buried her head in the hollow of his neck. She whispered words in his ear, but the noise of the helicopter made it impossible for him to hear what she was saying.

60

The commander sat behind the simple desk and gazed at them with a serious expression. Outside the windows, darkness had encircled the military camp.

They had been given a brief account of how the observation team, through Police Sergeant Muntadahr Hanif's informal network, had been alerted and successfully located them.

'Extremely regrettable,' said the man in charge of the military forces. 'We take security very seriously and take all necessary precautions. This incident had not been included in our analysis of possible threats.'

Wisting expressed his heartfelt thanks and praised their efforts.

'This is the kind of occurrence we don't like to be the subject of discussion,' the commander continued, opening a folder. 'I'd just like to remind you of the confidentiality agreements you signed when you arrived here.'

Wisting had no wish to have the incident more widely known about and gave a nod in reply. He was on an unofficial assignment accompanied by a civilian. In any case, it was a complicated situation. If it leaked out that their mission had brought Norwegian soldiers into hand-to-hand combat with insurgents, countless objections would be raised.

At the same time he felt frustrated that what had happened would simply be written off at the stroke of a pen. He thought it likely that dead bodies had been left behind in the mountain cave from which they had been rescued.

For posterity, it would be referred to as only an *undesirable incident* in the official military statistics.

The commander returned the confidentiality agreements to the folder, opened a desk drawer and put them away. He shut the drawer with a bang, as if to emphasize that the subject was now dropped.

'What are your plans for the rest of your stay?' he asked. Between the lines, Wisting could read that he was keen to get them off the base as soon as possible.

He gave Suzanne a sidelong glance.

'We'll have to discuss that and weigh things up, but I think we'll go back as soon as possible.'

'Your colleague is being treated at the field hospital in Mazar-e-Sharif. Transport has been arranged for him to Kabul tomorrow morning. The plane to Norway leaves at 16.00 local time. We can organize seats for all three of you.'

Wisting nodded. He did not like the idea of returning without having achieved what they had come for, but he saw no alternative. Afghanistan did not have to be a dead end. They had a name and an area in Gothenburg. That could be enough to work on.

'Is there anything more we can do for you?' the commander asked.

'There's one thing . . .' Wisting answered hesitantly.

The commander looked surprised.

'I have a son who flies helicopters down here. It would be nice to be able to say hello to him before we leave.'

'Do you know for a fact that he's here?'

Wisting shook his head. 'Thomas Wisting is his name,' he said.

'Lieutenant Wisting,' the man nodded in acknowledgement. 'Solid guy.'

The Norwegian reconstruction forces consisted of around two hundred soldiers, and the commander clearly knew his son. He noticed how proud the comment from the man in charge made him feel.

'In addition to the helicopter that brought you here, we have two machines in Mazar-e-Sharif. He must be with one of them.'

The commander stood up to indicate that the conversation was at an end. 'I can have him here by daybreak.'

The hot supper was tasteless. The distress caused by their experiences only a few hours earlier had stolen his appetite.

'You didn't tell me you have a son,' Suzanne Bjerke commented.

Wisting pushed his plate aside. An effort had been made to decorate the table between them with a paper napkin folded out into a little tablecloth. A small glass filled with toothpicks and a saucer containing tiny paper bags of salt and pepper made the table look a little more festive.

'Thomas and Line are twins,' he told her with a smile. 'They turned twenty-five in May. Thomas hasn't lived at home since he started as an army recruit five years ago.' He helped himself to a toothpick. 'It came as a surprise. He seemed to be such a Mummy's boy. He always went to Ingrid if something was up, while Line came to me.'

'You must be proud of them.'

He agreed he was. At work he had seen how easy it was for things to go wrong in the upbringing of children. There was no guarantee which road a child would take. He had colleagues with sons and daughters who had fallen by the wayside as early as primary school, with behavioural difficulties and adjustment problems. Others with youngsters who had come as far in life as Thomas and Line but had not made anything of themselves and lived on monthly hand-outs from social services.

'Coffee?' he asked, getting to his feet.

She accepted with thanks and he fetched two cups. The canteen where they were sitting was impersonal, but the subdued lighting encouraged conversation. As Wisting told her more about his children, Suzanne listened with some kind of longing in her eyes.

'What about grandchildren?' she asked.

Wisting laughed. 'I don't think that will happen for a while. Ingrid was really looking forward to it and was busy fulfilling her own dreams before they arrived on the scene.'

'Was that why she went to Africa?'

Wisting nodded and grew quiet for a moment at the thought of his wife. The prospect of grandchildren had become even scarier since he had been left alone.

'As long as he's down here, I don't think there will be much happening on the girlfriend front,' he went on. 'I think Line's too busy for a boyfriend.'

They had been sitting chatting for almost three hours when they agreed it was time to hit the hay. Wisting had opened up and talked to her about thoughts and feelings he had not shared with anyone else.

The small dormitory was lit only by a single lamp above one of the bunk beds. He pulled his sweater over his head and was standing bare-chested when she returned from the bathroom. She headed towards the locker where she had stowed her belongings but stopped when she passed him and placed her palm on his chest. He felt the warmth of her body and began to tremble at her touch.

Twelve hours ago they had been captive together in an underground cave and he had not known whether he would survive that day. Now he felt more alive and present than he had done in a very long time.

They toppled together on to the bed and made love as survivors do, intense and passionate, as if they both wanted to fight death and reassert life.

Afterwards she lay down and rested her head on his chest. He ran his fingers through her hair. He moved his hands down and lay stroking the skin on her back.

He had thought that on the day something like this came to pass he would feel pangs of conscience over Ingrid. Instead it felt like the start of something new and good.

61

Thomas was out of the helicopter before the rotor blades had stopped turning and ran towards him in a khaki desert uniform and flak jacket. He had grown a full beard that suited him well and made him seem both older and more grown-up.

Wisting put his arm around him and hugged him close. Thomas led him over to a barracks some distance from the noise of the engine.

'What on earth are you doing here?' he asked, smiling, as they went indoors.

Wisting explained as briefly as he could.

'I heard about the evacuation.' His son said, taking two cans of cola from a fridge. 'Things could easily have gone wrong.'

Wisting dismissed the incident with a wave of the hand.

'How's it going down here?' he asked instead.

'It's strange, to be honest,' Thomas said, taking a swig of cola. 'We're involved in a war which the authorities refuse to admit Norway is fighting. They call it peacekeeping efforts, but our very presence here just makes the enemy stronger and the opposition greater.'

'Do you regret it?'

'No, but I think Norway could have made more of a contribution to peace and reconstruction by using the resources in a different way. Instead of depending on military solutions, they should step up the humanitarian aid and concentrate on finding long-term solutions to the problems here.'

Wisting was not surprised to hear how thoughtful his son had become. It was like listening to his mother. He himself had only been in the country for a couple of days, but it was obvious that the civilian population needed a type of help other than armed troops in the streets. Decades of strife had turned the country into one of the poorest in the world.

'The USA spends 670 million kroner every day in hunting down terrorists and insurgents,' Thomas continued. 'Only a fraction of that goes towards reconstruction and development.'

They had an intense conversation until it was almost time for Wisting's departure for Kabul. Thomas shared his experiences and adventures while Wisting related the news from home.

Three hard raps on the door interrupted them. A soldier in full military gear addressed Wisting.

'There's a man at the main gate asking for Suzanne Bjerke,' he said. 'Can you pass on the message?'

'A man?'

'An Afghan,' the soldier explained. 'Do you know where she is?'

'I'll get hold of her,' Wisting said. He sprang to his feet and followed the soldier out of the barracks, Thomas at his heels.

Suzanne had packed for them both.

'There's a man at the gate asking for you,' Wisting told her, after introducing her to his son.

'Who is it?'

He shrugged, but in reality there were not many possibilities.

Rashid Athari was seated on a block of cement outside the gate, leaning on a stick. A cold wind blasted the wall surrounding the camp, whirling sand up into the air. Behind him, Khaled Athari was sitting in an ancient blue VW van loaded with hens in cages, rugs and hanks of colourful yarn.

'*As-salamu alaykum*,' Suzanne Bjerke greeted him.

The old man tucked the stick under his arm, reached out his arms and clasped her hands in his. A long stream of sentences ran out of his mouth as he spoke in a sorrowful, desperate voice. Suzanne Bjerke listened, made a few comments in reply and then went on listening.

When he had finished talking, Suzanne turned to face Wisting.

'He's heard what happened to us and is very sorry about it,' she translated.

Wisting took a step forward.

'He feels guilty,' she explained. 'He had talked to his brothers and some of the elders in the village about whether he should allow his grandson to go. The insurgents must have found out that we were expected back the next day and planned an ambush. At the village meeting they had talked a lot about the rich country in the north. The men who attacked us were probably after money.'

The rug merchant turned towards the van and called out to his grandson. Khaled Athari opened the sliding door and stepped out, carrying a travel bag.

Suzanne asked some questions and translated the answer: 'Khaled is coming back with us.'

The grandfather gave his grandchild several final instructions before patting him on the shoulder and sending him off with a nod of the head.

The rug seller's weary eyes told of how difficult the decision had been for him. He was sending away one of the dearest things he had in life.

Wisting wondered whether the old man could see something of the same in his own eyes and turned quickly to take his leave of his son.

62

Khaled Athari had been loaned a deck of cards by one of the soldiers who was on his way home at the end of his term of duty. He played card games with Suzanne Bjerke and solitaire the rest of the time for long stretches of the journey but had fallen asleep by the time the plane flew over Paris.

With refuelling stops and adjustment of time zones, they landed in the military area of Gardermoen at quarter to midnight. The floodlights were reflected on the landing strip, wet with rain, and they were drenched by the time they reached the terminal building.

They divided themselves into two taxis. Nils Hammer sat in the back seat of a spacious Mercedes and asked to be driven home to Larvik. He now had eleven stitches on his face and a bandage coiled around his head. Wisting had seen him clench his teeth when the pain became too much during the flight.

Another vehicle took Wisting, Suzanne and Khaled to the nearest hotel. They intended to get a good night's sleep and travel on to Gothenburg in a hired car the next day.

In reception, Wisting picked up copies of both *VG* and *Dagbladet*. The story was no longer on the front pages. The world was full of bad news.

Suzanne Bjerke shared a room with Khaled. Wisting was allocated the adjoining room, with a door between the two that he left open.

The boy found the TV remote control and clicked through to a channel broadcasting pop music. Then he moved to a basket filled with small bags of potato crisps and other snacks. He looked up at Suzanne with a question in his eyes and she nodded before giving him a quarter of an hour to get under the quilt.

'We have another long day ahead of us tomorrow,' she told him.

Wisting watched the boy carefully open a bag of crisps and take one out. He hesitantly crunched into it and stood savouring the salty taste.

Three months ago, TV, potato crisps and cola had been an everyday part of his life, until bureaucrats had turned his existence upside down. Wisting closed the connecting door and called Torunn Borg. He had given her an update on developments while they had waited at the airport in Kabul and arranged for her to give the Swedish police advance warning and information.

Her voice sounded tired and he understood that she too had had a long day. He had left abruptly and handed the investigation over to her when it was at its most demanding. He knew how that responsibility could physically exhaust and age a person by several years in the course of a few days.

'Did I wake you?' he asked.

'No, I was waiting for you to phone,' she replied, stifling a yawn. 'Are you all doing OK?'

'It was a long journey. I'll be glad to get a few hours' decent sleep.'

'I've made an appointment for you with Chief Inspector Lennart Mellander,' Torunn told him, giving him a phone number. 'You've to meet him at the police station in Ernst Fontells Plats tomorrow at noon.'

Wisting did some calculations in his head. The drive to Gothenburg would take around four hours. They would have to leave by 8 a.m.

He ended the conversation and went through to the room next door to let Suzanne and Khaled know. They were both fast asleep in front of dancing pop stars on the TV, Khaled under the thick hotel quilt and Suzanne on top of the bed, fully clothed. He found a blanket and covered her. Then he turned off the television and returned to his own room, where he stripped off, paid a visit to the bathroom and turned in for the night.

They were getting closer now, he thought, as he pulled up the quilt and switched off the light.

63

Wisting drove with his hands tightly gripped on the steering wheel. His eyes watched the rain hypnotically falling on the windscreen as the wipers worked rhythmically. The raindrops were swept aside, returned and disappeared again.

The motorway on the Swedish side of the border was of a high standard. Wisting defied the speed limit to make sure he would arrive in time for their meeting.

He dropped Suzanne and Khaled off at the Hotel Europa, where Torunn Borg had booked rooms for them. The hotel was situated in the city centre and was near a huge retail park where Suzanne could buy them some new clothes.

Lennart Mellander was a solemn man with a lined forehead. He must have passed fifty and was probably nearing the end of his career in the police. Wisting knew nothing about him except that he was a *kriminalkommissarie*, one of the highest ranks you could reach in the Swedish police hierarchy without a law degree.

His spacious office was expensively furnished and smelled recently painted. Wisting was made welcome and introduced to a senior female undercover detective, the leader of the drugs squad and an officer in charge of intelligence and analysis. They all sat around an oval table inside Mellander's office. Coffee, tea, mineral water and a dish of sliced fresh fruit were set out on a nearby sideboard.

Often this kind of meeting with colleagues was regarded as a nuisance that held up their regular work, but on this occasion Wisting could see that his Swedish colleagues were very interested. They made notes while he outlined the main points in the investigation and what had led them to Gothenburg.

Lennart Mellander rose from his chair when Wisting finished speaking, fetched the coffeepot and filled the empty cups.

'This corresponds with intelligence already on our radar,' he said as he resumed his seat. 'Afghans are behind most of the import and sale of heroin. They use their countrymen without residence permits as couriers. It's no surprise that they use children for the same type of work. These people are cynical and cunning.'

Wisting agreed wholeheartedly.

'Naturally you'll receive all the help you need,' Mellander added, with a nod in the direction of the undercover detective.

'If you succeed in pinpointing the apartment, we'll place it under surveillance,' she said. 'In addition, we have two teams that can keep an eye on the traffic in and out.'

The intelligence guy now spoke up: 'There are two pizza restaurants in the area we're talking about. We're checking the accounts and deliveries at the end of May. At the same time, we're tracking down any Afghans who live in the district or who own property there.'

These were opportunities Wisting had not foreseen and he felt elated at the prospect.

The Swedish police had allocated him an anonymous-looking hire car with tinted windows, and Wisting picked up Suzanne and Khaled from the hotel. They had eaten at a hamburger restaurant and were tired of waiting.

He ran through the simple formalities with them, things that he and Suzanne Bjerke had discussed before they left. She had been appointed his legal guardian and Khaled had to be prepared to repeat his statement about his experiences before a judge.

He and Suzanne had spoken about the ethical complications of placing Khaled in a position of which he himself did not appreciate the wide-ranging consequences. His witness statement could expose him to reprisals and threats. Without including Khaled in their discussions, they had also talked about the possibility of including him in a witness-protection programme, which would give him the right to remain in Norway.

The hire car was equipped with GPS, which allowed Wisting to find his bearings in the unfamiliar city streets. He felt his heart race as they approached the area they were focusing their search on, one filled with apartment blocks.

Suzanne Bjerke sat with Khaled in the back seat, and Wisting watched them in the rear-view mirror. The young boy's eyes were surveying his surroundings, his face stiff and impossible to read.

Heavy, lowering clouds still covered the skies. The rain had eased off, but the streets were wet and slick. All the streets and apartment blocks looked similar. The facades were all painted the same shade of pale ochre, though some were shabbier and more run-down than others. There were bare patches and piles of rubbish on the small grassy areas and the paint was flaking off the buildings. Some of the blocks were encased in scaffolding and around them were construction sites with clay and rubble and tarpaulins fluttering in the gusts of wind.

'Do you recognize this place?' Suzanne Bjerke asked guardedly when they had driven around a few times and arrived back at the main road.

Khaled nodded. 'It's here somewhere, but all the buildings look so alike.'

Wisting drove to the side of the road, where an opening between the tall buildings made it possible to look down towards the city centre. It was growing dark and Gothenburg was starting to glitter like a metropolis beneath them.

Khaled gazed out at the view. Wisting let his eyes wander without disturbing his concentration.

'Down there,' he said in the end, squinting at one of the apartment blocks with one hand raised in the air. 'It must be that one.'

Wisting set the vehicle in motion again. The GPS indicated that they were in Eklandagatan. He turned into a side road and ended up in Gyllenkrooksgatan. Here, Khaled nodded and pointed out an entrance in the nearest apartment block. Wisting drove past and parked at the kerb on the opposite side of the street.

'Fourth floor?' he asked, opening the car door.

'Yes,' Khaled agreed. 'The apartment in the middle,' he added.

Wisting pulled his lapels up to his neck and strode towards the building. His breath formed plumes of fog in the cool evening air.

Many international-sounding names were listed on the doorbells on the wall. Benny Skacke and the Larsson family lived on the fourth floor. The third doorbell had no name marked beside it.

Wisting took out his mobile phone and rang Chief Inspector Lennart Mellander.

64

Line was well wrapped up. She was wearing several layers of clothing, plus gloves, a scarf and a knitted hat that almost covered her eyes. These were all clothes left by her mother that her father had not yet cleared out.

'I didn't think you had a car,' she said to Tommy.

'Yes, of course I have,' he replied, drawing up one of the garage doors in the backyard. 'If you can call it a car, that is.'

An old Ford Fiesta was parked inside the oblong space – under a layer of dust and dirt, she could just make out an indefinable shade of blue.

'You don't really need a car when you live in the centre of town,' he explained. 'I use it mostly to and from the airport when I sign on with a ship.'

Line took a few steps to one side and stood looking at the car as Tommy reversed out. It was perfect for what she had persuaded him to go along with.

They drove out in convoy to Lamøya. Tommy backed the car up into a side road diagonally opposite the turn-off for the area that had once been an island and switched off his headlights. Line continued on and parked in the same place she had the last time.

She hooked the cordless mobile phone connection on her ear and called Tommy on speed dial.

'Are you there?' she asked.

'Yep,' he confirmed. She could hear him pouring coffee into a mug.

The plan was simple. She would keep Werner Roos's home

under surveillance, recording visitors and painting a picture of his associates and the network around him in an attempt to find leads to follow. This was traditional crime reporting and would probably turn out to be desperately boring.

Tommy Kvanter had insisted on accompanying her. She had not told Morten P. or anyone else about what she was thinking of doing and was grateful for his offer. Her editor only knew that she was working on a major narcotics story that could be connected to the beheading murder.

The lights from the extensive house shone between the trees like last time. The ground was wet, as it had been raining all day, but she found a cosy spot beside a thick spruce tree and set herself up. The distance to the fenced-in building was almost forty metres, but the telephoto lens brought her close enough to see everything in detail.

In the driveway, the same two cars were parked, a four-wheel-drive vehicle and a silver sports car. There was no movement to be seen in the house.

The four-wheel-drive was parked in such a way that she was able to take a picture of the registration plate. She walked a short distance through the woods to get a better look at the sports car. It was a Mercedes and she read the digits *SL 63 AMG* in the camera lens. She had no idea what model it was but felt convinced that when she managed to trace the number, she would find that Edith R. Suarez was the owner.

She retraced her steps to the spruce tree. Below the house she could hear waves crashing ashore. Sudden gusts of wind made the trees shake and the crown of the tree above her head creaked ominously.

Her hands began to freeze after only half an hour. She had chosen a pair of thin gloves to allow her to handle the camera and now regretted not bringing an extra pair. She flexed her fingers and clasped them together to stay warm, all the time keeping her eyes on the house. Ten minutes ago she had spotted movement in the living room. It had just been a shadow, but it did at least confirm that someone was at home.

She left the camera dangling around her neck and tucked her hands into her armpits. That helped.

Suddenly she saw it was Werner Roos in the living room. He was talking on the phone and when he ended the call he headed into an adjacent workroom.

Line managed to take a couple of photos before he switched off the light and returned to the living room. Then he walked into another room and disappeared from view.

Half a minute later the front door opened and he emerged, wearing a thick jacket and Wellington boots.

Line drew back to the tree trunk but knew it would be impossible for him to see anything from the well-lit courtyard, looking out at the darkness that surrounded the property.

He lit a cigarette, inhaled deeply and coughed.

Her mobile phone vibrated inside her layers of clothing. She adjusted the earpiece and whispered a response.

'A black Saab has gone by and could well turn up at your end,' Tommy told her. 'It's a Swedish registration. One man alone in the car.'

'OK, thanks,' Line said. Maybe she would be luckier with this trip than she had dared to hope. 'Werner Roos has received a phone call and has put on outdoor gear and gone outside. Perhaps he's expecting a visitor.'

'Be careful.'

Line smiled to herself as she wound up the conversation by sending a quick kiss down the phone line.

Werner Roos coughed again and walked round to the back of the house. Line moved nearer to the sea to keep him under surveillance. The forest floor was soft and covered in moss that allowed her to walk almost soundlessly as far down as the smooth coastal rocks.

The night fog drifted in dense sheets across the land, carrying with it the strong, salty tang of the sea.

Werner Roos walked out on to the jetty and stood in the pale light from a lamp hanging on the boathouse wall. He seemed to be waiting for something. Sheltering behind a cold rock, she took another photograph of him.

After a few minutes a man appeared. Werner Roos caught sight of him first. He had just lit up another cigarette with the first one before tossing the end into the water. He greeted the man, who came walking along the foreshore with a discreet nod of the head.

The newcomer stepped on to the jetty. Line took a picture of him in the lamplight and managed to make out that he was bearded before they walked together to the end of the jetty and stood with their backs turned in silhouette against the sea.

They conversed in hushed tones without looking at each other. Only occasionally did Werner Roos raise his voice. The other man dipped his head, as if he had no wish to contradict what was being said.

The conversation ended with a handshake. Line pressed the shutter release to preserve for posterity the dark contours of the agreement entered into under cover of darkness.

Werner Roos was left standing alone. Line withdrew into the woods and called Tommy as soon as she was sure she was out of earshot.

'The man in the Swedish Saab had a beard,' Tommy told her. 'It could have been him. He may have parked in a different place so that his car couldn't be seen from Roos's house.'

Line agreed. 'Could you follow him when he drives past?' she asked, hurrying back to her own car. 'And make sure you get the reg number.'

'What are you going to do?'

'I'm coming too.'

They kept the phone line open. The Swedish car drove out from the peninsula before Line was back in her car.

'He's driving towards the town,' Tommy said. 'I'll stay fifty metres behind him.'

'Don't let him see you,' Line warned him as she clambered into her car.

'Relax.'

They drove in silence for a few minutes. Line manoeuvred through the network of narrow tracks and picked up speed once she was back on the main road.

'He's driving out along Elveveien,' Tommy told her. 'It could be he's heading for the E18.'

'Follow him!'

'Sure, OK. There's a car between us now.'

Three minutes later, Tommy reported that the car was driving north on the motorway. Line noted the time and calculated that she was four minutes behind them when she drove on to the E18. She accelerated and, by the time they passed Tønsberg, she was only one minute behind. On the motorway bridge above Drammen she caught up with Tommy and overtook him. The Swedish-registered Saab was just over a hundred metres ahead of her.

Tommy rang: 'What are you actually planning to do?'

'Find out who he is and where the car is going.'

'The car belongs to Faryadi Zardad from Malmö,' Tommy said. 'I don't have enough petrol to follow him all the way home.'

'How did you find that out?'

'I rang the Strømstad police,' Tommy chuckled at the other end. 'Said someone had reversed into me and the car just drove off.'

'All the same, I'd like to know where it's heading,' Line said. 'There's a Swedish connection in this whole story. This could well be the missing link.'

'OK, I've probably got enough fuel to get to Uddevalla.'

They changed places behind the Swedish Saab but made sure all the time to have one or two cars between them. It was not difficult to follow him, as long as they were driving on the motorway. However, Line was prepared for it to become much harder when the car turned off and drove into the centre of some town or other.

They passed Oslo and continued on the E6 down through Østfold. Outside Moss, the Saab turned into a filling station and parked beside one of the pumps. They arranged for Tommy to drive on to the next petrol station, fill his own tank and pick him up again when he passed.

Line parked at the edge of the forecourt, trying to look as anonymous as possible among other cars. She slid down in her seat and located the man in her camera lens. He glanced over his shoulder a couple of times but seemed calm and unruffled.

After filling up with fuel, he walked inside and paid in cash. The assistant behind the counter reached out for a packet of cigarettes for him, explaining something and pointing down to the other end of the shop. The man nodded and walked over to the phone booth he had been directed to.

Line took a couple of discreet photos as he talked. It was a brief conversation and two minutes later she was on the road again. Tommy caught up with them at Rygge airport.

At 04.37 they crossed the border into Sweden.

65

The clock on the corner of the hotel TV had shown 04.38 when Chief Superintendent Lennart Mellander rang. Twenty minutes earlier, the surveillance team had seen the lights go on in the apartment on the fourth floor in Gyllenkrooksga-tan. A short time later a car had stopped outside and a man with a suitcase had gone in through the entrance.

The team had set themselves up in an apartment in the building opposite. Wisting had no idea what they had done with the family who normally lived there.

A man and a woman were sleeping on two separate settees in the living room. Two others sat in a child's bedroom with a camera attached to a tripod beside laptop computers that were in constant use.

'Down there,' one of the detectives said, pointing to an old white Opel parked some distance up the street. 'It's owned by an Afghan man in Malmö.'

The other detective, busy on a computer, showed Wisting the footage of the man's arrival. The suitcase he carried looked heavy. The Swedish police officer enlarged the image. The resolution was good and Wisting could see that the suit-case was covered in various stickers of dancing teenagers and the words *Disney* and *High School Musical*.

'The apartment is owned by a woman in Halmstad called Moqtada Begi,' the first detective explained, leafing through several documents. 'She's married to Zmarai Begi, who belongs to a faction within the political movement Hezb-e-Islami, with links to both the Taliban and al-Qaida. He served as a general under a warlord in North Afghanistan in the nineties, until the fall of the Taliban. Somehow he and his family gained asylum in Sweden. The War Crimes Commission, under the auspices of the Swedish police have, however, initiated a preliminary inquiry into him for breaches of international law.'

'A war criminal?' Wisting said in astonishment.

The policeman nodded. 'Amnesty believe he led forces that destroyed villages in the north during their fight against the Northern Alliance and killed defenceless men, women and children. The Swedish Security Service believe he is channelling financial support to the insurgents in his homeland and describe him as a possible security risk.'

Wisting sat down in an empty chair. Pieces of the big picture were falling into place. Those who sought asylum and protection in Nordic countries could include people who had themselves committed crimes against the rules of war. People who had participated in torture and execution of members of the civilian population. Through the narcotics trade, the militant Islamists in exile supported the struggle for power that still raged in their homeland. Children often became victims, as they had also been during the havoc caused by war. Beheading a refugee girl who got in the way of their business was almost part and parcel of their brutal methods.

'Aided by the information we've received from you, we have reason to believe that this is a headquarters for the resale of large quantities of narcotics to the Nordic drugs market,' the policeman continued, motioning towards the apartment on the other side of the street. 'Right now there are two or more of the operators gathered in there, with a suitcase stuffed full of heroin.'

'Are you planning to take action?'

'We have no choice. This is an opportunity we can't let slip through our fingers.'

'The suitcase might be headed for Norway,' Wisting suggested. 'What about tracking the delivery to expose the recipients and the people we hold responsible for two homicides?'

Supervised delivery was a passive investigation method that involved the police permitting the narcotics or other smuggled goods passing over land borders and being transported onwards to the recipient in order to expose the lines of communication and the link to the intended destination.

'That's not on,' the undercover detective dismissed the idea. 'As soon as the Emergency Squad is in place, we're going in to arrest those people and seize the drugs. So we'll take it from there.'

Wisting made no further comment. He was not in a position to become involved in what had become an operation led by the Swedish police. What was important was that he was present and able to pick up any threads that pointed to Norway.

He sat staring at the neighbouring apartment. It was still brightly lit but the curtains were drawn and it was impossible to track any movement.

All the surrounding buildings in the residential area began gradually to come to life. A newspaper boy was working his way round his route. Lights were switched on in kitchen windows and he observed people in their dressing gowns getting ready to face another day. The first workers emerged shivering into the cold morning.

'This is the third time,' said one of the detectives who had come in from the living room. He pointed to a black Saab 9-3 driving past in the street below and took a photograph. 'It has driven past here three times now.'

Another detective keyed in the registration number on a laptop.

'Faryadi Zardad from Malmö,' he told them. 'Listed in the registers for a few traffic offences.'

'He's not alone,' the man with the camera broke in. 'A dark blue Golf just went by in pursuit.'

Wisting moved as close to the window as he dared and looked down. The black Saab found a parking space left vacant when one of the residents had gone to work. The driver jumped out and strode to the entrance of the apartment block. Further down the street, the dark blue Golf parked on the opposite side. Wisting frowned. An uncomfortable, sneaking suspicion crept over him, making his mouth dry.

'Norwegian number plates,' the man with the camera told them as he read out the digits. 'Can you get that checked?'

Wisting did not reply. At that same moment a young blonde girl stepped out of the car. One of the Swedish detectives gave a wolf whistle.

'Who can that be?' the man with the camera mused aloud as he pressed the shutter release.

'I know her,' Wisting said. 'She's a Norwegian journalist.'

'What the hell is she doing here?'

The police radio crackled as the Emergency Squad announced that they were ready and standing by. Line walked across the street, heading straight for the entrance that the man in the Saab had disappeared into. She read the names beside the doorbells just as Wisting had done the day before.

Wisting took out his mobile phone and located Line's number. He had no inkling as to how on earth she had found her way here. He himself had travelled halfway round the world to reach this point. All the same, he had to get her away from Gyllenkrooksgatan before the police moved into action. She could sit in her car and still take photos that would land on the front pages of her newspaper but, no matter what, he was desperate to make her move away.

He saw her adjust an earpiece as her phone began to ring. At that very moment the door behind her crashed open and two men dragged her into the hallway. Wisting was left standing with his mouth open, listening to the engaged signal at the other end.

66

She tried to scream but the hand covering her mouth meant she could not utter a word. She wriggled and struggled to open her mouth for a bite but the man who had grabbed her held her in an iron grip, clamping her jaws together.

She could smell the foul odour from his mouth and felt his bearded face against her ear and the side of her neck. He was using his whole body weight to hold her.

Another man grabbed her kicking legs and she was pulled into the lift. They moved slowly up while she stood squeezed against the wall. The counter above the door eventually stopped at four and she was hauled in through the nearest door.

In the middle of the room, a boy she guessed to be in his early teens stood in outdoor clothes. He looked ready to travel and had a large suitcase at his side. Also in the room were two other men.

The man holding her shouted out clipped orders. The boy was pushed into an adjacent room and one of the men fetched a roll of sticky tape. He used it to cover her mouth, winding the roll a couple of times around her head. Then he bit off the tape with his teeth and bound her hands tightly behind her back before forcing her to her knees and taping her feet together.

Line toppled on to her side and stared up at the four men, who were engaged in a heated discussion in another language. One of them rummaged through her bag. He pulled out her press card and the temperature in the room shot up another few degrees.

Line fought to gather her thoughts. Somewhere along the way, the man in the black Saab must have grown suspicious. However, she simply could not understand why he had not shaken her off in the city-centre streets instead of leading her here to what must be the same apartment where both Khaled and Layla had been held captive. Then it dawned on her. They had no intention of letting her leave here alive.

Wisting stood like a helpless onlooker as decisions were made and commands flung out. On autopilot, his mind raced through an analysis of the situation. The killers had already shown how ruthless they were. They made use of children in their drugs trafficking and executed anyone who got in their way. As Line was now.

The police radio crackled to life again as rapid instructions were fired out and he understood the Swedish detective knew there was no time to lose.

Down in the street, two Emergency Squad vehicles were rolling in from either end. Eight men moved in formation towards the apartment block entrance. They were dressed in dark coveralls and helmets, bulletproof vests and knee protectors, with semi-automatic pistols at their hips and holding two-hand-grip machine guns in their hands.

The driver of the black Saab was clearly in charge. He produced a pistol and sent one of the other men to the room into which the boy had been bundled. This man dragged out a thick, patterned rug in contrasting colours into the living room. His accomplice stepped back to make space on the floor so that he could roll it out.

The leader held his gun down by his side and barked out a series of brief orders. Line was pushed into the middle of the soft rug. She felt her heart race as she contemplated what was about to happen – they were preparing to carry out an execution. Her pulse rate soared and her breathing grew laboured and ragged.

The man holding the gun took a step on to the rug and aimed the weapon straight at her. He shouted more commands and two of the men turned her round so that she was lying with her forehead down. She screwed up her eyes and waited, unable to sort out the thoughts spinning through her head.

One of the men called out something from the kitchen that caused a sudden reaction from the others. As boots tramped across the floor, Line opened her eyes and glanced to one side. The man who had yelled now stood by the window, gesticulating wildly with his arms and repeating the same thing over and over.

Seconds later the door burst open and six policemen in bulletproof vests and helmets stormed into the room, spreading out with their weapons raised. Animated voices and authoritative commands ricocheted loudly off the walls. The Saab driver raised his pistol towards them but one of the police officers responded at once with rapid gunfire. The ringleader whirled round and tripped over Line's legs as warm blood sprayed over her face.

67

Wisting stood in the centre of the room, gazing at the blood that was barely visible on the rug. Some of the droplets had splattered the grey suitcase. Fresh blood had soaked through the white sheet draped over the body.

Line was sitting in the kitchen being examined by a paramedic before being taken to police headquarters for interview. Wisting had already checked her out and reassured himself that she was OK. She was tough and strong, but he knew from experience that an incident such as this would come back to haunt her in nightmares for a long time. She had explained how she had ended up in Gothenburg, but he had not entirely understood the whole context, least of all why she was here with Tommy Kvanter, who was still waiting in a car a few blocks away.

The other three men who had been in the apartment had surrendered and been carted off. The boy who had been locked up in one of the rooms had also been taken away. Who he was and where he came from had not yet been established. What his captors had intended for him was more obvious: there was a Swedish Rail ticket for departure from Gothenburg that same day at 08.02 on the coffee table. That had been fifty-three minutes ago. Wisting picked it up and inspected it more closely. The proposed journey was a haphazard one, involving changes at Laxå station and on northwards through the country until the railway line met the connection from Stockholm. That train would not arrive in Oslo until 14.36. From there the train took just over two hours to reach Larvik, at 16.51. They actually had plenty of time.

He turned to Chief Inspector Lennart Mellander, whose main concern was to get everyone out so that trained investigators could examine the apartment.

'Do the media know about this?' he asked.

Mellander nodded in the direction of Line, who was sitting on a kitchen chair answering questions.

'Apart from her, I mean,' Wisting added.

'No.'

'Can we put a lid on it for the rest of the day?'

'That could prove difficult,' Mellander said. 'We've shot and killed one person. It's bound to be the main news item by lunchtime.'

'How long would it be possible to hold it back?'

'With a good reason, we can keep the details out of the public eye for twelve, maybe sixteen hours. The guys we've arrested will be interrogated by the Security Service. They can always find reasons to avoid the press. What's your thinking?'

'I need to get to Oslo,' Wisting said, without providing any further explanation. 'I have to catch a train.'

Wisting managed to extricate Line from her interview. The plan he was concocting depended on news of the arrests in Gothenburg being suppressed. There were eight hours until the train would arrive in Larvik. If the intended recipients were not warned off in the meantime, someone would be standing on the platform, ready to pick up the suitcase. Experience told him that arrangements were made well in advance for a narcotics delivery and that both sender and receiver endeavoured not to have any contact with each other on the day of a delivery. If anything unexpected were to occur, then the police would find it difficult to track down any possible connections.

327

He held nothing back when he explained to Line what his intentions were and could see that she was giving this a great deal of thought. She had shaken off the shock of her experience and was back on the job.

'Sole rights?' she asked, with a smile.

'Exclusive, guaranteed,' he promised.

68

The train pulled out from Oslo Central at 14.43 on the dot. Wisting had reserved eight seats as far forward as possible in the first-class section so that they could sit undisturbed.

The details of the plan were finalized in the car from Gothenburg. En route they had received information from the Swedish police, who had interviewed the boy they had found in the apartment. Fourteen years old, he was from Iraq and had been picked up in Skien. He had agreed to cooperate and revealed he'd been told to deliver the suitcase to a man with a yellow rucksack at the railway station in Larvik. He would receive 1,000 kroner in return and a ticket for the next train to Skien.

In simple terms, the ad hoc plan was based on Khaled agreeing to help by taking up his role of six months ago. He was to alight from the train carrying Suzanne Bjerke's suitcase, which had been decorated with stickers that had come free with a comic she had bought for him. He had to look out for a man with a yellow rucksack and place the suitcase at his feet before moving away. As soon as the man had put his hands on the case, the undercover officers would take care of the rest.

If everything proceeded according to plan, they would be able to put an immediate end to this entire investigation. If not, he was prepared for severe criticism for involving a minor in a covert operation.

When the train passed Tønsberg, they left the first-class section and their reserved seats and found new ones in the middle section of the train so that they would not appear to be travelling together. Four plain-clothes officers had also come aboard and split up into other carriages.

Khaled sat on his own with the suitcase at his side. Wisting was seated opposite him, while Suzanne was in front. They passed open fields, small farms and paddocks with horses. It had started raining again and long drips of water were trickling down the windows.

It was scarcely half an hour before the train would arrive and Wisting felt the seriousness of and responsibility for the situation weighing him down. Usually he liked to run through every eventuality before an action plan saw the light of day. Various possibilities would be discussed at lengthy meetings. In this case, there had been no time for anything like that. He had merely relayed messages and orders by phone.

The train rattled into Sandefjord station and waited for a couple of minutes for a connecting train. Then they were on the move again. Next stop: Larvik.

He saw Suzanne shift restlessly in her seat. The darkness outside was settling over the changing landscape.

Wisting's mobile peeped with an incoming text message from Nils Hammer. He was signed off on sick leave but had not been able to stay away.

All units in place, he read. *No yellow rucksacks to be seen.*

Wisting glanced at his watch and sat with the mobile in his hand, waiting for an update. They would arrive in eight minutes.

The conductor walked through the carriage, nodding to familiar faces that had been present for the entire journey. A few paces behind him followed a short man in his thirties with a beard, deep-set eyes and a hard, weather-beaten face. His hair was wet, as were his jacket lapels: he must have boarded the train at the previous station.

Only when he had passed by did Wisting spot that he was carrying a yellow rucksack.

The man was surveying the rows of seats, his eyes flicking back and forth. He walked five steps past them before turning on his heel and sitting down in the empty seat behind Khaled.

Wisting fixed his gaze on the window, which reflected a vivid picture of what was going on in the carriage.

The man leaned forward and said something. The noise of the rails made it impossible to hear what it was. Khaled looked around in confusion. Wisting tried to nod his head imperceptibly as a signal to him that he should continue to follow the instructions he had been given.

They had discussed the possibility of something unexpected happening and the consequent need for improvisation, but this scenario was not one they had considered.

Suzanne Bjerke sat up straight in her seat. He gained the impression that she too had understood the situation, but she remained passive, as per her instructions.

All of a sudden Khaled sprang to his feet, dragging the suitcase with him into the middle aisle and moving forward in the train. The man with the yellow rucksack remained seated for a few seconds longer before getting up and following the boy. Wisting went on sitting. It was too early to intervene. At present the man was officially only a fellow passenger on the train. Only when he put his hand on the suitcase could he be linked to the crime.

Khaled pulled the suitcase out to the passageway beside the toilets and the hot-drinks vending machine. The man walked slowly after him but stood inside the sliding doors at the end of the carriage, staring out into the darkness, as if he were waiting for something.

Wisting glanced again at his watch. Five minutes remained

before the train would arrive at the station. It would seem conspicuous if he got up and made preparations for disembarking. A trip to the toilet would also look suspicious. He chose to remain in his seat and observe, but he did not like the situation.

Suddenly the man lunged forward and pulled on the emergency brake. Wisting was thrown forward in his seat as the wheels screeched under them and the train juddered to a halt at the disused station at Lauve. The man with the yellow rucksack bounded into the passageway, grabbed the suitcase, forced open the exit doors and leapt off the train before it had stopped completely.

Wisting ran after him. The man was making straight for a waiting car. The heavy suitcase was a hindrance to him and Wisting was catching up with every step, but the distance was too great.

The man yanked open the back door, throwing in the suitcase and jumping in after it. The driver tossed a cigarette out of the window as he revved the engine.

Wisting acted without really thinking. He stretched his arms into the open car window. His hands curled around the steering wheel just as the car moved off. He was dragged after the vehicle as it picked up speed and felt the driver struggling to release his grip on the wheel. With a jerk he pulled the wheel towards him before letting go and rolling around on the road surface. The car continued to accelerate for a few metres before smashing into a concrete block.

The man with the suitcase was sprawled on the back seat. The driver tried to force the door, but the collision had made it impossible to open. Instead he crawled over to the passenger seat and was on his way out of the car wreck when the undercover police officers who had occupied other seats on the train arrived on the scene. Pulling their guns, they ordered

the two men in the car down on the ground before handcuff-
ing them.

Wisting staggered to his feet. It felt as if something had
come to a conclusion at last. He raised his head to the skies
and saw that the rain had changed to sleet. Autumn was turning to winter.

69

It was past midnight when Wisting switched off the light in his office and let himself out of the police station.

In the hours that had elapsed since the arrest, many pieces of the puzzle had fallen into place, The man on the train and his accomplice had been armed. Both guns had been traced to the theft Cato Dalen had committed. In the vehicle, they had found a two-day-old rental contract in the name of Edith R. Suarez and Nøysom AS for an apartment in Sandefjord. There was reason to believe that they had stayed somewhere in Lågendalen prior to that. Their mobile phones had been frequently recorded in the coverage area of an outlying mobile phone mast on the hillside behind the cabin that had recently burned to the ground. The call logs of their phones showed correspondence from the previous day with the number found on the men who had been arrested in Sweden.

Their names were Mamhood Khan and Izmat Shafi. One of them had a cut on his hand that had turned septic. Espen Mortensen was fairly confident that a DNA analysis would link him to the trace evidence of skin and blood he had found on the wooden stake Layla's head had been placed on.

The copious circumstantial evidence was solid and would become stronger as the days went by. Wisting was convinced that clinching evidence would fall into place as soon as they began the forensic work.

The Police Security Service had been reticent but confirmed that they had folders on both these names. They were asylum-seekers from Afghanistan who were waiting for their applications to be considered.

A fine layer of snow had fallen, muffling all the night sounds. Wisting brushed his windscreen clean and started the car.

He had an appointment.

Suzanne was waiting outside the entrance to the children's residential unit in Bøkelia where Khaled Athari was now sleeping in the same bed that he had been forced to leave behind three months earlier.

She got into the car with a smile on her face and they drove through the silent streets without either of them speaking a word.

Outside the small modern villa in Byskogen he drew to a halt and stopped the engine. She let them in, switching on a couple of lights, and showed him where he could hang his jacket.

Wisting moved through the house, taking in the fragrance of the woman who lived here, and lingered at the panoramic window in front of the terrace. The night outside was bleak and quiet as he surveyed the town centre below and the fjord that stretched out into the black distance and the skerries beyond.

His phone buzzed and he took it from his pocket, deciding to switch it off. He would just read the message first. It was from Line: *Aren't you glad it's all over?*

It was far from over, he thought, gazing out into the night again. The narcotics that flooded into the country would go on demanding their victims, but something was different, all the same.

He turned to look at Suzanne, who was approaching with two glasses and a bottle.

It was not over.

This was the start of something completely new.

NEWS EXTRA

Dramatic arrests in Norway and Sweden
Five men arrested for BEHEADING MURDER
Man shot dead by Swedish police
By Line Wisting

Larvik (VG): A total of five men have been charged with the murders of Layla Azimi (14) and Ahmed Saad (37). The five were
arrested yesterday during a coordinated police operation across
the territorial borders of Norway and Sweden. Norwegian officers took part in the action in Sweden, where a sixth person was
shot and killed.

WAR CRIMINALS charged with
the beheading murder
By Line Wisting

Oslo (VG): The Police Security Service confirm that the two
Afghans who were arrested and charged with the murders of
Layla Azimi (14) and Ahmed Saad (37) were wanted for war
crimes during the Taliban regime at the end of the nineties.

Neo-Nazis sold murder weapons to Islamists
By Line Wisting

Larvik (VG): Police sources confirm that the firearm used in
the murder of Ahmed Saad (37) has been traced to the theft
of an extensive collection of guns committed by the Patriotic
Front.

International narcotics gang behind
BEHEADING MURDER
By Line Wisting

Gothenburg (VG): Swedish Police have revealed that during the arrest of three men in an apartment in Gothenburg, a considerable amount of heroin was seized.

Prestigious SKUP prize awarded
to young VG journalist

Oslo (Norwegian Press Agency): The Association for a Critical and Investigative Press has awarded this year's prestigious SKUP prize to the young VG journalist Line Wisting, for her outstanding work in journalism.

Shocking murder linked to Norwegian
narcotics network
By Line Wisting

Hamburg (VG): Police in Dresden have reopened a three-year-old case after fresh information came to light in the wake of the clearing up of the Beheading Murder in Larvik. The homicide in Dresden has also been linked to an unsolved murder in the Czech Republic.

Property company built on narcotics money
By Line Wisting

Larvik (VG): The Economic Crimes Unit of the Norwegian Police has charged a property investor in Vestfold with the import and sale of narcotics. The police suspect that he has built up his entire fortune with the help of proceeds from the sale of narcotics.

621 asylum-seeker children disappeared

Oslo (Norwegian Press Agency): Since 2000, 621 children have gone missing from Norwegian reception centres for asylum-seekers. Only a very few of them have been traced. Last year, eighteen children disappeared from reception centres in Norway without giving a forwarding address. Whether or not the cases are investigated is dependent on which police district the child lives in, and in many cases no investigation is initiated at all.